Flash 5:34

A Haunting in Highland, Book 2

Andrew Carmitchel

To Dave,
my friend
Andy
Carmitchel

iUniverse, Inc.
New York   Bloomington

Flash 5:34
A Haunting in Highland, Book 2

iUniverse books may be ordered through booksellers or by contacting:

iUniverse
1663 Liberty Drive
Bloomington, IN 47403
www.iuniverse.com
1-800-Authors (1-800-288-4677)

*Because of the dynamic nature of the Internet, any Web addresses or links
contained in this book may have changed since publication and may no longer be
valid. The views expressed in this work are solely those of the author and do not
necessarily reflect the views of the publisher, and the publisher hereby disclaims
any responsibility for them.*

ISBN: 978-1-4502-2755-1 (sc)
ISBN: 978-1-4502-2756-8 (dj)
ISBN: 978-1-4502-2757-5 (ebk)

Printed in the United States of America

iUniverse rev. date: 5/28/2010

October 2nd - 5:34 P.M.

It came and went too fast, technically, for human comprehension. It was an infinitesimal piece of a moment-already history before any coherent thought could be formed; yet all who experienced it knew, deep down somewhere, that something as significant as it was inexplicable had just happened. Something that in some mysterious way had never happened before...

Bart Melleville was driving home from work to his home in Highland, heading east on Interstate 270 from St. Louis into Illinois. For him, it was a bright flash that was long gone by the time he was able to even form a thought. He involuntarily grimaced, grit his teeth hard and instinctively took his foot off the accelerator, waiting for whatever was next. An explosion? He held his breath and watched with widened eyes, but nothing happened. Five seconds went by. Then ten. He put his foot back on the gas pedal tentatively, suddenly aware that he was dangerously slowing on a high-traffic highway. He checked his mirrors then and saw quickly that there was no danger. All the other cars had slowed too.

Jim Ray Crawford, after a long day of construction work, was outside in the dusk on his farm near Alhambra pouring feed for his cattle when it happened. For him it was like grabbing hold of an electric fence. He was aware of what seemed to be a microsecond of light, then felt an unpleasant tingle from head to toe. He too found himself gritting his teeth. He had been in the process of pouring grain into a trough when it happened. The jolt made him spill some, and he quickly took several steps back. The cows at the trough quit feeding and looked up at him. Jim Ray looked first up at the darkening Autumn sky, then out across the pasture behind the animals. He saw nothing unusual. He realized then that he was holding his breath, for some reason, so he took a deep one and tried to reason out what had just happened. His mouth felt dry. He looked at his cows, and they looked back at him. Whatever had happened had affected them too.

He took another deep breath, poured the rest of the grain into the trough, then turned to go back toward the house. He looked back before he got to the back door. The cows still weren't feeding. They seemed, instead, to be intently watching his every step.

Brenda Crawford dropped the bowl of mashed potatoes that she was carrying to the table when it happened. "Earthquake!" was her first thought, though nothing was moving and all was silent after the bowl shattered. Brenda stopped and stared at the mess on the floor, then at her own hands. They were shaking. She listened intently, expectantly, for something. She heard only the ticking of the kitchen clock. Then it hit her. Her daughter! Where was her daughter?

Before her mouth could even form the word "Marsha!" and yell it loud enough for it to be heard in her upstairs bedroom, the 8 year-old came running into the kitchen, seemingly out of nowhere-and then past her mother towards the back door. She opened and went through it so fast that she nearly collided with her father, who was on the bottom step of the back porch, on his way in. She ran past him without a word, and he turned and watched with amazement as she sprinted toward the cow pens.

Brenda was still standing there, frozen over her dropped mashed potatoes when the back door opened again and her husband Jim Ray walked in.

Officer Ben Christopher was sitting in his "speed trap position" on St. George Road in Highland when it happened. He wasn't thinking about catching speeders, He was instead day-dreaming about the cold beer and good dinner that was to be coming his way soon, and was just checking the time to see how close he was to finally being off-duty when he felt his scalp tingle sharply, and saw the hairs on his arm stand up as if suddenly electrified around his wristwatch. He winced, closed his eyes and pulled back into his seat. For him, it was a horrid, instantaneous flashback to his time in Iraq. It was the millisecond before the bomb went off.

When nothing happened in the following few seconds he opened his eyes and saw all the rush hour traffic on St. George Road slowing, at once and together. A jeep even pulled off the side of the road, and into the ditch.

Bobby Meachum had just taken the first toke on his second joint of the young evening. He was sitting by his open second-story bedroom window, as usual, to make sure all the smoke drifted out and away from the house. His mother, who was cooking dinner in the kitchen directly below him, smelled it anyway, as usual. She simply turned on the oven's overhead fan, as always, so that no trace would be left when Bobby's father got home. She was long past the fight with Bobby.

When it happened Amanda Meachum felt a quick, sharp pain, as though she had somehow burned herself; even though she was walking away from the stove and toward the dining room table at the time. She stopped in her tracks, turned quickly and shot an accusatory glance at the innocent and happily cooking little stove. After a few seconds of confusion and alarm, she simply walked back over and turned off the vent fan. She had no idea what had happened, and didn't know what else to do.

When the moment came for her son Bobby, who was sitting by his open bedroom window upstairs, he quickly exhaled the smoke that he'd been holding in his lungs. He held up the new joint and took a close, wondering look at it. The stuff, it seemed to him…was amazing. What a hit! "WHOA!" he finally said happily.

Jonathon Parker was grading papers at his kitchen table when the moment came. It caused him to make a long red pen mark across the first page of Alice Benson's essay. He immediately stood up and turned toward the glass door that led to his deck out back. His skin was tingling. He found it hard to take a breath. He took three tentative steps toward the door and looked out back at his yard and the pasture and woods beyond it. He saw nothing unusual, but stood and stared anyway. Seconds went by, all was silent, but he didn't move. He could hear his own breathing, and feel his whole body trembling.

Police Chief Rodney Thomas was at his computer at the time. He was typing the last line of a report he wanted to finish before heading for home when the screen went dark. At the same time an odd, ominous feeling (not quite shock, but something close) came over him, and he quickly and instinctively jerked his hands away from the keyboard. The lights in his office flickered, but didn't go out. Still, the room seemed dimmer, somehow.

For at least a minute afterwards he sat looking at the black computer screen in wonder, trying to figure out what had just happened. One of Highland's legendary power outages? Some kind of sonic boom that somehow…? Nothing made sense. He found himself listening intently in the sudden silence that now engulfed his office. Though he knew that there was undoubtedly a logical answer to this, he couldn't help having an eerie feeling about it. Maybe he was just tired…but it was as though he had somehow been transported, very suddenly, to a different place. A far away place.

Then he heard a dog; somebody's dog that undoubtedly lived close to the police station. He sat listening. It was an unusual sound. An unnatural sound. It was somebody's big dog, and it was howling, not barking. A long, mournful, wolf-like howling. He listened quietly in the dim light, waiting for it to stop, but it kept going. And it seemed to be getting louder.

Then Chief Thomas' phone rang. It was jarringly loud, and he jumped about a foot.

★   ★   ★

The phone kept ringing well into Chief Thomas' evening. Friends, other police officers, the mayor, two city council members and even a sprinkling of Highland citizens that he didn't know kept him busy for hours. Police Chief Rodney Thomas believed that the public should have open access to their top law-enforcement officer. His phone number was in the book, and he had his cell-phone set up to take the "roll over" calls that came to his home. There were times, of course, when he regretted his own philosophy, and this was quickly turning into one of them. He simply didn't know what had happened, couldn't find anyone who did know, and so was left with having to repeat himself over and over again: "We're not sure what, if anything happened at this point, but I can assure you that we're looking into the matter," or words to that effect.

People were reporting that not only their TV cable was out, but that even their radios weren't working right. It made no sense, he had no answers, and the calls kept coming. "Why couldn't their damn phones quit working," he mumbled out loud at one point.

But it was not to be, and for another hour in his office, then in his car on the drive home, and even later, sitting at his kitchen table trying to get down a few bites of cold dinner, he took calls. And when he wasn't answering calls (as patiently as possible) he was making them. He called the city manager and urged him to look into whether or not some kind of electrical anomaly had taken place. He called each of the four officers that he had out on duty at the time to get their take. He called his friend Joe Blanton, the County Sheriff, to see if he'd heard anything (he learned that the "incident" appeared to be county-wide...which made him feel better, for some reason).

In the end though, as he walked into the living room to talk to his wife Joanie for the first time since early morning, after the last call had been made and all possible information had been gathered from every source he could think of, he knew that he really didn't know a damned thing. Not yet.

Joanie was cuddled up on the couch with a blanket over her, with eyes closed, as the TV blared out white noise. Rodney walked quietly over to turn off the television, then over to his sleeping wife. When he sat down at her feet and began to rub them her blue eyes opened, a bit reluctantly, and she smiled. "Just resting my eyes," she said sleepily. It was an old joking line she used since the early days of their marriage, to cover her penchant for falling asleep in front of the TV...no matter what was on. It was a habit that at one time, long ago, had irritated the hell out of her young husband.

"Sure you were," he played along, "Just resting your eyes." He could see that she wouldn't be awake long. Indeed, her eyes were closing again. He reached over and gently brushed her disheveled blond hair off of her face and tucked it behind her ear. She smiled again. "Joanie honey, did you notice the... thing, a few hours ago? Did you notice anything unusual? About 5:30 or so?"

At first she didn't move, even as he continued to caress her. He thought that was too far gone, and hadn't heard him. But then she surprised him. Her eyes snapped open, she brushed her own hair back, and she squirmed halfway up so that she was resting on her elbows. "Yea. What was it, Rod?" she asked, suddenly fully awake.

He hesitated before answering. His first instinct was to quote the party line about an "ongoing investigation." But this was his wife.

"I don't know," he said finally, and a bit more irritably than intended. "But tell me what you noticed, hon? What happened with you?" He looked at her intently. He knew he'd get the unvarnished truth from her. Maybe even an insight into something. He was tired, and all the stories he'd heard, even his own experience, was all getting jumbled together.

She looked into his eyes for a moment, and the away toward the television. Her smile was gone. "I don't know either, really," she said distractedly, almost sadly. It was almost like a...bomb going off, or something. Only there was no sound. Nothing at all." She looked back at him, "Except for that dog of yours," she said sarcastically. "He went absolutely nuts!" She looked away again. He thought he saw her shiver slightly.

"What do you mean, nuts?" he asked. Then he turned to look at the foot of the couch, the floor below him, then quickly around the room. "Where is Mitzi, anyway?" he added. Despite her "your dog" charge, Mitzi was never, ever very far away from Joanie. At night in front of the television she was always at his wife's feet at the end of the couch, if not on her lap.

"She's in the basement," Joanie said tiredly, but in a way that told him there was more to it than that. "She ran down there right after it happened, and hasn't come up since," she added.

Rodney could see in her eyes that she was more than a little bothered by it. Her voice, at least to others, could be deceptive, but after all their years together, he could read her like a book. She was worried. He got up to go downstairs to check on their dog. Stupid thing.

"The worst part though...was the howling," his wife added before he could get to the basement door. "She wouldn't quit howling."

Rod stopped to turn and look at his wife. She was staring vacantly at the television picture that she couldn't hear or see. Her voice had sounded different to him; as though she was talking to someone else, even herself, when she described the howling. He watched the back of her head for a long moment, but she didn't say anything more. She didn't move at all. She just sat there as if engrossed in the best TV show ever made.

So Chief Thomas turned back to open the door to their finished basement. He flicked on the light, and could hear Mitzi's low growling before he even took a step down the stairs.

Chapter 2
October 3rd 3:39 A.M.

When Bart Melleville finally realized he was awake, he found himself sitting up on his side of the bed, breathing heavily, and with his heart racing a mile a minute. He was terrified, relieved and confused; a mix of feelings that only those who have suffered the most vivid of nightmares can attest to. "Jesus!" he exclaimed aloud between gasps of breath, temporarily forgetting (and perhaps not really caring) that his wife Nancy would be awakened by his outburst. He wiped at his forehead. It was covered with sweat. His heavy breathing was barely slowing down. He reached out for Nancy with his other hand, wanting to wake her now. Needing her now. She wasn't there. Knowing he was disoriented from the dream and the dark, he felt for her again. Then again with both hands. The sheets were cold. She wasn't there.

Normally, there is a familiar, rapid, and ultimately reassuring progression that takes place in the fevered brain of those who wake after suffering a nightmare. Each second back into the conscious world brings blissful, predictable reality back into sharper focus, while, simultaneously, the once vivid land of dreams fades into harmless wisps of increasingly ludicrous, half-forgotten fantasy. Bart Melleville though, sweat -soaked and hyperventilating as he grasped blindly in the night for the love of his life, was the exception. The absurdity of his state-of-mind at that moment, which any "normal" dreamer might find both embarrassing and perhaps even humorous in a matter of seconds, completed eluded the successful banker from Highland, Illinois. Each second that passed, in fact, made it worse. His confusion only deepened, and each second of this mystery caused his panic to grow, his face to grow more flushed, his heart to beat more wildly, and his sense of reason to recede further and further away.

So, eventually, Bart Melleville just screamed. It started as a desperate cry for his wife Nancy, but his brain was running far too many frantic calculations to send that clear an order to his tongue. In addition to trying to locate his wife, he was feverishly searching for safety, order, reason and light; so his primal scream came out as a loud, jumbled "NAHENOAHH!!"

Nancy Melleville, who was sitting at the kitchen table in her own world of distress holding a cup of lukewarm coffee and a lit cigarette, couldn't have been blamed if she had made straight for the door when the Indian Warrior-like scream came. She didn't though, as she had the advantage of having been up, wide awake and in the well-lit world of rationality for the last 45 minutes. Though startled enough to spill her coffee, she just as quickly regained her composure and got up quickly to head for the bedroom and her husband.

When she turned on the bedroom light she saw Bart sprawled sideways on his stomach on their bed, struggling mightily to (apparently) beat up the sheets and one of the pillows. The sudden light caused him to become even more frantic for a few seconds, then reason and understanding seemed to flood over him all at once. He froze in the new light, then a moment later dropped his head face down onto the bed in sweet resignation.

"What in God's name happened, honey?" Nancy asked as calmly as she could. His arms and the back of his neck were so red that it alarmed her. She could see that he had soaked through his t-shirt too. "Are you OK, Bart?" she asked a few moments later when he still hadn't moved.

Bart finally took a deep, very audible breath and with great effort rolled over onto his back. He stared up at the bright bedroom light for a few moments, then closed his eyes again. He could still see the light bulb, now dancing in red behind his eyelids. He took another deep breath. "I think I just had the worst nightmare of my life," he said.

His voice was higher pitched than usual, and sounded surprisingly emotional. Nancy was concerned enough to temporarily table her own reason that she was up in the middle of the night, and walked softly over to the bed. She sat down by his head and reached a hand out to stroke his graying, dampened hair. "There, there honey," she cooed soothingly. "It's all over now."

Bart kept his eyes shut, and nothing more was said between them for a long minute. Nancy continued to stroke his forehead lovingly. She looked over at the clock on the nightstand and saw that it was 3:46 A.M. It was going to be a long day at work tomorrow.

"Why were you up, Nancy?" Bart asked suddenly. He had opened his eyes and was in the process of awkwardly trying to sit up from the skewed position he had been lying in. For some reason he felt an urgency to look at her face, her eyes, when she answered his question.

Nancy looked down, then up at him. She forced a sheepish smile that didn't quite work. "Nightmare," she said simply.

Bart studied her intently. Despite her lighthearted posture, it was obvious to him that something had really upset her. She didn't look like she wanted to talk about it, and avoided his eyes. He couldn't ever remember her getting up in the night before, at least since the kids still lived at home. "What kind of nightmare?" he finally asked.

She shook her head and made a dismissive gesture with her hand. "Oh...I don't know. It was silly," she said. She stood up and did a stretch and yawn, a gesture that was obviously meant to diminish the whole episode. "I can't even remember much of

11

it, to tell you the truth," she added. She started walking casually for the door and kitchen. Even in his miserable state, Bart could see that for whatever reason, she really didn't want him to probe any further. But before she'd gotten very far, right before she got to the bedroom door, she stopped suddenly and turned to look back at him. "I'm sorry, honey. I guess I'm not thinking straight. Tired... Tell me about your nightmare, or whatever happened. You scared me half to death!"

Bart stared at her for a long moment, then looked down at himself. He pulled at the soaked t-shirt that was clinging to his skin, then over at the clock. A shower and a lot of coffee were in his immediate future, he thought. There would be no more sleeping that night. No way.

"I don't remember," he said as he struggled painfully to his feet (can a nightmare make you sore?). He looked at her standing there in the doorway. He could see the bags under her eyes and her deep worry lines even from where he was standing across the room. And he knew that he probably looked even worse.

He looked down and away. "I know it sounds crazy, Nancy, but I don't remember a thing right now. I just know that it was terrible...something terrible."

★   ★   ★

When Bobby Meachum finally made it down to the kitchen for breakfast, only his mother was there. She was furiously scrubbing a pot from the last night's supper, and didn't even look at her son when he walked in. "Hurry up and get yourself some cereal or something Bobby. If you aren't careful you're going to miss the bus again," she said mechanically (she'd used those same words many times before).

Bobby scratched at his long, matted hair (which should have been washed the previous night) and looked absently around the kitchen. He was in no hurry, as usual. He really didn't mind missing the school bus. In fact he rather enjoyed it, if the weather was decent, as it was that morning. He rather enjoyed being late, very late, for school too. So he stood there in no hurry, trying to think what he was hungry for, or if he was really hungry. "Where's Dad?" he asked as he yawned.

Amanda Meachum kept scrubbing the pot that was well past clean already. "He couldn't sleep," she said over her shoulder. "He decided he might as well go into work early. Hurry up, Bobby!"

Bobby rubbed his eyes. He was still sleepy. "Couldn't sleep?" he asked, more rhetorically than not, "That's weird." He stretched and yawned again, then crossed the kitchen to the counter where an open box of Raisin Bran was sitting. Getting out a bowl, the milk and the sugar seemed like too much work. So did walking to school. He reached in and grabbed a handful of dry cereal and popped it into his mouth. "She ya!" he said with his mouth full, and then turned and within a few seconds was out the door.

Most mornings Bobby smoked a joint on the way to the bus stop. It made his morning go better, he had discovered long ago. He had been doing it since the 8th grade. At first the paranoia it caused dampened the mellow effects of the drug, and he was an inconsistent user. Gradually though, when he saw how really bad the teachers and principals were at detecting "the stoned ones" (or didn't care), it became a regular habit. Now, in his junior year, he was pretty much a public toker. He didn't really worry about such things anymore. Not much.

He was only a half-block away from home when he stepped into an alley and lit up. It was only after he took the first drag that he heard the growling. It startled him, but when he turned he saw immediately that it was only the Bensons' little beagle. Bobby couldn't remember his name (memory was somewhat of a problem, sometimes), but he knew he was male and less than a year old. He had pet him often when the kids took him out for a walk, and had even played with him a few times when he was in the mood. Now there he was, tied to a tree in the Bensons' back yard (which seemed unusual in itself) growling with teeth bared, and looking right at him.

The sight was so unusual and confusing that Bobby's first instinct was to turn and look behind him to try to see what the dog was really growling at. There was nothing there though, other than a garbage can or two. No squirrel. No nothing. He turned back around, took another toke on his joint, and looked at the dog. It was still growling... and apparently at him...fiercely growling, with his bared teeth dripping saliva. He was beginning to put his full weight on the leash, trying to break free.

Even as he felt the drug begin to work its calming magic, Bobby felt an unwelcome chill begin to work its way up his spine. There was something so...unnatural about it. This dog wasn't like this. And what was spooky was that he wasn't going crazy, and jerking repeatedly against the leash, like dogs do. It was pulling, straining steadily, snarling with hatred, and staring at him murderously.

"What's the matter little doggie?" Bobby said aloud nervously, and immediately regretted it. The growling intensified, and its fight against the leash grew suddenly frantic. It was terrifying to see, even in a small dog, and loud enough to draw attention. Someone was going to hear it, and look out their window. "God damn!" Bobby cried as he threw his joint to the ground, stepped on it, then sprinted out of the alley and down the street toward the bus stop. He didn't slow up until he was a half-block from the stop, when a coughing fit made him pull up. After a half-minute of hacking, he managed to walk the rest of the way, stopping to cough intermittently. None of the usual kids were there waiting. He was sure that he'd missed the bus.

He was still breathing hard, bent over with hands on knees when the bus did come. It squeaked to a stop and opened its doors. Bobby stood up, took a deep breath and climbed up the steps. The bus, usually a packed cacophony of chaos by the time it got to his stop, had only two other students on it.

★　　　★　　　★

Jim Ray Crawford was standing at the window, nursing a cup of coffee and looking out back at his cattle when his wife Brenda came out to the kitchen.

"Well, there you are!" she said in her best good morning voice.

Jim Ray half turned and gave her a thin smile in response, then turned again to look outside.

Brenda looked at the back of her husband's head. His hair seemed lately to be thinning more every day. He was worried about something, which actually wasn't unusual. Between his suddenly "part-time" job at the construction company, the slowdown in her business at Frey Realty, and the diminishing number of beef cattle he had to sell off, times were even rockier than usual. And he'd always worried about money, even before all of that. But today, and last night, it was different. He was too quiet, even morose, and she didn't know why. It made her uneasy.

"Is something wrong Jim?" she asked him.

Jim Ray took a sip of the coffee that he held with both of his hands. "Not really," he answered without turning around. "Something's wrong with them cows, though," he added. "Even little Marsha knows it." Their eight year-old had run out to the cow pens the night before, after the "flash thing" had happened. She had gone out and stood, and stayed there with the cows. They had had to make her come in, eventually. In a way, she had acted as oddly as their cows. It was harmless, her parents supposed, but it had bothered both of them.

Brenda looked at him a moment longer, then walked over to the coffee pot and poured herself a cup. Something being wrong with the damned cows was not what she meant by asking, and she felt like he knew that. He could be so...reclusive sometimes. She knew from experience that the more worried he got, the more quiet and the more reticent he became. It was probably just a "man" thing, but it aggravated the hell out of her. She sat down at the kitchen table, and decided to try again.

"How long have you been up, Jim? I woke up at 3:00 and you weren't in bed."

"Since a little before that. 3:00, I mean. Couldn't sleep," he said.

He still didn't turn from the window. It aggravated Brenda, but she was used to it. She also knew how to get to him a bit.

"What's wrong, honey?" she asked plaintively, her voice (from much practice) sounding suddenly close to tears.

Jim Ray, oblivious to her tactics as always, turned around fully to look at his wife. He looked into the almost-tearful green eyes that he had loved so much, every day, going all the way back to the days he followed her around in grade school like a puppy. "It's nothing honey, I swear to you. I just had a nightmare, baby. That's all." He walked over then and put his arms awkwardly around her. He gave her a too hard hug ('...now don't muss my hair!') then stepped away. He took one more glance out the window, then sat down at the table with her.

"What kind of nightmare?" the suddenly fully recovered Brenda asked.

Jim Ray looked down at his work coarsened hands. He shook his head. "I don't know how to describe it," he said. "It was...like a warning...and there was a face, but..." he looked up at her suddenly. "The cows. They won't eat, Brenda. They're just ...standing out there. Just standing there, looking up at the house."

Brenda looked into Jim Ray's dark eyes. There was something alarming in them, she thought. They weren't quite the same kind, but worried eyes she knew so well. There was something else there. There was something new. A fear...

She was worried now. She closed her eyes and sighed, then looked over to the window where Jim Ray had been standing. She stood up suddenly, intending to go wake her daughter up and start the morning routine, but after hesitating, went over to the window to have a look at the cows first.

★　　　★　　　★

Chief Rodney Thomas was late for the "urgent" meeting that he himself had called, so all heads swiveled in his direction when he opened the door to the City Hall conference room. Mayor John Bander, City Manager Janice Granger, County Sheriff Joe Blanton (he was a surprise), and two of Rodney's patrolmen who had been on duty the night before all looked at him expectantly as he stepped into the small room and closed the door behind him.

"Sorry fellas...and Janice," ("fellas" was a habitual word that he knew he had to stop using. After all, he had three female officers on his staff now. 'Old habits of old men die hard,' he always said). "I'm sorry to be late. Had to get this taken care of." He held up his bandaged hand as evidence while glancing up at the clock to see just how late he was. It was 9:25. The meeting had been set for 9:00 sharp.

"What the hell happened to you?" Mayor Bander asked, in his usual boorishly direct manner. He had a way of making everything sound like an impatient demand. They didn't call him "Crash" for nothing.

"Dog bit me. Twice. My own dog. Can you believe it?" the Chief answered as he quickly moved toward his seat.

"Mitzi?" City Manager Granger asked in disbelief. Janice and his wife Joanie were in the same book club and had become good friends, a fact that made Rodney uneasy, though he would never say anything to Joanie about it.

"Yeah, Mitzi. She went crazy last night. I'm gonna have to put her down, I'm afraid."

"Oh no! You can't!" Janice Granger cried.

"Yeah, well..." Rodney mumbled. Her plea embarrassed him for some reason, and he really wanted to ignore her and move on. So he did. "I don't know about the rest of you, but I've had a pretty strange last 12 hours or so, and I still don't know what the hell happened." He looked at the faces around the table. All were basically expressionless; all anxiously staring back at him. Waiting. "I know we've all talked to each over the phone, several

17

times, to try to get a handle on this...this thing that happened, but, well, uh...I just thought it would be good to get together, face to face, to figure out what's going on."

Rodney sat back, and again looked around the table. No one said anything. He could hear the clock ticking. Nothing else.

"You mean you called us here to tell us you don't know a damned thing?" the Mayor finally asked disgustedly. "Jesus, Rodney!" he added for emphasis. His words, as always, were jarring. This in itself wasn't unusual as, in general, everything the Mayor said was too loud (many suspected a hearing problem, but no one ever had the courage to ask). But his words here, coming in the midst of their collective gnawing anxiety, managed to irritate them all.

"Hold on there Mayor," Sheriff Joe Blanton said. "That ain't hardly fair. Nobody's been working harder on this than Rodney... hell, harder than all of us. Makes sense to get people into a room. See what we can come up with, or what," he said forcefully, if awkwardly.

The others around the table shifted their glances from the Sheriff's droopy handle-bar mustache to their corpulent, red-faced Mayor. It was good to have someone in the room who wasn't beholding to him. The Mayor seemed too surprised to respond so the City Manager swooped in to re-direct, as she usually did. "Why don't we start by sharing everything we know up to now?" she asked.

"But we don't know a damned thing!" the recovering Mayor blustered. "He just said so!"

Janice ignored him. "We know that the utilities people say there was *no*, I repeat, *no* electrical anomaly that they could detect."

"You mean no power outage? Speak English!" the Mayor demanded.

This time Janice shot him a dirty look before continuing and the Mayor actually seemed a bit chastened by it. He reddened even more and looked down at his meaty hands.

"There was no detected electrical anomaly, yet we have had dozens of complaints from people who say they were shocked," the City Manager said.

"Same way up north of Highland," Sheriff Blanton interrupted. "I got complaints...I guess you'd call them complaints...reports, maybe. Anyway I got reports of weird stuff like shocks or whatever, from Marine, Alhambra, Grantfork...and places out in the middle of nowhere."

"But nothing from Edwardsville, or anyplace east of there, or southeast of there, isn't that what you told me?" Janice asked. The Sheriff's poky way of getting to the point irritated her.

"So far. That's right, so far..." he answered, a bit more ominously than necessary.

"So we have a Highland area phenomena, it would seem," Janice concluded.

"So far..." the Sheriff added again. "It's only been a few hours since it happened!" he added in answer to her irritated glance.

"But what happened, besides the damned cable going out?" the Mayor yelled.

"All right, look," Rodney broke in. "We're in the, uh, what do they call it...the Fog of War moment here, and..."

"Fog of what? What the hell?" the Mayor cried.

"Just let me finish!" the Police Chief demanded. Rodney rarely, if ever raised his voice, so it had the natural effect of silencing the room. "By Fog of War I mean that this 'event' we had...well, we're too close to it to know what happened yet. But something did happen. Something that affected people. The people we serve. And what's more, we all went through it."

"Not me," Sheriff Blanton (who lived in Edwardsville) said. Soon it was his turn to redden and look down, as just about everyone in the room gave him an irritated glance.

"I want us to all, in order, go around the table and tell what you experienced last night. And what you saw others experience, as in the case of Officer Christopher here. He was on traffic duty at the time. And let's listen to each other...and try to put the pieces together a little bit. None of the experts seem to know anything. At least not yet. So let's give it a try. OK?"

All nodded their heads, except for the Mayor. "Sure, I'll go along," he said, "but has it occurred to anybody else that maybe we're jumping the gun a little here? I mean, maybe it was just some weird thing that the electrical boys didn't catch. And it ain't gonna happen again. I mean, it's a beautiful, sunny day out there, right?"

Rodney gave the Mayor a long look. Even when he tried his best to be patient with this man, he inevitably found himself grinding his teeth. "Yeah, it's a beautiful autumn day, John," he said. "You know the Superintendent of Schools don't you, John? Bob Warner?" The Mayor looked puzzled, but nodded. "Bob gave me a call when I was driving over here from the Dr.'s office. On this beautiful autumn day, he tells me that more than half-*more than half* of his kids... didn't show up to school today. But that's not his biggest problem. Three-fourths of his teaching staff lives in the Highland area. Half of them didn't come to work today. Some didn't even call in sick. You have to call in, or you could get fired. But they just didn't show." Chief Thomas looked from the Mayor to the other now stunned faces around the table. "We've got some kind of a problem here, folks," he said.

Chapter 3

It was the best morning of school that Bobby Meachum could remember-at least since the time when he was in 6th grade when they let school out right after everyone had gotten there because of an impending snowstorm (that never came).

The halls of Highland High School seemed, actually were, virtually empty. It was confusing but, for Bobby, exhilarating too. Teachers and administrators walked around with worried looks on their faces. The other students who were there all looked tired, and as worried and serious as the adults. There was a part of him (a small part) that wondered, from the time that he boarded the virtually empty bus, if something had happened...or if he had somehow missed something. It was certainly possible. He never listened to anything but his i-pod, so there could have been a nuclear war for all he knew. But when he entered the building and saw the frown on the normally smiling, sickeningly upbeat Principal Grayson, he decided he didn't really care. Hardly anyone was there! They couldn't possibly hold normal school!

The only bummer was that none of his fellow burn-outs were there either. There was no one to talk to. So he got his usual Mountain Dew, sat at a table in the cafeteria by himself, and watched and waited. Surely, he thought, someone he knew would come staggering in soon. Or better yet Old Grayson, who was nervously walking around with folded arms rushing up to talk to every teacher that came in, would perhaps get on the P.A. and call the whole thing off. That would be the best scenario, he thought.

But it didn't happen. In fact, for the next 15 minutes nothing much at all happened. A few more kids and teachers walked in, but that was it. The cafeteria area (they called it the Commons, like it was English or something) was just eerily quiet, and there was no one to talk to. It made Bobby wonder...but just a little bit.

First period was great. Bobby's English class had only five students show up, and his teacher Mr. Parker wasn't there. Mr. Parker was the one teacher he liked (and the one who *never* missed school), but to Bobby's way of thinking, this was a situation to take advantage of. He quickly warned the other four meek students to keep their mouths shut as soon it was apparent that they were leaderless. Then after gingerly walking over to the classroom door to have a look down the hall to make sure no one was coming, he returned happily to his seat, and put his head down on his desk to get some much-needed sleep. He was interrupted though ten minutes later when Principal Grayson came in and ordered them to join the English class next door. It was Mr. Bonner, whom he hated from unfortunate experiences from the year before, along with seven sophomores. Bummed out at first, Bobby quickly recovered his optimism when it became obvious that Mr. Bonner wasn't going to do anything. He announced that the class would be a quiet study hall that day. He looked pale and shaken as he spoke, even to Bobby. "He needs some blood or something," he thought.

When the announcements were read and Mr. Bonner had returned to his desk the students dutifully got homework assignments or books out, and Bobby happily laid his head down and went quickly to sleep. He was in this state 20 minutes later, having an erotic dream about Mary Ellen Carson (senior cheerleader), when he was awoken by a sharp poke to his ribs. He jerked his head up to act instantly awake, as he had done so many times before. It took him several groggy moments to realize where he was, and to remember the situation he was in. Mr. Bonner was standing at his desk in the front of the room giving him a familiar look of disapproval. Bobby blinked several times, then gave a quick glance around to see that the other students were looking at him too. Had he been snoring?

"As I was saying," Mr. Bonner said, acting as though nothing had just happened, "I think we need to talk about this. After all... all of us went through that, electrical...or whatever it was, thing last night. Isn't that right?"

Bobby was completely dumbfounded. He looked around at the others. They all were expressionless. One girl, a sophomore who he didn't know, was nodding her head at Mr. Bonner's words. And she was smiling. "Weird," Bobby thought.

"I myself had a rough night," Mr. Bonner continued. He was pacing back and forth now nervously in the front of the room, not even looking at the students as he talked.

"Crazy bastard's talking to himself," Bobby whispered, too low for anyone else to hear.

"That thing happened...and for some reason, well, it was a rough night. That's all." The teacher suddenly stopped pacing and looked directly at his reluctant audience. "Did anyone else have nightmares last night?" he asked almost pleadingly.

Bobby looked around. No one that he could see was nodding their head. They all just stared ahead in wonder, looking a little worried. The one girl was still smiling though. It seemed creepy to him. Why in the world was she doing that? Was she enjoying this?

"And...and," Mr. Bonner was frantically rolling his sleeves up, "...look what my cat did, kids? Look at this!"

Both arms were covered in scratches. It was ugly, and one of the girls let out a short, but fairly loud scream. It made everyone jump. Bobby stared at the freshly scarred arms. It made him a little nauseous, but he couldn't look away.

And it made him think about something he didn't want to think about: the eyes, and the horrible growling sound made by the Bensons' dog earlier that morning.

★　　★　　★

Police Detective Darrin Crandle and his new bride Marilyn 'Kramer' Crandle had just arrived at Lambert Airport in St.Louis from their week long honeymoon in Cancun, Mexico when Darrin's cell-phone rang. It caught him especially by surprise because he had just pressed the icon to turn it back on, and because he had not heard it ring for a week. He nearly dropped it, but managed to recover, open it and put it to his ear by the third ring.

It was his boss, Police Chief Thomas. "Darrin? Are you still on vacation?" he asked.

"Honeymoon, Chief. We just got back from our honeymoon. I'm at the airport right now," Darrin answered. So much for getting away from the boss...

"Oh, hell! I forgot! Damn it!"

Darrin had to smile. He could almost see the Chief leaning back in that desk chair of his, running his hand through his thinning hair in exasperation. It was good to be back, he supposed, in a way. "It's OK, Chief. Party's almost over. How can I help you?"

"Well...I'm sorry. When do you come back to work anyway, hotshot? We've got a bit of a problem." The Chief had been thinking of Darrin, off and on, all morning. He had almost called earlier, but the chart in the office had said "VACATION" by his name, and he'd let it go for a while. But now... the fast rising detective had become his go-to guy on so many things. He had more than proven himself to Chief Thomas, despite his relative inexperience. He was known as the cop with "poster boy looks;' but Rodney knew he also had "poster boy brains." He was a natural.

"I'm supposed to be in there tomorrow morning," Darrin answered. When the Chief didn't respond for a few seconds though he added "Do you need me before that, Chief?"

There was another long pause. Darrin looked up at Marilyn, who smiled at him and reached her arm out for his. "No...no, it can wait, Darrin," the Chief finally said. "Just make sure you talk to me first thing when you come in tomorrow. OK?"

Darrin squeezed Marilyn's arm, and returned her smile. He thought about the surprise new car, a shiny Ford Focus, that he had waiting for her in the garage of their new house. But, at the same time, his curiosity was up too. Especially with the Chief hesitating so much. He seemed so unsure of himself. Uncharacteristically so.

"OK then Chief," Darrin said as he and his new beautiful raven-haired wife walked arm in arm happily toward the baggage return. He almost ended the call there, but hesitated himself for a moment, then asked "Is there any kind of heads-up you can give me on the, uh, the situation you got there?"

For a few moments there was nothing, and Darrin was afraid the Chief had beat him to it and hung up. But then: "I wish I could. I don't know, really...I'll talk to you tomorrow, Darrin."

And then he really did hang up.

★   ★   ★

Father Mcgahee had already had a long, grueling, frustrating day with many of his parishioners, and despite all the listening he had done and advice he had dispensed, he didn't really understand why. Person after person from his flock at the St. Rose Parish had either called him or had actually come in to see him. Some had just came to church looking lost, and seeking sort of vague comfort, and were not particularly looking for a priest. But in sensing the general need, he had talked with many in that category too. Something was wrong, but despite all his efforts, they had mostly left without seeming to be comforted, and without ever really giving him a clear understanding of what they wanted.

So he was in truth somewhat irritated (despite just having prayed for patience and understanding) when he saw yet another person standing just outside his office/study, obviously waiting for him just as he was preparing to walk to his comfortable quarters for a late afternoon drink and dinner. He sighed, and actually thought about brushing past her on his way out-but quickly dismissed the idea.

She looked familiar, but he didn't associate her with the church. An attractive face he'd seen somewhere, yes, but not one he'd seen in the pews. He walked toward her, held out a hand and tried to smile benignly. "Hello, I'm Father Mcgahee," he said simply.

"Hello Father. My name is Janice Granger, and I'm not a Catholic," Janice said as she shook his hand. She immediately blushed.

Father Mcgahee chuckled. "Well, I'm glad we got that out of the way!" he said.

"I'm sorry. Long day," Janice said sheepishly. "I'm the City Manager here in Highland," she said. "You may know me from that. Perhaps you've seen my picture in the paper?" Then she blushed again, even more deeply.

"I thought you looked familiar," Father Mcgahee said patiently; kindly. "How can I help you, Janice? Conversion, perhaps?" He couldn't resist.

"No, no..." Janice smiled and looked down, obviously embarrassed. "I just wondered if I could talk to you for a few minutes." She looked back up and into his eyes. She hesitated a moment, then plunged ahead. "...About what's happening. What happened last night...what you've heard from people today..."

Father Mcgahee chuckled again, but his smile was having a hard time accompanying it. "Well, non-Catholics only get five minutes," he said half-jokingly. Then his smile disappeared altogether. "I'm afraid I won't be of much help to you." He looked past her and toward the (finally) empty church. "I probably have more questions than you do." Then he looked back at her sharply. "What happened last night?" he asked plaintively. "I was in St. Louis until late. Did something happen that I should know about?"

Janice looked back at him with surprise. "You really don't know? Didn't any of your, uh, flock tell you?"

Father shook his head. "Not really," he said.

Janice sighed, and looked away from him and out at the empty church for a moment. Father Mcgahee watched her intently. He could see already that even she, an important city official, was confused…and more than that… frightened. But of what? He could also see that she was tired, perhaps as tired as he was. He imagined that she must have talked to many, many more people than he that day.

She looked back into his eyes. "Do you think we could sit down for a minute?" she asked.

★   ★   ★

Detective Darrin Crandle looked out of the living room picture window (*his picture window!*) of his new home with a broad, unabashed smile on his face. Everything, finally, was just right, and he couldn't help himself. It was all perfect, in fact. As he watched the dusk of evening slowly descend on the Devonshire cul-de-sac, its newest resident couldn't help but think about how fortunate he was; how wonderful his world had become in just the last two years. 'If ever there was a time for self-congratulations," he thought, "this is it!"

Since the time, not all that long ago, that he had graduated at the top of his class at the police academy until this current moment as a first day proud, new husband and homeowner, it seemed to him now that nothing but good things, the best one could hope for, had come steadily his way. He'd found a job, immediately, that he loved. He had excelled in it, by any measure, and had already been promoted. He was respected-even admired-by his peers at the police department. Most of all, he'd met, courted and just married the most wonderful girl in the world. Marilyn was his true soul-mate (a romantic concept he would have cynically dismissed as impossible not all that long ago). He also had just had the best honeymoon ever, was a new home owner...and now... he could smell their first (and undoubtedly delicious) dinner cooking from where he stood giddily surveying his new world.

He was about to turn away and go try to help (bother) Marilyn in the kitchen when he saw his new next door neighbor, and now good friend, Jon Parker come out of his front door and walk toward the street to check his mailbox. "I'm gonna go say hi to Jon, honey! Be right back!" he yelled.

Marilyn was either too busy to answer, or didn't hear him, as some insistent oven alarm was going off at the time. Darrin was only going to take a minute anyway, so he proceeded out the front door and yelled "Hey Jon, what's up!" as soon as the door closed behind him.

Jon was already headed back up his driveway, flipping through his junk mail as he walked. Darrin's greeting seemed to startle him. He jumped a bit, dropped a piece of mail, then turned and tried to make out who had called out in the gathering dusk. It took him a disoriented moment or two to figure it out, but when he finally saw that it was his good friend advancing across the lawn he recovered quickly. "Darrin! When did you two get back? Congratulations! Welcome home, buddy!" he yelled out effusively.

A little too effusively, Darrin thought. Not in those exact words, of course. Darrin knew his friend Jon very, very well. They had worked on Darrin's first case together. He had been an invaluable, unofficial...and sometimes very unwilling... participant in the biggest case in Highland history. They had figured it out together (though it was still, technically, unsolved, of course). All their time together had taught Darrin to be able to read Jon like a book. And so as he walked over to shake hands with his old partner now he knew from even the few words that Jon had spoken; from the tone and ever so-slight tension in the sound of his voice-that Jon was upset about something.

It wouldn't take him long to find out what it was.

★   ★   ★

Chief Rodney Thomas was on his way home just after dark when City Manager Janice Granger called. They had talked a half-dozen times since their semi-successful group strategy meeting that morning.

"Yeah, Janice, what ya got?" he said in answering the phone. He appreciated the fact that she was so concerned about the "incident," when it technically had very little to do with her job. Indeed, as the day had worn on he had sensed that everyone else he worked with and talked to was increasingly inclined to put... whatever happened...behind them. He'd seen that before. The natural instinct of most people, in his experience, was to always gravitate back to comfortable normalcy as soon as possible, no matter what the trauma. Like a whole nation did after 9-11. Janice though, was different. She was smart; inquisitive, and she wouldn't rest until she had some kind of answer for all this. Just like him.

"I just left the church. Thought I'd stop and talk to the priest there, uh...what's his name?" she asked.

"Father Mcgahee? Father Franklin? Why did you go see a priest?"

"That first one you said. McMillen, or whatever. And I just thought I'd see if people were coming to see him today. See what they were telling him," Janice reported.

"Pretty smart," Rodney thought. "And what'd you find out?" he asked aloud.

"Not much," she said. "He was all worried about confidentiality and stuff, and he wasn't even in town last night when it happened."

29

"Did he give you anything at all?" Rodney asked. This was beginning to sound like every other conversation he'd had in the last 24 hours. A lot of vagary.

Janice didn't answer right away, but right about the time the Chief thought his phone had dropped another call she said "Sorry. I was pulling into my driveway. Hard for me to do two things at once sometimes."

"Know the feeling," he said patiently. Ironically, he was pulling up to his own house at the same moment.

"He...he did say something interesting though, finally, when I got him to trust me a little bit." She paused again. Looking for her keys? Then she came back: "Sorry again. Anyway, he said that more than one person complained about nightmares, and that they were reluctant to share the details about it. I thought that was strange...and he said several people talked about their pets. He said that they seemed more worried about their pets than anything. Weird, huh?"

"Yeah, weird," Rodney said. Weird, but nothing new, he thought. He had just parked his car and was getting out to walk up to his house. He found himself suddenly wanting to wrap up this conversation and walk into some normalcy for a while. If the damned dog was back to normal, that is. "Well, nothing helpful on my end either," he said. "I must have talked to every electricity expert in the..."

Janice screamed loud enough to make him rip the phone away from his ear. He stopped in mid-stride and stared at the offending i-phone as a chill raced through his body. He stared at it a moment, then gathered himself to tentatively pull it up to his ear again... but this time, the other ear. He heard nothing at first. "Janice?" he cried, "Janice? Are you there? What happened?"

There was a short, stifled sob, then "I'm...I'm sorry," she said once again, but this time choked with emotion. "My cat...my cat is dead. I'll call you back, OK?" And she hung up her phone.

Chief Rodney Thomas stood there on his front sidewalk for a full minute trying to calm his racing heart. She had temporarily scared the hell out of him... but the call had also activated something deeper in him too. A fear that he didn't want there; that would not easily go away. Something was very wrong. He knew it in his bones.

He eventually got himself together enough to walk up to his door. He heard fierce barking coming from right behind it, and a sense of dread crawled into his stomach again. He hesitated. But this was his house, damn it! He took one deep breath, then opened the door. Mitzi jumped onto his legs...and began licking him in frantic greeting, like she always did.

"Mitzi's better, Rod!" Joanie yelled happily from the kitchen. "Isn't it wonderful?"

Chapter 4
October 4th – 6:02 A.M.

Jim Ray Crawford woke from a blissfully sound sleep in a snap. He had been exhausted, had slept like a rock, but was fully awake the second his eyes opened.

It was still dark. 6:02. He reached his right hand out to feel for Brenda. She was still sound asleep and he could hear her breathing deeply. He quietly pulled back the covers, swung his legs around, grabbed his pants and shoes, then slipped silently out of the bedroom. He closed the door carefully, then finally took a natural breath as he walked out to his kitchen. Mission accomplished. He didn't want her awake when he went out to check the cattle.

They hadn't eaten, or even moved much since *it* had happened. They didn't even make noise. They just stood there, staring. Jim Ray knew, of course, that cows weren't too smart. He knew they could get sick. He'd worked with them since he was little, and he'd seen a little of everything over the years. But this? He'd never seen anything like this before. Not even remotely.

He poured a half a cup of newly-brewed coffee, took a few sips, then walked over to the door to put on his jacket and boots. "If they don't eat today, we call the vet," he whispered to himself. "...whether we can afford it, or not."

He got his flashlight out of the pantry (Brenda had long battled his penchant for putting his things in there, but finally, years ago, gave up and gave him a shelf), took another long sip from his cup, then turned on the back porch light and walked outside into the cool autumn morning air.

When things were normal, the very act of him turning on the light would be enough to elicit some rustling around and mooing from the cattle pens. At this time of year he could always hear them before he could see them. Now though, he heard nothing, and it made his heart sink a little-again. Something was very wrong. He knew it in his bones. Yet, as he crossed his back yard and approached the animals, he was hoping beyond hope that somehow they would look better, or show him *some* sign of normalcy, once he got there. Something!

A few steps later, still about 20 yards from where the cattle were, Jim Ray stopped in confusion. He was flashing the light in the area of the feed trough, the trough that they had been standing dumbly by for a day and a half...but they weren't there. He moved the light around, then back and forth. Nothing. "What the hell?" he muttered out loud.

He walked the rest of the way over and stopped right outside the fence. He made a long, slow sweep with the flashlight over the whole area, searching every place that his cows could be, from one end of the pens to the other, and then beyond. His anxiety began to build by the second. He could feel his heart beating faster, and he felt flushed. He kept moving the beam methodically, looking carefully at every inch it lit. There were no cows. There were no holes in the fence, or open gate. Nothing unusual. Nothing at all.

There were just no cows.

Then his flashlight flickered, but came right back on. Then it flickered again, and went out. "Damn it!" he cried. He shook the flashlight. It flickered. He turned toward the light coming from the back porch so he could see what he was doing.

Then the damned thing came on again. He had it pointed toward the house and at an upwards angle. It caught some kind of movement toward the top of his house when it came on, so he steadied it, and brought it back to that spot.

It was his little daughter Marsha, standing there in her nightgown, looking out of her bedroom window. She was smiling down at him.

★   ★   ★

Detective Crandle walked into the Chief's office at precisely 8:00 A.M. Chief Thomas was in his usual pose: feet up on his desk while studying the ceiling, with one hand holding his cell phone to his ear while the other ran nervously through his thinning black (though now gray-speckled) hair. He glanced over at Darrin when he entered, gave a weak smile, and motioned awkwardly with his elbow for him to have a seat. "Uh-huh...that's good. Uh-huh. OK. I got it," he said as he listened. He swung his feet down to the floor and put his elbows on his desk, but whoever he was listening to didn't take the obvious "let's wrap this up!" hint. So the Chief picked up a pencil and started tapping it impatiently on his desk, and kept on listening.

Darrin looked around the office while he waited. Rodney's office was as sparsely decorated as it was furnished, with only an obviously dated picture of his wife Joanie and another of his dog Mitzi adorning one wall, while the other three remained bare, years after he had occupied it. Darrin looked at the pictures for about the umpteenth time, and wondered to himself how in the world the Chief got away with having no kids (a thought that had never occurred to him before). Marilyn wanted at least three of them. She'd made that very clear, already.

"That's good news...very good. Yeah...listen Bob, my other phone's ringing. Yeah...gotta go. OK, then...talk to you soon!" Chief Thomas closed his phone with a loud snap and looked up glumly at Darrin. "The Superintendent of Schools just plain talks too much, ya know it?" he reported irritably. "You know him? Bob Warner?"

"Haven't had the pleasure," Darrin answered. "What did he want?"

"Oh, I called him actually," Rodney said as he leaned back in his chair, put his feet up on the desk, and resumed his normal office posture. "I wanted to check his attendance. About half his kids and teachers were sick, or weren't at school anyway, yesterday. He tells me that this morning everything is looking normal again, at least as far as he can tell." The Chief looked away from Darrin and up to his favorite spot on the ceiling. "And that's good," he added.

"What the hell happened, Chief?" Darrin asked.

Chief Thomas looked back down at his officer. "You don't know? You haven't heard anything yet?" he asked. The look on his face told Darrin that the Chief wasn't really looking forward to explaining things to him. And that made Darrin even more curious.

"I've only talked to one person...besides Marilyn, since we got back..."

"Oh yeah, congratulations on that, that marriage... by the way," the Chief interrupted.

"Thanks...anyway, I had a brief talk with my new neighbor, Jonathon Parker. You remember him, don't you?" Darrin said casually.

Chief Thomas couldn't help but snap his head back down from the ceiling to Darrin, but the rest of him didn't move. It was almost involuntary, as though he didn't want Darrin to see the visceral reaction he had had when that name was mentioned, but it didn't help. Darrin saw that his boss had very quickly turned pale, and he just as quickly surmised why.

"Sorry," was all he could think of to say. Then "Of course you remember," a few tense moments later.

The case that involved Jonathon Parker was one that no one involved would ever have a chance of forgetting. It had happened two summers ago, and it still occasionally invaded the dreams of Darrin, Chief Thomas, Jon Parker, and many of the town's residents; especially those who lived on Devonshire. It had involved the bizarre death and mutilation of policemen and animals alike. It was the first case, and the most notorious one that Darrin had worked on...and it was still unsolved; still technically on the books.

And there was no forgetting. Especially since Jon Parker had written a book about it. Or about most of it. It was the part he left out, the part that only Jon, Darrin and the Chief knew about - that still haunted them.

"And what did Mr. Parker tell you," Chief Thomas asked Darrin coldly. He still hadn't moved.

Darrin wriggled a bit in his seat. "He just said that some weird thing had happened about dinner time the night before I came home," Darrin said dismissively. He wanted to make the boss relax, but it was too late for that.

"And...?" The Chief asked through a penetrating stare.

"Nothing much else. He said it was like a flash, and it made him feel sick. Said he didn't go to school that day. That's all. We didn't talk for very long."

Chief Thomas glared at Darrin for another few moments, then looked back up at his ceiling, leaned back in his chair a little further, and seemed to visibly relax. "We still don't know what the hell happened," he told Darrin. "Still don't know...I talked to every expert I could think of, had a big meeting, sent people out to interview folks-everything I could think of." He looked at Darrin again. Darrin was looking at the Chief's bandaged hand. Funny, he hadn't noticed that before. "All I can tell you was that there was some sort of momentary...flash, I guess you'd say, and everything seemed different right afterwards. Everybody around here felt it," the Chief said.

"Anybody get hurt? Is that what happened to your hand?" Darrin asked.

Rodney looked at his bandaged appendage as though he was seeing it for the first time. "This...no...dog bit me. Mitzi, can you believe it?" he asked. Then he paused before adding "And that's another thing, by the way. This, this flash thing...it seemed to affect animals more than people. At least it seems like it. I know it sounds crazy. All I got is, all my evidence for saying that, is, ah... anecdotal...is that the word? Piecemeal evidence. Like me hearing dogs howling right afterwards, my dog going temporarily nuts...and Janice Granger, the, uh, City Manager?" he clarified needlessly, "...she found her cat dead with a broken neck, lying right inside her apartment door. Like a welcome mat or something."

Darrin couldn't help grinning, not at the Chief's tortured attempts to explain the unexplainable, but at the prospect of having a dead cat for a welcome mat. "Have you talked to any of the veterinarians yet?" he asked as he tried to choke back his smile. "You know, to see if this animal thing is widespread?"

The Chief resumed his glum stare at Darrin. "Glad you're back, you know it?" he finally said. "Do that first thing this morning, will ya?"

"Sure," Darrin answered.

"First though, let me fill you in on everything we have done; everybody we've talked to," Chief Thomas said as he leaned his head back again, "even though everything seems to be back to normal this morning." The Chief studied his ceiling and seemed to think it through for a minute before beginning. "I mean, whatever happened, it looks like it's...it's done now, you know what I mean?" he asked a bit sheepishly. "But it sure was a strange thing though, ya know?" he added a moment later.

★   ★   ★

The last thing that Sheriff Joe Blanton expected to see lying in the middle of the road that morning (or any other morning, for that matter) was a dead cow. True, it was a little-traveled country road. And true, he was used to seeing opossums, raccoons, rabbits, skunks and even the occasional deer lying with guts strewn on these country hard roads. But a cow? And here in the middle of nowhere, with woods on one side of the road and a yawning cornfield on the other? And without a farmhouse, electric fence or cattle pen in sight?

"Good Lord," he said aloud as he slowed his car down to pull over and have a look. He was both amazed and puzzled. Could it have fallen out of a truck somehow?

He slowed to a stop, put his car in park, and left the motor running. He wasn't planning on staying long. Just long enough to have a look.

The cool, crisp autumn air had a bite to it despite the bright early morning sun, so right after stepping out of his car the Sheriff reached into the back seat for his jacket. He had retrieved it, shut the door, and was in the act of quickly putting it on when he heard a low, but very distinct, growling. He froze there in position with his jacket half on, and listened intently. After a few seconds, the growling stopped. It seemed to have come from the woods by the side of the road, to his left, and whatever it was, it was close. Coyote?

After listening intently for half a minute more, the Sheriff quickly put his jacket the rest of the way on, unstrapped his weapon, then opened the front door of his car and reached in to turn off the engine, all the while trying to never take his eyes off the spot in the woods where he thought the growling had come from. After he shut the door, and with the car's engine now off, the world around him was suddenly plunged into a natural, if a bit eerie, silence. His ears strained to catch any sound at all. There was nothing but a distant cardinal's call. He stared into the woods and brush, looking for any movement at all, but saw nothing unusual. He kept his hand on his gun anyway. A rabid animal, of any kind, was dangerous...and crazy.

A minute went by. He gave a quick glance over to the dead cow, then looked back at the woods. Did that bush just move? Or was it just his vivid imagination...

After another minute, he began cautiously walking over to the dead animal in the road, while never taking his eyes off the woods for more than a second or two at a time. When he got within a few feet he could see it clearly, even though the animal was facing away from him. The head was at the wrong angle from the body. The neck was broken, and even from where he stood he could see that the throat had a deep gash in it. Thick, deep red blood was still oozing steadily out of the wound, and pooling around the head. "This thing just got killed!" he said aloud, and then quickly stepped back to avoid stepping into the rapidly spreading blood and gore. "God almighty," he mumbled to himself a few moments later, after taking a deep breath. "Scarin' yourself, Joe boy," he added in self-admonition.

He shook his head, reached for his phone to call in a dead cow, of all things, and was turning to walk back to his car as he did so when the growling started again. It was a low, menacing snarl, louder than before, and close. His eyes shot to the woods, and this time he saw (and heard) movement in the bushes. For sure. He froze right where he was and watched intently. The growl stopped as abruptly as it had started. The bushes stopped moving, too. All was silent again.

Slowly, carefully, he put his phone back in its holster, and drew his gun.

Chapter 5
October 4th 9:33 A.M.

"There's a police officer here to see you, Dr. A Detective Crandle?"

It had always irritated Doctor Norton when Gloria, his receptionist/assistant for nearly 20 years, ended her statements with a question. It irritated him, but she had been doing it more often than not for the whole time she had been working for him, and he knew it would never stop. He had confronted her about it only once, on a particularly bad day many years before, and she had cried for almost a week. Dr. Norton, as mild-mannered and non-confrontational as he was sensitive, vowed to himself way back then that he would never do anything, or say anything, to ever hurt her again. And he never had. Still, did 'A Detective Crandle?' mean 'Do you know this guy?' or 'Are you expecting a policeman?' or 'Should I show him in?' or 'Do you think that's his real name?' or what?

It was a relatively minor aggravation that he was bound to live with, but, nonetheless it made him want to take an immediate vacation. "Show him in, Gloria. Thank you," he answered meekly.

"I'm Detective Crandle," Darrin said as they shook hands 90 seconds later.

"James Norton," the veterinarian answered. "Hope everything's OK?" he added awkwardly. Darrin had seen the doctor turn very red the moment he had walked into the office, and as he shook the man's slightly shaking, sweaty hand, he wondered why.

"Everything's fine, I'm sure," Darrin answered. "I appreciate you seeing me. I'll just bother you for a minute. Just have a few questions, if you don't mind."

Dr. Norton invited him to sit down. His office was as plush and heavily decorated (ornamented really) as Chief Thomas' was plain, Darrin noticed. There didn't seem to be one space on the wall that didn't have a diploma, award or picture and the expensive leather chair he was invited to sit on was so comfortable it felt like physical therapy. "Vets must really clean up," Darrin thought.

Rather than sit next to his guest, the doctor moved to the more modest chair behind his desk. When he got there and was situated he asked the inevitable, obvious question. "How can I help you, sir?"

Darrin could see that this guy wanted to get this over with in the worst way. He saw him glance at the clock before Darrin could even respond."First of all, have you noticed anything...let's say, unusual in any of the animals you've treated in the last day or so?" Darrin asked.

The doctor's magnified eyes blinked behind his thick glasses. He seemed a bit confused by the question, or at least took an inordinate amount of time before answering.

"No," he finally said.

"No?" Darrin asked. The doctor nodded firmly. Darrin could see that he would have to find a way to put this man at ease if he was going to get anything at all. He took a deep breath, looked up at a picture of a beagle with a medal around its neck on the wall behind the doctor, and gave it a try. "Something happened here in Highland, and in parts of the area surrounding Highland the other night. No one seems to know exactly what it was...some of the guys are calling it a 'flash,' but others say that doesn't really describe it. Anyway, there's more we don't know than know about

41

what happened...did you feel it by the way Doctor? The 'flash' thing?"

The doctor stared at him through the thick glasses. He offered no response. He may have been trying to formulate a careful answer, but Darrin had no way of knowing. He thought it more likely that the old boy was stonewalling, for some reason, so he decided to push on to the meat of the matter. "Anyway Doctor ...one thing that we have noticed, is that after the thing happened, some animals -dogs and cats...you know, they started acting strange. Getting aggressive like..." Darrin said awkwardly. The doctor just looked at him, with only an occasional huge blink disrupting his stare. "My boss for instance," Darrin continued, "his dog, a really nice dog, just attacked him. Bit the hell out of him!" Despite the fact that the doctor remained expressionless, Darrin immediately regretted using the word "hell" in his last sentence. Somehow, the doctor looked like the kind of guy who would be offended by it. "Anyway," Darrin trudged on, straining toward the finish, "we wondered if you had anybody report that kind of thing to you... or maybe brought their animal in? Anything?"

Darrin stopped there and waited. Dr. Norton looked at Darrin and blinked, but said nothing. Darrin looked back at him and waited. He was beginning to get angry with this veterinarian. Why was he so nervous? Why be so uncooperative? Was he afraid he would give away animal secrets or something? It was ridiculous.

The doctor's intercom buzzer buzzed and Darrin almost jumped a foot. After a long moment the doctor slowly, reluctantly reached over and pushed the button. "Yes?" he said.

"Doctor, your 10:00 appointment is here at 9:45. Mrs. Beastley? And Cookie?"

Dr. Norton sighed. "I'll be with them shortly," he said. He leaned back and looked at Darrin briefly, and seemed to be about to say something when he instead abruptly leaned forward again to quickly hit the button. "And thank you, Gloria!" he said, in a much louder voice than he had used before. Then he leaned back again, and to Darrin's surprise, actually said something. "Four," he said, and then paused, as if searching for more than one word.

Darrin's patience was disappearing, so he thought he would help him. "Four what?" he asked sharply.

As the doctor cleared his throat and squirmed in his seat Darrin thought "If I ever get a dog I'm gonna let it die before takin' it to this guy."

"Four cases of animals that bit, or attacked people," the doctor finally said. "All of them yesterday. None so far today."

Darrin waited. When the doctor didn't volunteer anything else in the next few moments he asked, "Is that unusual?"

"Very!" the doctor answered immediately. "I've never seen such a thing. I know these pets. The attacks weren't in, uh, character, for any of them."

"What do you think happened, Doctor?" Darrin asked. He was trying to be careful with his questions. Now that the pump was primed, he didn't want to accidentally shut it off.

"I don't know," Dr. Norton said resignedly. For the first time he looked away from Darrin. He seemed to be studying one of the diplomas on his wall. "My own dog went wild for a while too. Better now though." He shifted his glance from the wall back to Darrin. He leaned toward him and put his elbows on the desk and looked at him intensely. "If I were you, I'd check with the medical doctors, and the dog pound...the animal shelters. People who get hurt by animals don't get patched up by me. And they only bring their pets to me after being attacked...and only sometimes, if they love them. Many would just get rid of their animals." The doctor sat back again, appearing to be exhausted by his little speech. "I should be getting back to my patients now," he added a few moments later.

Darrin looked at the doctor in wonder, for a long moment. This guy was a strange birs alright, but, at least a bit helpful in the end."OK, Doc," Darrin responded. He stood up and offered his hand to Dr. Norton. The doctor seemed confused for a few seconds, then realized he was supposed to shake hands again and did so, though awkwardly. Darrin held onto his hand a little longer than usual so that he could look him in the eye and ask one more question. "Level with me Doc," he said, "Why do you think animals, or some animals, were affected, and people weren't?"

Dr. Norton pulled his hand away and looked down. He looked, suddenly, visibly upset. His face turned bright red again. "I think, perhaps, people were affected just as much," he finally said, "but maybe...maybe we just don't realize it yet."

★　　　★　　　★

Bart Melville stood in his plush National Bank office in downtown St. Louis and stared out the window onto the street below. He had been at work for three hours (having gotten there an hour before he had to) and he still hadn't accomplished a thing. He couldn't, and knew deep down that he wouldn't. No matter how hard he tried.

It was arguably worse at work than at home. Here at the bank there was no one to talk to. There was no one who would, or could, understand. The one (quickly aborted) attempt that he had made to confide in someone else had been a disaster. Jerry Clemons had listened to him patiently all right , but was undoubtedly left puzzled and more than a little alarmed by an executive who wanted to talk about a "horrible flash moment" that almost made him get in a car accident, and about a horrible dream that he'd had afterwards that "almost gave me a heart attack!" That conversation, that reaching out, had been a mistake. He knew that right after he tried. He was sure now, in retrospect, that Clemons wouldn't hesitate to bring that up around the water cooler. He was pretty sure he'd already gotten some strange looks from a couple of his co-workers.

But as he stood there aimlessly watching the people walking busily down the sidewalk below him he also knew that Clemons and the rest of them weren't all that important. In fact, for the last two days - his whole job didn't seem that important. He was miserable. Increasingly so. He felt like he was going crazy. The dream (which he'd had twice in two nights), the lack of sleep... the terrible thoughts. He had to do something.

Bart's cell phone rang. For him, in the state of mind he was in right then, it was like a perfectly timed call to action. He checked to see who it was. It wasn't his wife, Nancy, so he didn't answer it. Instead he walked purposefully over to his desk, sat down at his laptop, and Googled the words "psychiatrist" and "St. Louis."

★   ★   ★

"Someone stole your cows? Is that what you're telling me sir?"

The Sheriff's Office Dispatcher made it sound ridiculous by repeating it, as he knew it would. "Yes ma'am. At least that's what I think happened," Jim Ray Crawford said. "I don't see how they could have though, to tell you the truth," he added confusingly.

"And you live just off of County Road 24, just south of Alhambra. Isn't that what you said, Mr. Crawford?"

"Yes, that's what I said. That's where I live," Jim Ray answered. This whole conversation embarrassed him terribly, but he didn't know what else to do. He hated conversation in general, but one like this, where he was made to feel like a fool, was a nightmare.

"How do you think they did that, Mr. Crawford? Steal your, your cows I mean?" Jim Ray didn't answer right away, so she continued. "I mean, were there truck tire tracks around where the cows were? Was there a gate left open? Are you sure the cows haven't just...wandered off somewhere?"

After she said that Jim Ray distinctly heard a muffled giggle. It made him blush with anger and embarrassment. "No, the cows aren't out playing hide and seek, ma'am," he fired back. "They don't do that. My gates are closed, my fence isn't broken. They're just gone," he added in exasperation. "Can you just report that please? Can you tell Sheriff Blanton, please?"

The Dispatcher didn't answer immediately. Jim Ray imagined her wracked with laughter, holding her hand to her mouth in a desperate attempt to keep him from hearing. "OK, Mr. Crawford," she said finally. He didn't hear any smirking in her voice. "I haven't been able to raise him yet today, but as soon as I do, I'll let him know."

"Thank you," a miserable Jim Ray said.

"We'll get him, or a deputy out there as soon as we can," the Dispatcher promised.

★   ★   ★

It was on the walk home, right after he'd gotten off the school bus, that Bobby Meachum thought about the Bensons' little beagle. He'd actually had a dream about the thing the night before; straining at the leash to try to get at him, black eyes looking crazed and vicious. There was a part of him that wanted to stop in that alley and check it out. And there was also a part of him that really, really didn't want to.

It was his need for a joint to mellow out the day that eventually won him over to the "why not check it out" part. It had been what he liked to term a "half and half" day (half bad because all the teachers and kids were back, and it was school as usual-and half good because they had gotten out at noon because of a teachers' institute), and that was all the excuse he needed to sneak into the alley and toke up before he got home. Besides, he reasoned, the dog probably wouldn't be tied out there anyway.

But the dog was. Bobby was already several steps into the alley, and had already stopped to light up before he saw it. An instant, but very brief chill ran down his spine, like in the first moment one unexpectedly sees a mouse scuttering across the floor. But it left him as quickly as it had arrived, because the dog was wagging his tail, and seemed to be almost smiling at him!

Bobby let out the long stream of smoke he'd been holding in his lungs with as much relief as pleasure. "Thank God," he said aloud a moment later. "Little dog's back to normal."

He took another toke and watched the dog as it laid down on its stomach in the ancient act of submission to master, with its tail wagging away. It was obviously begging for attention; to be petted. "Feeling better today, little guy?" Bobby said in the same baby talk voice that everyone seems to use when addressing pets. "You recognize Bobby now, don't you? Don't you little puppy?" he said as he walked over to the happy beagle. Bobby looked up at the house to make sure no one was looking out. It was dark. All the curtains were closed. No one at home.

He reached down to pat the dog's bowing head. Its tongue lolled out in appreciation of Bobby's gentle stroke. "There you go beagle baby. You're just a wittle wittle doggy aren't you?" Bobby cooed.

The bite came so fast and so hard, and shocked him so badly, that he could do nothing at first but watch in horrified shock and silence. The dog's mouth, its grip, almost completely covered his suddenly blood covered hand, and would not let go.

In dumb shock, Bobby actually witnessed his own blood begin to pool rapidly on the ground beneath the dog's jaw. Only when the first paralyzing shot of pain raced from the shattered bones in his hand, up his arm and then through his whole body- was he was finally able to scream.

Chapter 6
October 4th 4:27 P.M.

The 4:00 afternoon meeting didn't start until nearly 4:30. It was again Police Chief Thomas' fault. He was late for two reasons: he had had to interview young officer Ben Christopher about (of all things) a dog attack, and then shooting, and he had taken a disturbing call from the State Police on his way to the meeting.

Darrin was actually twiddling his thumbs when Chief Thomas entered the conference room. There were only two other people there-Janice Granger and himself.. It was disappointing, but not surprising. "Afternoon fellas," the Chief said, once again inadvertently insulting the female in the room. "Sorry, I'm late. Couldn't be helped. Had an officer to interview about a dog attack, believe it or not." He moved to his seat at the long table. "Had to shoot the damned thing. Anybody else coming?" he asked, looking at Janice.

"The Mayor said he was too busy. I'm not sure about Sheriff Blanton and the others," she answered quietly. She looked a little despondent. It had been her responsibility to notify everyone.

"Well, Sheriff Blanton won't be here," the Chief said grimly. "Just got a phone call a few minutes ago from the State boys. "Seems that they found his car, abandoned, on a country road by some woods between Grantfork and Alhambra. Out in the middle of nowhere, fellas. Looks like he'd stopped there to look at, or maybe he even hit... what they said was a half-eaten cow lying beside the road."

Janice and Darrin stared at the Chief in surprise. Janice was the first to speak. "Oh no!" she said. "What do they mean? Is he considered, uh, missing?"

"Half-eaten cow?" Darrin asked. "They said 'half-eaten cow'? Out there?"

"Yep. Had to be coyotes. I know Joe, and my bet is that he saw them, and went traipsin' off after them," the Sheriff said. His words were more reassuring than the tone of his voice. "He'll show up. I know Joe. He'll come back with two dead coyotes and a big, silly grin on his face, wondering what all the fuss is about," he added.

Darrin wasn't buying it. "How many coyotes would it take to eat half a cow? Why wouldn't he call it in, even if he was going after them? Do you think we should go up there and help search?" His mind was working too fast, and he didn't really expect an answer to his questions. He just knew that things were getting increasingly bizarre; increasingly alarming. Especially when it came to animals, and their behavior. It didn't make sense.

"First of all," the Chief said patiently, "It's not our jurisdiction. Secondly, we haven't been asked. Not yet. Like I say, Joe knows his way around. If he still hasn't shown up by morning, then, well..."

But Darrin was hardly listening. He was thinking instead of the odd interviews he'd had with people all day long, and how, in a very weird way, this latest news fit. He was sure that when he heard from Janice, and then the Chief in the next few minutes that their stories would have the same tenor as his own - people were shook, but didn't know why. Not really. Nightmares that no one wanted to talk about (even if you could get them to admit that they had them in the first place), bizarre, unaccountable animal behavior (Officer Christopher had had to shoot a dog that bit a kid's hand half off just a few hours before). And worst of all, there was a feeling out there-still vague and largely unspoken, yet unmistakable - that something *larger* was wrong; that something had changed, and changed for the worse. It was an inexplicable darkness that he couldn't quite see. But it was growing, even if everyone wanted to avoid it...to make it go away.

His mind phased back in to listen to Janice, who had been giving her report to the Chief, because the tone of her voice had changed. "...a couple of people have admitted, the nightmares to me. That they had them. But they won't describe them." She paused then and looked hard at Darrin, and then Chief Thomas. Her eyes and mouth gave away the strong emotion that she was feeling, but trying to control. "I had a nightmare too, guys. A few hours after I found Socks," she said shakily. She paused before continuing, studying the both of them, as though desperate to get reassurance from them. The Chief nodded calmly and without expression.. Darrin was temporarily confused, frankly wondering what finding her socks had to do with nightmares; but quickly enough remembered the "cat as welcome mat" line that the Chief had used. Belatedly, he nodded for her to go on too.

Janice sighed, as if already regretting what she was about to say. "I don't know what it has to do with anything," she began apologetically, 'but since there's just the three of us here. I think I need to get this out. Maybe it'll help somehow...I don't know...I can tell you that it was the worst nightmare I ever had. Nothing else comes close. And it keeps coming back. Even during the day, in flashes, like." She spread both of her hands out on the table and looked at them. Finally, shehe went on, with a steadier voice: "It...it's hard to put it into...narrative form. I still don't know the order of things; in the dream I mean. I can only do that when I get one of those 'flashes'." She blushed slightly. She studied her hands, and wouldn't look up. "There were dead animals all around me, but they were still walking around. You could tell they were dead, because they had terrible wounds, missing limbs-even heads. And...and the ones with heads, their eyes were all red." She shuddered visibly, took a deep breath, then went on: "The worst part though, were the children. There were dead children too." She choked slightly when she said this, and she pressed her outstretched hands down on the table harder and harder. She couldn't know it because she wouldn't look up, but the other two were staring at her, mesmerized.

"The children....they were floating around me," Janice said hesitantly "They were smiling...they were white...too white, and their eyes were all red, and dead looking. And their hair was... wild. Not combed. No one was helping them, or caring for them. And they were, well, growling... and some of them were eating the animals. And I looked down, and one of them was chewing on my arm. I couldn't get away! I just looked at it, and it was eating me... but they were little children!"

At this, Janice stopped, sobbed once, then stopped. Darrin knew she was done then, and was afraid she was about to burst into tears. Chief Thomas unexpectedly got to his feet and walked around the table. Janice was still staring at her hands and taking deep breaths, obviously trying to regain her composure. The Chief awkwardly put his hand on her shoulder to try to comfort her. Darrin thought that his boss looked as pale and shaken as the City Manager.

For that matter, he wasn't feeling too hot himself.

★　　　★　　　★

"She's a good person, Janice is. She does good work, and she's the only one around here that sees the big picture, sometimes. But I'll tell ya...that surprised me," Rodney Thomas said. The Chief's feet were back up on his desk as he sat in the comfort of his own drab office, not twenty minutes after Janice had confessed her horrific nightmare. He was struggling to answer Darrin, who had silently followed him back to where the Chief felt the most comfortable, and had broken a long silence by asking his boss what he had thought about Janice's outburst. "I don't know what to think, Darrin, to tell you the truth," the Chief added.

Chief Thomas was a rational man who prized common sense and solutions. He was at his worst, or at least the most uncomfortable, when something didn't fit the script; when something illogical or emotional stood in the way of the "facts." Darrin had realized this way back when the two first worked together, over two years ago now. The case of the murders on Devonshire (or the "Haunting in Highland," as it became known) had almost undone him. It still bothered him. And now, the way things were beginning to happen; the strange, illogical series of events... and with the totally unexpected nightmarish confession of a sensible City Manager that he thought the world of, the Chief undoubtedly felt like he was wobbling off center. Darrin knew all of that, just by looking at him. And he felt much the same way.

"Chief, I've got to bring this up," Darrin began carefully.

Chief Thomas snapped out of his easy-going countenance immediately, and looked hard across the desk at Darrin. "Don't go there, Darrin!" he growled in anticipation, "I don't want to hear it!"

His quick reaction startled Darrin, but probably shouldn't have. He knew the Chief too well. The old guy was way ahead of him.

Darrin let a few moments pass in silence, before deciding he wasn't going to follow this particular order. And they both knew that, too. Still, he let the Chief cool off a few seconds before trying the same thing - from a different angle. "What do you know about Scott Air Force Base?" he finally asked.

"What?" the Chief asked with irritation and confusion.

"I think Janice, uh...did her thing out there, you know, told us about her dream, because she thinks...well now she knows, that a lot of people are having that trouble. Dreams, I mean."

"I know that," Rodney snapped defensively.

"Well, just listen a minute," Darrin pleaded. He felt like he was fighting for time. He didn't know how much fuse was left to burn before his boss went off. "Suppose they did something, inadvertently, or experimentally in one of those jets flying out of Scott? They're only what, 20 miles away? Maybe they tested some kind of new, I don't know...whatever they test, and it made a new kind of sonic boom, maybe. And maybe that was the flash. And the flash, or whatever it was, kind of threw everything out of whack. Our dogs and cats go nuts first, because they can hear it better, right? It messes them up. and the people? Well, they don't realize it, but they're affected too. They start having dreams and..."

"You're full of shit, you know it?" Chief Thomas interrupted. Then he half grinned at his detective. "You're good at what you do, but sometimes you're full of it, boy."

Darrin smiled back at him sheepishly. "Well, hell...you never know, right?" he answered defensively, "I'm just saying, that if things keep going like this, we've got to think creatively, right?"

Chief Thomas leaned back in his chair, smiling more broadly now, and at least temporarily looking more relaxed. "I suppose you're right, Darrin," he said breezily to the ceiling. "Keep thinking boy, keep thinking..." then he shot a mild warning glance at his young detective. "Just don't do any more thinking about those... ghosts, or whatever, in those woods behind Devonshire, OK?" he asked, forcing a chuckle as he did.

★　　　★　　　★

Bart Melleville was nervous, and it showed. Dr. Goldstein could see the thin layer of perspiration on his upper lip, and his forehead was creased with worry. He guessed, quite correctly, that this handsome middle-aged banker had never seen a psychiatrist before.

"Thank you for seeing me on such short notice, Doctor." Bart said politely. "It is Doctor, right?"

Dr. Goldstein smiled at the question. It was a common one at initial sessions. "Yes, that's right Mr. Melleville. I am a doctor. And you're welcome."

The doctor then went on to talk about procedural matters, and saying things designed to make Bart feel more comfortable for the next five minutes. Bart fidgeted and appeared to only half listen. Dr. Goldstein could see that. Anxiety, both physical and emotional, in a new patient was understandable, even normal.

But this patient appeared to be particularly nervous and distressed, and so the doctor wasn't particularly surprised when he immediately and vehemently jumped in as soon as he saw an opening.

'…so Mr. Melleville, if you'd now like to tell me about…"

"Dr. Goldstein, there's nothing really wrong with me," Bart began. "I'm happily married, we *mutually* decided not to have kids, I'm happy with my work, my father didn't beat me, and I had a wonderful mother who did not spoil me. I think…I think we can skip over all of those parts, OK?"

The doctor was not surprised. In fact, based on the physical clues his new patient had been giving him, he'd expected as much. He smiled benignly, looked briefly down at his clip board, then up at Bart. "OK, Mr. Melville, why don't you relax, and tell me what you'd like to talk about today."

Bart looked at the doctor for a long moment, then abruptly sighed, loosened his tie and leaned back into his chair. He seemed suddenly resigned, and perhaps a little relieved at not getting the verbal confrontation he'd expected. "It's a nightmare that I've had. Twice now. The last two nights. A nightmare worse than any I've ever had. Thought I was going to have a heart-attack afterwards. I really did." He raised his head up long enough to look the doctor in the eye. "This is going to sound crazy you know," he stated flatly. The doctor merely nodded. "I guess you're used to that though, huh?... Crazy, I mean?"

Dr. Goldstein smiled warmly again. "Go on Mr. Melleville," is all he said.

Bart laid his head back again. He closed his eyes. "Something strange happened the other night, on the 2nd. I was driving home, only about 15 minutes away from the house, something…like an electrical charge or something happened. For a second I thought I was going to lose control of the car. It was bad, but I can't tell you exactly what it was. I really can't. Whatever it was, it affected the other drivers on the highway too. Everybody slowed down. A few cars even pulled over. So I'm not nuts on that part. I wasn't the only one." He looked up at the doctor again briefly, then laid his head back again. "Anyway, I'm telling you that part because that was the night of the nightmare. Just a few hours later. Somehow, over the last couple of days...it seems like the two things might be related. It seems like a possibility, somehow." Bart paused. He sighed aloud again.

"Go on," the doctor urged after a few moments.

Bart took another deep breath. He closed his eyes again, tightly. "OK, here's the crazy part. That night I dreamed I was in some kind of hilly field. There were woods close by. I could see everything very clearly. Even the blades of grass I was standing in. Not like in most dreams. Anyway, I'm standing there when I suddenly start to notice that there are animals, dead animals, mostly wolves, I think...but all kinds-all around me in the grass. And they're dead...but they're still moving, like baring their teeth, which they weren't doing when I looked just a second before. They would suddenly stand up and walk toward me. Then stop and lay down again. Like that." Bart paused and swallowed hard. Then he went on. "Well, I'm pretty horrified at all this. I mean they're closing in on me, gradually, and its not like a normal dream, where you know you're going to wake up. Where you *know* you're dreaming. Not like that at all. But...that isn't the worst part. I...I suddenly get a hard tap on the shoulder, or a shove in the back like- I don't remember. Anyway, I turn around and...God it was horrible, horrible! I turn around and there's all these kids... children. They're...they're dressed in white robes, and just floating there... smiling, with these glowing red eyes...I mean, I think they were dead too. And about the time I notice that they're floating towards me, which was horrifying, I feel this incredible, sharp pain in my stomach. I don't want to take my eyes off them, but the pain in my gut is killing me, so I look down...and that's when I see one of them, a little girl, actually eating my stomach, and she looks...oh God...she looks up at me with this bloody smile... and..."

Bart opened his eyes and sat bolt upright. He was shaking and, the doctor could plainly see, suddenly perspiring heavily. "I'm sorry...sorry," Bart gasped as fought for breath. "I'm OK. I'm sorry," he mumbled helplessly.

Dr. Goldstein didn't answer, or offer any of the comforting, reassuring words he might have been expected to give to this traumatized patient. He just sat in stunned amazement, looking past Bart Melleville and in the general direction of the wall behind the gasping banker. He was wondering, in astonishment, how it was possible to have the exact same nightmare described to him, by two new patients...in one day.

★   ★   ★

It was getting very late in the afternoon and getting darker by the minute under the trees where he was searching. He hadn't eaten all day, was bone tired, and he was about to give up to head out of his section of woods when his cell phone rang. It badly startled Deputy Sheriff Harvey Milton. He was very upset as it was, and half-spooked, being alone out in the middle of nowhere desperately looking for his boss and life-long friend, Sheriff Joe (as he always, affectionately, called him). He was angered by the jarring noise, so when he pulled his phone out he was more than prepared to be cross with whoever was bothering him at a time like this. But when he looked at the number that was calling and saw-to his overwhelming relief and joy-that it was Sheriff Joe himself-he was suddenly happier than he could ever remember.

"Where in God's name have you been, you old fart!" he practically yelled into the phone as soon as he could bring it up to his ear. "We've been tearin' up hell lookin' for ya!"

He didn't hear anything, so he moved a few paces and readjusted the phone on his ear. "Joe?" he asked. Nothing. Then he tried "Hello?" a few moments later. He heard nothing. Under normal circumstances Harvey would have impatiently hung up by now. But this call was different. Far different. "Joe?...You there Joe?"

Then he heard something. It was faint at first, and it stopped and started several times. He stood still there in the darkening woods and listened as intently as he could listen. "Joe?" he asked hopefully once again, even though he was getting a sinking feeling in his stomach.

Very suddenly, the sound was back. It was much clearer now, as though, inexplicably, it was now right next to him. He listened, and as he did, he began to feel almost sick...and then, gradually... deeply frightened.

It was the sound of a child. Then several children. He couldn't tell if it was boys or girls. But they were laughing into the phone, giggling together-over and over again.

Chapter 7
October 4th 5:33 P.M.

Detective Crandle went home soon after his office talk with Chief Thomas. Despite the growing uneasiness he was feeling with the things he was hearing and with the seemingly bizarre events that had taken place, his mind kept turning back to Marilyn. Their honeymoon had been wonderful, but too short, he thought, and despite everything else all his idle thoughts that first day back to work had been spent on fantasies of going away with her again. She had become everything to him, and that fact had been wholly reinforced by having, basically, a depressing day of interviewing depressed people. He couldn't wait to walk in his front door, grab up his new wife, kiss her, and hug the hell out of her.

But she wasn't home. He remembered why as soon as he pulled into the driveway. "Remember honey, I have a teachers meeting after school tonight," she had told him that morning. "I'll be home late." Late for her usually meant 5:30 or so, which wasn't late for him, so he hadn't really paid much attention. Another example of him being a "selective listener," as Marilyn often said.

He parked his car in the driveway (the garage had too many unpacked boxes in it to hold two cars) and walked toward the street to check the mailbox. It was a wonderful early October early evening. After having spent so much time each day in the sun, on the beach or lounging on the veranda of their honeymoon suite, it was hard, especially in the waning days of a beautiful fall, for him to be sentenced to the indoors again. He took his time, standing for a while at the mailbox, looking over the mail (Bills? Already?) while breathing in the crisp, chilly air.

"What's up, Darrin!" His next door neighbor and best friend, Jon Parker, was walking out to check his own mail. Jon taught English at the high school, and Darrin's first thought was: if Jon's home, why wasn't Marilyn?

"How come you aren't at the teacher meeting?" Darrin asked.

Jon slowed, and gave a confused look at his neighbor. "What teachers' meeting?" he asked.

"Marilyn's not home because of a teacher meeting. Aren't you a teacher?"

Now Jon understood. "She's a grade school teacher, dipshit," he said smiling. "I teach high school. We don't go to the same meetings."

"Oh," Darrin said, as though he understood.

"Boy, we can't stand to have the little woman very far away, can we?" Jon teased. He opened the mailbox. No mail. He closed it again and turned back to Darrin. "Hey, why don't you come over for a beer? A welcome home beer."

Darrin hesitated. Without thinking, he actually looked up the street to see if she might be turning into the cul-de-sac, which of course provided more ammunition for Jon.

"Don't worry, we'll sit by the window so you can come running out when your little darling comes home," he said.

"Shut up," Darrin snarled. He looked up at beautiful early evening sky. The few high clouds that were there were starting to turn purple as the sun headed for the horizon. This was supposed to be the last nice day for a while. Rain was moving their way. "Yeah, I'll have a beer," he said definitively. "But only if we can sit out on your deck while we're drinking it." He smiled. "Like the old days," he said.

★   ★   ★

Brenda Crawford was trying to tell her husband (who wasn't really listening) how concerned she was about how their daughter Marsha was acting "different" in the last few days when their doorbell rang. Jim Ray jumped up from the table like a runner hearing the starting gun to get to the door first. He had no competition, as his totally absorbed red-cheeked wife continued to pour out her thoughts even after her attention-challenged husband had bolted from the room, and his daughter was no where to be found.

Jim Ray opened the door to a frowning, bedraggled looking gray-haired man in a noticeably wrinkled and dirt-stained Deputy Sheriff's uniform. "I'm Harvey Milton, from the Sheriff's office," he said almost distractedly. Then, reluctantly: "I've come about your missing cows?"

Jim Ray had been prepared to light into whoever finally showed up from the Sheriff's office. It had been, after all, seven hours and fifteen minutes since he had made the call. But that all changed by the very appearance of the man standing before him. He recognized stress, and exhaustion from hard work when he saw it. He made an instant change-of plans.

"I'm Jim Ray Crawford," he said as he stepped outside into the porch light over his front door and closed it behind him. "Let me show you where they were. Do you have a flashlight? Its almost dark, and we may need one. Mine keeps going out."

The Deputy Sheriff simply nodded. He walked out to his car, got his flashlight and then followed Jim Ray around the old farmhouse, through the back yard, and back to the empty cattle pens. At Jim Ray's insistence, they walked around the pens, the closed gates and the unbroken fence. It all proved nothing, of course, but it made Jim Ray feel better for him to see.

"That's the way it was when I came out early this morning," Jim Ray said. "I swear. Them cows had to have been stolen, cause there was no way out."

"Did you search for them anyway, Mr. Crawford, before you called it in?" Harvey asked wearily.

"Course I did!" Jim Ray said. He expected the question, but it still got his dander up a bit. "My land, and everybody else's around here. No sign of 'em."

Deputy Sheriff Milton shined his light absently around the same area they'd just walked. Jim Ray supposed he was looking for tracks, or clues of some kind. "Did you find any tire tracks, or hear anything unusual in the last couple of days," he asked, "or anything else that I, er, we could use in looking for your cattle?" he asked.

"Nothing," Jim Ray said. "Nothing at all." Jim Ray had decided beforehand that he wasn't going to report that his cows were acting oddly, and not eating, or for that matter that his daughter was pretty much acting the same way. He didn't have to listen to Brenda to know that something odd was up with little Marsha. She had seemed so concerned about the cows after it first happened, for instance, and that was *very* unusual...but now, she didn't seem to even care that they were gone.

But he wasn't going to share any of that. It was bad enough to be made fun of by that lady on the phone.

"We found a dead cow today," the Deputy Sheriff said nonchalantly, "but it was miles from here. Too far away to be one of yours. And it was just one cow." He looked out over Jim Ray's field. "Doubt if you could identify it though. It was pretty torn up." He looked at the cattle pens again, then turned toward Jim Ray. "Ever have trouble with coyotes out here, Mr. Crawford?"

Jim Ray found himself getting quickly irritated by what he considered to be an irrelevant question. "No. Not at all. And as far as I know, they ain't too good at opening gates and then closing them again, are they?" he snarled.

Then, as if to answer, a chilling, very close-sounding coyote howl, then another, then another, suddenly shattered the rural stillness of the young evening. The howls seemed to be coming from all around the two men, who were just as suddenly struck with confusion, awe and alarm.

The two of them were too stunned by the suddenness of it to be frightened. Deputy Sheriff Milton's flashlight swept erratically first toward one howl, then another, but it caught nothing unusual in its beam.

★   ★   ★

"I didn't see anything, unusual or otherwise, out there. I didn't hear anything either. Nothing!" Jon said definitively-and with obvious (if slightly feigned) irritation.

Although Darrin, without a doubt, thought he was being subtle with his approach, Jon could read his friend like a book. Always had been able to, he thought. He knew what was coming before it got there. The big clue was when Darrin's cell rang and it was his precious little wife. Instead of running right home, as he'd been prepared to do not a half-an-hour before, he told her he'd be home in a few minutes, closed up his phone, and asked for one more beer. It was all too obvious.

They had been talking, naturally enough, about what was quickly becoming known around Highland as the "Flash." Darrin had started it by sharing at least part of what he'd been investigating with his friend. Then he had complained that it was hard for him to believe a lot of it, partly, perhaps, because he had been out of town when it happened, and therefore didn't experience it. Then he had started with the questions. "How did it affect you, Jon?" "What kind of things have you been hearing from the kids and the other teachers at school?" That sort of thing.

Then, as they sat in their deck chairs watching night fall on the notorious pasture and woods behind Jon's house, he told Jon about the dream that a "co-worker" had told him about. That's when he circled in for the kill. The references to "red-eyed" seemingly dead children made the obvious connection, although Darrin acted as though he was oblivious to it. He was feeling for; he was looking for, any connection to - "A Haunting in Highland," - Jon's now famous work of fiction... a novel that in large part, they both knew, was all too true.

It was a story from the past, and one that Jon, upon completion of the book, had refused to ever discuss again. Darrin knew that very well. So when he asked, very carefully, if Jon had happened to see or hear anything unusual coming from the woods behind his house the night of the "flash," Jon was ready.

"Don't think I don't know what you're getting at," Jon said cooly but tensely. "That dream...you could have made that up. Probably did, knowing you. This...this flash thing, was way different than it was back then, Darrin. It was worse, in a way." Jon glared at his friend, who's features were gradually fading in the oncoming veil of night. "Look...look, just leave it alone, alright?"

Darrin nodded, but he wasn't going to do that, and Jon knew it. Not by a long shot. Darrin was relentless when he thought he might be on to something.

For the next few moments though, both sipped their drinks in silence and returned their eyes and thoughts to the darkening pasture lying before them.

★   ★   ★

Janice Granger was getting ready for bed, and she was depressed. As the hours had gone by she had become more and more convinced that confessing her nightmare to the Police Chief and Detective Crandle that afternoon had been an idiotic, very spur of the moment-mistake. She had unburdened herself of what was undoubtedly a totally irrelevant, personal matter, and she had showed her emotions while doing so. She had broken her own rules; rules that any single career girl instinctively knows, or soon learns, in trying to make it in what is still too much of a man's world: don't ever "act like a girl." And she had, in her own opinion.

She had shown weakness. And it was gnawing at her mind; and had been growing worse by the hour.

Janice studied herself in the bathroom mirror after brushing her teeth. It had been the kind of day that she liked the least; one where her confidence was shaken by something that happened or that she did, which led to inevitable feelings of insecurity and self-doubt when she was (as always) home alone at the end of it.

She looked into her own brown eyes. There she was, a still relatively good looking 43 year-old, a woman at the top of her profession, independent, living alone and loving it, but still insecure, and too often unsure. She knew it, knew she had a tendency to over think things and make them worse, but couldn't help it.

She sighed, mentally told herself to buck up and get over it, then turned off the bathroom light and headed for her bed and a good book to fall asleep by.

It was less than a minute later, just after she had pulled back the covers and turned on the reading light, when she heard it. A faint, but unmistakable sound that was as familiar as any sound in her house up until only a few hours ago, really. It was the loud purring, and soft meowing... of her cat.

Janice froze where she was and listened. Nothing for a few moments... then there it was again. Very faint, but definitely there. She listened intently. She was trembling now. It was Socks. It had to be. But then...silence again.

Then there it was! Louder, and coming from the direction of the kitchen.

She was terrified, in a sense, but also felt a sudden, overwhelming sense of grief. How in the world...how could this be? "But Socks is dead," she said out loud, perhaps in the hope that the sound of her own voice would return some semblance of sanity to the moment.

It was quiet for a few moments after she spoke. It was as though her voice made it go away. Then, very clearly, it was there again. It was higher pitched now, and was exactly the cry Socks used to make when she wanted to be let in the house from the back yard. Janice's mind was racing to try to find logic, comfort, reality. Could it be another cat? A bizarre mental illusion produced by a tired brain after a hard day? Could it be related to her horrible dream somehow? ...The beginning of mental illness?

The high-pitched meowing continued. Janice gritted her teeth and decided. She put her book on the bed and walked determinedly out of the bedroom and down the darkened hallway toward her kitchen, and hesitated only briefly at the light she would need to turn on to look out of the glass door that led to her patio out back; the door that Socks had gone in and out of so many hundreds of times.

She took a deep breath, flipped on the light, and stepped bravely out far enough to see out the glass door.

There was nothing there. She stood there watching; staring. No cat, and now, no sound. After a few seconds she breathed again. Her shoulders sagged and a wave of pure relief engulfed her entire being. She walked shakily over to her kitchen table and pulled a chair out to sit down. She kept her eyes on the glass door as she did so. "I'm going nuts," she said aloud. "Nuts."

Chapter 8
October 5th 9:33 A.M.

This time Janice called the meeting. And again, it was just the three of them. Detective Crandle and Police Chief Thomas were asked to come to her office for an "urgent" meeting at 9:30 A.M., the descriptive adjective here being the result of her own overreaction to the previous day's slight by all the others who didn't show up to her last call for a conference.

Chief Thomas was the last to arrive, and asked "What's urgent, Janice?" before even sitting down.

Janice didn't respond immediately. She instead waited patiently for him to sit down and get comfortable. Then she cleared her throat and said in as authoritative voice as possible "I want to apologize to you two." She briefly made eye contact with each of them, then, as was her habit, looked down at a spot on her desk to better concentrate. "I had no business making such a big deal out of some silly dream I had; a dream that has nothing to do with... business. It was unprofessional, and I'm sorry," she said evenly.

She stopped there abruptly and again looked at each of them. An awkward few moments ensued. The Chief and Darrin looked briefly at each other, then back at her. Janice said nothing more, and the other two seemed baffled as to how to proceed.

Chief Thomas finally broke the silence. "No need to apologize, Janice," he said. He smiled widely at her. "Heck, I had a nightmare myself last night! It was a doozy too. Be glad to tell you two about it, if you want to hear it."

Janice frowned slightly and looked back down at her desk. She said nothing.

"I don't think you need to apologize for anything," Darrin said firmly. When Janice looked up he looked directly into the City Manager's tired eyes. "In fact, I think what you told us could be very important. Very important."

"How's that?" Chief Thomas asked.

"Well, for instance, I had a long conversation last night with my neighbor," (he temporarily left out the neighbor's name). "He teaches at the high school," Darrin continued, "and although he didn't want to talk about it much, he eventually admitted that he'd had bad nightmares too. Bad enough to keep him up all night, and cause him to miss work. Starting on that same night by the way, Janice. The night that that flash thing happened. And he said it had happened to some of the other teachers and students."

"That's what the priest told me too. People having nightmares, I mean," Janice added eagerly. She was both relieved, and warming to the discussion.

"And a few of the doctors I talked to yesterday, though they're so damned guarded that they don't give you much," Darrin said, "told me about animal bites and nightmares. Nightmares!"

Chief Thomas frowned and squirmed around in his chair. "So what are you saying?" he asked irritably.

"I'm saying that Janice did what no one else has had the guts to do yet, and that's important. We tend to ignore, or at least not talk about, the psychological part of this. You know what I mean? Probably because we don't understand it. Can't control it," he said as he looked at the Chief. "I mean its circumstantial so far, or whatever the right word is...but I think there's a lot of people out there, right in our community, that are having bad dreams too.

And that 'thing' that made the animals go crazy...I'm just saying maybe it affected people too. More than we think."

Darrin stopped there. He looked at the other two anxiously. Janice nodded at him with a tight smile. Chief Thomas, after an uncomfortable attempt to study the ceiling while sitting in a straight-backed chair, was squirming around as though his underwear was in a particularly tight bunch. "So what are we supposed to do, Darrin? Call people in to tell us their dreams, for God's sake?" he asked.

"No. I didn't say that," Darrin answered patiently. "I'm just saying that.."

"We've got a County Sheriff who's still missing," the Chief said as he stood, "and God knows what else going on!" He glared at Darrin, then over at Janice. "I've got to get to work," he said curtly. "I think we all do."

With that, he pivoted and walked purposefully toward the office door. He slowed though as he approached it. He reached for the doorknob, turned it halfway, then stopped. Slowly, almost reluctantly, it seemed, he turned back around. "Sorry guys," he said to them sheepishly. "I really didn't get much sleep last night."

★   ★   ★

County Sheriff Joe Blanton was now a Missing Person. Technically, the law said that that could not be the case for 48 hours, but technicalities do not apply to small children and important officials.

Besides Sheriff's office personnel, the Illinois State Police, off duty or loaned police and even some fire fighters from towns within the immediate Madison County area, and a plethora of volunteers (many of whom were old friends of Joe's) were all crowding into the rural area where the Sheriff's car had been abandoned. A preliminary contact had been made to the F.B.I.

Detective Crandle and Chief Thomas saw, and were amazed by, the extent of the search operation already in place, and the speed with which it had been organized. They had driven the eight miles north from Highland about 45 minutes after their meeting with the City Manager to have a look at things for themselves, out of curiosity as much as concern. The Highland Police Department had no jurisdiction outside the city limits, and their help had not been asked for. At least not yet. But when the squad car carrying two officers pulled up to the search site, professional courtesy easily got them past the road block at the perimeter, and they were treated with deference once on the ground at the scene.

And it was a strangely eerie scene. The missing Sheriff's car was still there, pulled only slightly off the center of the road. It looked, to the imaginative mind not concerned with ascribing feelings to inanimate objects, forlorn and lonely sitting there as it was; a sad, still and quiet island in the center of the beehive of activity that surrounded it. But it also struck one as stubbornly loyal-waiting there patiently, if a bit naively, for its Master the Sheriff to emerge from the woods and routinely hop back in and start the engine, as always.

Darrin and Rodney were soon standing within a few feet of the abandoned car, which was cordoned off with drooping, poorly staked yellow police tape. The two men looked around briefly at the bustle of uniformed activity around them, and then back at the isolated car.

"Seems kind of lonely just sittin' there, doesn't it?" Darrin asked, effectively crossing the magic barrier between imagination and cold reality.

Chief Thomas gave an irritated glance at his Detective. "You've seen too many Disney movies, Darrin. Cars don't get lonely." He looked briefly back at the car, then away to try to find someone he knew, or someone who looked to be in charge that wasn't too busy. After a minute he spotted a tired looking Harvey Milton, a Deputy Sheriff, standing off by himself looking aimlessly into the woods. He knew Harvey, but not as well as he knew Joe. Good enough though. He left Darrin without saying anything and walked directly over to Harvey.

"Whatta you know Harvey?" he said as he approached. Harvey looked even worse when you got up close. Like he hadn't slept, which he hadn't.

Harvey seemed totally surprised that somebody was addressing him, and did a defensive half-whirl toward the Police Chief. He was more than a little on edge, Rodney could see.

"Oh...hi Rodney," Harvey said after a confused moment. His shoulders slumped. "Sorry. A little rattled I guess." He looked away from Rodney then, resuming his aimless stare at the woods.

His appearance made Rodney uncomfortable, and the better part of him knew that he should leave the man alone, and that it wasn't his case, but he wanted information even more, if there was any. "Any clues at all, Harvey? Any progress?"

Harvey again looked as though he was snapping out of a trance when he realized he'd been asked a question. It was like waking a man up from a dead sleep, the Chief thought.

Harvey took a long moment before answering. "No, not really," he said. His words sounded as lost as his gaze. "Too early, maybe. No sign of him. They swept the inside of the car and all around it. Don't know why they don't take it away. They took the damned cow away." He turned his head around to look at Rodney, his face suddenly alarmed; in pain. "You should have seen that thing, Rodney. Half of it eaten to the bone. Horrible. Must have been a big pack of coyotes, is all I can figure. Huge pack. Never seen anything like it..." His voice trailed off, and he looked away absently again.

A noisy pick-up truck was coming up the road, temporarily drawing the Chief's attention along with everyone else's. It had three men riding in the front seat and four or five standing in the open back. A hat flew off one of them right before the truck pulled up to a stop, and mercifully, shut off the engine. It was hard to tell if they were returning from a search or just arriving, very enthusiastically, to join one.

Darrin had walked over in the meantime. "Anything we can do to help?" he asked Harvey. Harvey turned toward Darrin reluctantly. He gave this new stranger a glassy-eyed look but said nothing.

"They haven't found out anything. There's been no sign of him," Chief Thomas said, a bit impatiently.

The three of them lapsed into a silence then; with the two Highland officers joining Harvey in watching quietly, helplessly, from the outskirts, as the high-purposed, confusing machinations of the search for a missing Sheriff stumbled on through the gloriously sunny autumn morning.

★   ★   ★

Bart Melleville, still in his pajamas though it was nearly noon, watched the cat as it ambled through his back yard. It was sure taking its time. The view was perfect (for stray cat-watching, among other things) from where he sat sipping coffee at his kitchen table. As he watched, the cat paused it's slow gait and stopped for a moment. Then it turned its head very gradually, almost unnaturally so, toward the glass door that Bart sat behind, as if carefully studying the threat level of the pajama clad observer. Bart knew that with the way the late morning sun was shining into the door there was no way the stupid cat could see him...but still. There was something chilling about it: the way it looked at him. It reminded him, just a little...just enough, of the dream. It held its head so still. And was it showing its fangs?

"I'm going to run up town to pick up the rest of your prescription, honey," Nancy Melville said breezily as she strode into the kitchen.

Bart was about to take a break from his stare down with the cat to take a sip of coffee at that moment, and the surprise caused by the unexpected volume and proximity of his wife's voice caused him to violently jerk his hand enough to, in effect, pour half a cup of hot coffee down the front of his pajamas and onto his chest and stomach. He stared dumbly at his steam rising from his chest for the moment it took to feel the first surge of pain, then leaped wildly to his feet, bumping his left knee hard on the underside of the table in the process.

"God damn it!" he cried as he frantically tried to pull his soaked pajama top away from his skin with one hand and rub his knee with the other, all the while hopping madly around the table.

Nancy jumped back in surprise and confusion herself at her husband's reaction to her words, but quickly ran to his side when she fully understood what had happened. There was much apologizing, soothing and patting to follow.

A few minutes later Nancy brought him some dry clothes, and he changed right there in the kitchen. Shortly, thanks in large part to Bart's natural tendency to find humor in the worst of situations (a trait Nancy had always loved in him; and one that had been completely missing in recent days), they were both laughing at the ridiculousness of it all, as Bart imitated himself in hopping around in pain over and over again.

"Is there anything else I can pick up for you when I'm out?" Nancy asked him a little later, after the laughs were exhausted and during the obligatory last-minute search through her purse.

Bart was back in his accustomed seat at the table, redressed and nursing a new cup of coffee. He suddenly felt better than he had in days. It was like some sort of steam valve had released all the pressure. "No, honey," he sighed, "I'll be fine." And he meant it. Maybe it was the medicine, although the doctor said it would be several days before it kicked in. Maybe it was the coffee spill, or the sunny day. He didn't know, or at the moment care why. He just knew he felt better than he had in what seemed like a long while.

Nancy looked at him sitting there looking out for a few more moments, then she walked over to him and kissed his cheek. He was already staring out into the back yard again, and was already too distracted to return her affection. But he was still smiling. and that made her smile. "See you in a while, honey," he said absently.

"Bye, sweetie," Nancy said, and with that she walked out of the kitchen and into the garage.

Bart heard the door shut, the garage door open, and the engine of his wife's car start...but only as the vague, dream-like background noise that you put no conscious thought into; like the sound of the neighbor's lawn mower running while you are reading the paper on a Sunday summer morning.

Bart though, wasn't reading. He was looking intently for the cat; the stray black and white cat that had so captivated his attention just a few minutes before. Where could it have gone? And come to think of it, how had it gotten over the privacy fence and into his back yard in the first place?

Where did it go? And why did he give a damn? The medicine?

He got up from the table and walked to the glass door leading out to the deck and back yard. He couldn't see the cat. There were two small corners of the yard that he couldn't see from where he had been sitting; one to his left and one to his right. With his nose practically touching the glass, he looked first in one direction, then the other. No cat. He stepped back, took a sip of coffee, and let his eyes scan the entire yard one more time. The damned cat was gone.

Bart took another sip of coffee and had just begun his turn to head back to the kitchen table when he was stopped by a screaming meow. Though it startled him, this time he handled it better. He pushed the coffee cup out away from his body and only spilled a couple of drops onto the linoleum floor. With his cup under control, he turned again to look out into the yard.

No cat. His eyes quickly scanned the whole yard, but he could see no sign of it.

Then the loud, urgent meow again.

This time he looked down. There, at foot level on the other side of the glass door, just inches from where he stood, was the cat. It was just sitting there, looking up at him.

But...how...?

The wonder of how it had gotten there lasted only a few seconds. A look at its face, up close, changed all that instantly for Bart. The cat that stared up at him had one all yellow eye with no discernible pupil. The other eye was black, and was hanging precariously out of its socket, held by some kind of red, bleeding, fly-covered muscle. Its mouth was twisted back in a kind of deformed, grotesque smile, with yellowed fangs permanently revealed.

Bart felt his heart begin to beat harder, and a nauseating chill start in the pit of his stomach that quickly spread over his whole body. He couldn't move, and he couldn't quit looking down at it.

Then the cat moved. It looked down, and very deliberately bumped its head against the glass. Then it looked up at Bart, let out a loud, surreal sounding cry, then bumped its head against the glass again.

It wanted in.

Bart willed himself to look up and away from it. He had to look at something else. Anything else. His eyes saw it immediately. In the back corner of the yard, by the fence. A tall man. Just standing there, looking at him. Smiling at him.

Then walking toward him.

Bart blinked his eyes, then shut them. It wasn't real. It couldn't be.

Another loud meow. He opened his eyes and looked down again.

The cat stared up. He saw the fangs.

He couldn't feel anything now. He was numb...so numb.

As he returned the stare, his hand-he saw his own hand out of the corner of his eye, without any conscious direction from him-as if it was completely disembodied and on its own- move up to the door handle.

Chapter 9

"It's Bobby Meachum, Dr. Bledsoe. We've had...a bit of an emergency with him. We think you need to see him right away."

A very tired looking Dr. Bledsoe looked up from the orders he was signing in the nurses' station at St. Joseph's Hospital. It was unusual for Nurse Raymond, or any other nurse, to even speak to him when he was trying to finish up his shift and go home, much less make a request. The nurses knew from experience not to. But he had detected a slight bit of alarm in her voice. Enough to get his reluctant attention. "The kid that lost his fingers to that dog?" he asked wearily.

"Yes," she said as she nodded quickly. "That's the one."

Even in his exhausted, irritable state the doctor could see the stress on the nurse's face. Still, he couldn't imagine that anything was seriously wrong. The kid had had a terrible, traumatic experience, and had lost a lot of blood, but he was more than stable now. Minus most of his hand, yes-but young and strong and about ready to be released. "What seems to be the trouble?" the doctor asked, hoping against hope that it was something that he could solve from where he sat.

Nurse Betty Raymond fidgeted as she stood there, rubbing her hands together and nervously looking away. She hesitated way too long for the doctor's pleasure. "What's the trouble?" he repeated more firmly.

"He bit Nurse Grimwold," she finally blurted out. She looked directly at the doctor. "He hurt her...and then he tried to bite me." With that she looked away again, and began rubbing her hands together even more urgently. Her face had turned red.

Dr. Bledsoe stared at the distraught nurse for a few moments. He was, in fact, very tired. He was also annoyed. Yet, between Nurse Raymond's alarmingly uncharacteristic behavior and the short, bizarre report that she had just given, well...there was a trace of plain old curiosity working at him too.

He finally looked away from her, sighed heavily (to give the audible warning that this "better be good,"), and reluctantly closed the folder in front of him. Then he stood up, stretched, yawned and scratched at his full head of gray hair.

"OK. Let's go have a look," he said.

★　　　★　　　★

Rookie Highland Police Officer Ben Christopher was only three blocks away driving on routine patrol when the emergency call came in. It was a 911 call from an address on Keeven Street, called in by a Nancy Melleville. Some sort of unintelligible distress situation was taking place at her household. Officer Christopher answered the dispatch, did a u-turn, put on his lights and raced to the address.

Ben Christopher knew who Bart Melleville was, at least vaguely. He had met him once, but wasn't sure where. Rotary Club? Anyway, he knew the basics: Highland native, involved in the community, well known and respected, successful banker in St. Louis, middle-aged...but was he the skinny, graying tall one, or the balding heavier one?

All this and more ran through his mind as he raced toward Keeven. A fairly new policeman in town has to try to remember a thousand things. Geography first, of course, but as his mentor

Darrin Crandle had emphasized, knowing the people, their stations in life, and even their habits wasn't far behind. Every bit of knowledge could someday help you down the road, he'd emphasized over and over again.

So Ben was working at it. His knowledge so far was partial and too often sketchy, and there were huge holes (was Nancy Melleville Bart's wife? His daughter? Did he even have the right Melleville?), but yes, he was working at it.

He whirled onto the quiet street of Keeven with lights blazing. No traffic. Right away he saw that he didn't have to double check for the right address. He could see the woman from a block and a half away, jumping up and down and waving her arms frantically in her front yard. He hit the gas hard and screeched up to her house within a few seconds.

He wasn't prepared for what came next (he was a rookie after all). Nancy Melleville was absolutely hysterical. She practically threw herself onto his car as soon as it had stopped. She was screaming at him, with eyes bugging out frighteningly, and soon pounding on the passenger side window.

He couldn't understand a word she was saying. What he saw in her eyes made him, honestly, a little afraid to get out of the car. He hadn't seen this before.

He drew his eyes away from her, took a deep breath, then called for an ambulance and back-up. Then he told himself in stern terms to get a grip, gritted his teeth hard and got out of the car.

She was all over him, immediately. She ran over, hugged, clawed and cried.

"Calm down Ma'am...please...PLEASE," he pleaded as he tried to hold her away. "What's wrong?" he asked urgently as he forcefully held her face away from him. She clutched harder and started moaning. "What's wrong? Tell me what's wrong! Did someone hurt you?" he asked desperately.

She gulped, choked and sobbed convulsively. She was beyond hysterical, and obviously incapable of anything resembling lucid speech. She clutched him even harder.

Officer Christopher was overwhelmed himself. He couldn't think straight, and had no idea what to do next. So, gradually, he gave up and did what was easiest and that felt the best. He held her and patted her back reassuringly... as the sirens heading their way grew louder and louder.

★　　　★　　　★

"And how are we doing today, Mr. Meachum?" Dr. Bledsoe said breezily as he forcefully swept his way into his patient's room. His long ago learned practice (acquired from observing other doctors in medical school many years before) of turning up the volume, being overly enthusiastic and always seeming to be in a hurry when visiting patients had served him well over the years. It created the impression that the doctor, though undeniably nice as well as humane and concerned, was far too busy for anything trivial, and by all means needed to be given the most important information quickly before sweeping out of the room again. Patients were inevitably intimidated, and inane questions or concerns were swept by the wayside.

And it almost always worked...if the patient was engaged.

Bobby Meachum was not. He did not move a muscle to acknowledge Dr. Bledsoe's grand entrance, and so slowed the doctor's purposeful steps toward his bed. The puzzled doctor, in fact, was eventually forced to stop altogether at the teenager's bedside, without having received any physical, much less verbal, sign of recognition.

His patient was sitting up straight in bed and looking out the window, which was in the opposite direction from where the doctor stood. He appeared to be smiling, and he was talking to himself, it seemed, and in a voice low enough for no one else to hear.

Not only the manner, but the appearance of his patient gave Dr. Bledsoe reason to pause, uncharacteristically, there at the bedside. The boy was alarmingly pale. His long hair was well beyond unkempt. It was tangled and shooting out in all directions as though someone had purposefully done a bizarre experiment on it involving huge amounts of static electricity. And the talking to himself...the mumbling, really, sounded more like a rhythmic chant with each passing second. And the voice didn't sound like that of a teen-aged boy.

Dr. Bledsoe watched and listened, mesmerized, for a full minute. What he was witnessing completely riveted and absolutely baffled him. He stood slack-jawed and inert until a strategic forced cough from Nurse Raymond (who was standing and waiting well behind him) snapped him back to the medical problem at hand.

The doctor closed his mouth, turned and smiled gratuitously at the nurse, then turned with renewed (if now a bit feigned) confidence toward Bobby Meachum again. "I say how are we doing today, Mr. Meachum?" he asked happily.

Bobby didn't react at all. He still stared out the window, smiled and chanted in that low, deep voice.

The doctor smiled also, benignly, but his now wide awake mind began to race over the wide range of possible conditions that the symptoms he was witnessing suggested. But there were too many things that it could be, and the bizarre posture and behavior of the boy made it all the more confusing. Infection? Fever?

He tried to keep his bedside manner. "Let's take a look at that hand..." he hesitated here to look quickly at the chart, "...Bobby. Shall we?"

The second Dr. Bledsoe's hand touched the teenager's bandaged one Bobby's head whipped around to face the doctor, Nurse Raymond gasped. The doctor, whose attention was absorbed with beginning to examine the wound, did not see it. He was startled though, by Nurse Raymond's sudden intake of breath, and so turned to look at her. He saw a woman who had gone instantly pale, with her eyes widened in horror.

The doctor quickly turned back to see what had so frightened her.

Bobby was looking directly at him. He was grinning even more broadly, and his eyes were a frightening, unworldly pale yellow. The doctor froze, unable to speak, release the wounded hand, or even move. After a few breathless seconds, the boy's lips began to stretch back, showing even more of his teeth. His tongue lolled out briefly, then shot back into his mouth. A sound, a deep growling sound came from somewhere deep within him.

Then, moving with a speed that was too fast for either the nurse or the victim to comprehend, Bobby's head shot down to bite through and then, with another lurch, to completely engulf the doctor's hand.

Chapter 10 -
October 5th 3:33 PM

Chief Thomas and Detective Crandle looked at the body for a long time in silence. Though both had been witness to the horrible physical remains of gruesome murders before (it was unspoken, and would remain so, but the grisly Devonshire homicides couldn't help but come crashing back into both of their minds upon their first sight of the body), this one seemed uniquely horrible.

What was left of the highly respected, universally well liked Bart Melleville was lying in pieces before them, at their feet by the now blood-stained glass door leading out to the deck, right there in the poor man's own home. His head had been decapitated. His neck appeared to be missing altogether - unless the long piece of bloodied skin lying by the wall several feet away was some part of it. One eye had been gouged out. There were scratches, deep scratches, all over his bare arms. The shirt he had been wearing, or what remained of it, clung to his torso in blood-soaked shreds.

And there was fur, or what certainly appeared to be tufts of animal fur, dancing lazily everywhere in the breeze created by the open glass door.

It was an amazing, horrifying and surreal sight-even for an experienced, hardened homicide investigator, and neither the Chief nor Darrin felt anywhere near that.

So the two of them stood and looked at the crime scene without words, as others took pictures and samples around them. Having been summoned from standing by impotently while observing the search for the County Sheriff, to now look helplessly at this hellish scene, completely unnerved the both of them. They were, in those first few minutes especially, in a state of shock.

"Chief Thomas? Janice, the City Manager is here. She wants to know if she can come in." The young officer's words (truthfully, any words now) seemed grating. Rodney felt exactly like he was being rudely awakened from a deep sleep, and all the confusion (and then anger) that comes with that feeling came to him now.

"Hell no!" he shouted, once he had gotten his bearings. He could feel the blood running in his temples. "No one should see this! It's not her job, anyway!" he added forcefully.

The Chief's harsh words seemed to shake Darrin from his own dream-like shock. He whirled on the Chief. "She's the City Manager, for Christ's sake" he said angrily. "She needs to know what happened, Chief!"

The two furrow-browed men looked challengingly at each other for a long moment, then away from each other and back at the dismembered body, at the same time.

"This hair...fur, whatever it is. Somebody's bagged up some samples of that, right?" the Chief asked impatiently.

"Yes, sir," the still red-faced young officer answered.

There was another long silence.

"Tell the City Manager she can come in," Chief Thomas said brusquely. He turned and looked at the officer. "But tell her what's... tell her what's in here first, for God's sake."

The young man nodded and left.

"We don't need a woman fainting in here," the Chief mumbled to Darrin.

★   ★   ★

"What do you mean, 'she didn't get off the bus'?'" Jim Ray asked his wife Brenda. "I mean, are you sure she got on it in the first place?" His second question was meant to replace the silly first one, and to try to calm down his hysterical wife, and also to give himself a moment to think.

Brenda had come running out of the house in a panic. He could see her alarm long before he heard it, as he had turned away from his task of chopping wood that they would never use (little Marsha was allergic to wood smoke) when he heard the back door slam. He hadn't seen his wife run in years, and here she was doing her hobbled version of an all out sprint toward her husband. And even before she got to him and, red-faced and fighting for breath, delivered the news, he knew somewhere deep down that it had to do with their Marsha.

The child hadn't eaten for two days, as far as he knew. And she was acting, well, very strangely. She either stayed in her room, or went somewhere else on the little farm (by herself, all the time) seemingly just to get away from them, her parents. She wanted to be alone. All the time. Jim Ray knew kids went through stages, but this was a baffling one: an eight-year old that seemed happy (if anything, happier than before), but didn't want to be with or talk with her parents. A kid that didn't want to come to dinner, and worst of all, creepiest of all...a kid that they could hear talking to herself, saying things that they could never quite make out, well after the lights were out at night.

"Of course she got on the bus!" Brenda yelled impatiently as she fought for breath. But Jim Ray could see that she wasn't sure. "She was at school...and they say she got on the bus...the secretary said, and..."

"Have you talked to the bus company? The driver?" Jim Ray asked as he laid down his axe. It was coming on slowly, but his own deep fear was beginning to gather force.

"No!...No! Not yet..." Brenda said between gasps. Her husband's simple questions seemed to confuse her; to make her angry. "She didn't get off the bus! She's lost!" she cried.

"Now look," Jim Ray said with as calm a voice as he could muster, "don't panic, OK?" He reached out his hand to gently hold her arm. "You get back in there and get on the phone, and I'll take the pick-up and go look for her. If she got off that bus, she can't be far away." With that he pictured his poor little girl wandering aimlessly, frightened, around the countryside. His heart sunk. "I've got my cell," he said grimly as he pulled his hand back and reached in his pocket for his keys. "Call me if you hear something. I'll do the same."

With that he strode away purposefully toward his truck. He turned a few steps later to tell her it was all going to be all right, but Brenda was already running toward the house.

★　　★　　★

"Say that again?" Chief Thomas demanded. He was on his cell, and holding his other hand up to cover his other ear. He listened for a moment, then walked out of the kitchen and away from the others into Bart and Nancy Melville's living room.

Janice had not fainted. She was emotionally overwhelmed by the scene at first, like the rest of them, but got her balance back rather quickly. And when she did, it was the fur (cat hair, she suspected from experience) that drew her interest.

"Somebody's going to find out what kind of fur that is, aren't they?" she asked Detective Crandle shortly after the Chief had walked out.

Darrin was distracted again. He was kneeling over the torso of the body, looking closely at some of the scratch marks, being careful not to touch anything. He looked back briefly at the City Manager. "Yeah. We'll know what it is pretty quick." He looked back at the body again. "What in God's name?...it doesn't make any sense..." he mumbled more to himself than anyone else. He looked up at the blood-splattered glass door. "Could somebody have broken in...with a dog, or..." he looked around for Officer Christopher. He found him sitting at the kitchen table, still looking stunned. "Hey Ben, these folks didn't have a pet did they?" he asked.

Officer Christopher shook his head slightly without making eye-contact with Darrin. He looked pretty bad.

"Did they?" Darrin repeated, a bit louder.

"I don't think so," the young officer said. He looked as though it took all his strength to verbalize the answer.

Darrin, still kneeling over the body, glared at him. The kid had had a rough day, but that was no excuse. "How about you get off your ass and find out?" he snarled. "And while you're at it, check with the neighbors. See if anybody is missing a pet."

Officer Christopher now looked at Darrin. He looked like a hurt little boy. But he jumped to his feet after a moment, said "Yes, sir," and quickly left the room. He almost ran right into the returning Chief Thomas as he did so.

Chief Thomas walked into the kitchen and then down to where Darrin was kneeling and Janice was standing. He stood beside Darrin until the Detective looked up at him.

"I don't know what the hell is happening. I swear I don't," the Chief said.

The tone of his voice, oddly shaken and up a key or so, got Darrin's attention. He stood up and looked at his boss. "What's up?" he asked.

The Chief glanced at Janice and hesitated. She could see that he was unsure if he should go ahead. A moment later though, he did: "You know that kid that had his hand bitten, that lost a couple of fingers to that dog?"

Both Janice and Darrin nodded.

"Well...it seems he just bit off most of Dr. Bledsoe's hand down at the hospital."

What?" Janice said. Darrin just stared at his boss.

"The officer said..." he glanced apprehensively at Janice again, but continued, "...the officer said that he, uh, well, ate it, they think. The hand. Most of it, anyway." The Chief paused. He looked at Darrin and then Janice. They both just stared at him.

"And get this: the kid got away afterwards. Crawled out the window and got away. Can you believe that?"

Again, the other two were too stunned to respond. They stared at the pale Police Chief as he looked over at the body by the glass door. The disembodied head of Bart Melville had been turned onto it's side, for some reason, and the one good eye seemed to be staring at them from across the room. Janice looked at it for a moment, then turned away. "What in God's name is happening?" she asked.

Chapter 11
October 5th 5:03 P.M.

"It was cat hair. I know it was, Darrin," Janice Granger said firmly. She was staring into her drink as she said it, sitting in a booth at Michael's Restaurant. Detective Crandle, whose idea it was to meet there, sat opposite her, listening to and watching her.

Darrin had solved the Devonshire case two years before (or had come as close to solving it as was humanly possible) with creative, out of the box thinking, as much as anything else. He had, in a sense, thrown the manuals away. And he had used a civilian, not another policeman, to get there. His neighbor and now best friend Jonathon Parker had been his "partner" that time. Jon was smart, was vitally involved, and helped him eventually stumble onto the right, if highly improbable, path.

Now, with everything that had happened on that day alone (a still missing Sheriff, a totally mystifying and gruesome murder, apparent teenaged cannibalism and escape at the hospital and, in the last hour, a report of a missing eight-year-old girl) Darrin felt that everything that made sense-all the certainties that grounded their simple, peaceful lives in Highland-were under attack. And an attack of the worst kind, because it was, so far, totally indefinable. And what you can't understand, what you don't know, is the scariest thing of all.

"Cats...have a smell. Only its not a smell, really," Janice continued. She looked up at Darrin, then down at her drink again. "I don't know what in the world happened. Who could have done such a thing. But there was a cat in there when it happened. I know that much..."

Darrin watched her nervous, fluttery hands playing with her glass and waited for her to go on. She didn't. He looked at his watch. 5:05. Should be heading home, he thought. He took a big swig and downed half of his remaining beer.

"Can I ask you something?" Janice said as he was returning the mug to the table. She was looking at him now, finally. Pretty brown eyes. It made him wonder, briefly, why she was alone.

"Sure," he answered. "Shoot."

She looked down again, and blushed slightly. Painfully shy. Maybe that's why, he thought.

"Why did you ask me here? For a drink, I mean?"

Darrin's mind suddenly revisited that sickening feeling that begins somewhere around the 5th grade, when some ugly girl that you've accidentally been nice to asks "Do you like me? Because I like you?"

But that was silly. Janice was smart, and definitely not ugly. She was genuinely curious. For the right reasons, he thought.

"Well, to tell you the truth, I saw the way you looked" (whoops!)"uh, the way you looked at things there, at the murder scene," he said. "And I could see that you see the whole picture. I've noticed that. Probably what you have to do in your job, right? As City Manager, you know, uh, that something big, something bigger is going on." Darrin squirmed. He realized that he was being about as clear as mud. "I...I just wanted to hear what you think of... of all this."

Clear as mud. But Janice looked at him as though she understood perfectly. Thank God.

"What do you think the headlines will be tomorrow? In the newspapers, I mean?" she asked casually as she looked back down at her drink. This time she swirled the ice cubes around.

Darrin wasn't expecting that one. "What do you mean?" he asked without a clue.

"I mean there are three, maybe four, *huge* stories out there. All of them took place in, or near, Highland. Every one of them. All of them in the last 24 hours, and that doesn't even begin to cover it." she looked up at him. "I mean, little dogs don't bite kids so hard that their fingers come off. Cattle don't just disappear. Or little girls..." she looked absently over toward the bartender. They were his only customers, and he seemed to be doing nothing more than standing there anxiously awaiting their next order. "...and cats don't just fall over with a broken neck and die, either," she added absently.

Then she turned back and looked directly at Darrin again. "Which headline would you choose?" she asked. "They're all bad. All bad for Highland. This is the city I'm supposed to be promoting. Bringing business to. How the hell do I do my job when...when this stuff is happening?"

Darrin was a little taken aback by her sudden show of strength, and the underlying anger there.. "Hell, its not my fault!" he thought, but didn't say.

"We've got to get to the bottom of it, is what I'm saying," she continued, "There's...there's a logical explanation here, right?" This last sentence sounded plaintive. Like a quick trip back to her insecurity.

Darrin took his time before answering. He finished the rest of his beer, then raised his hand to signal for another. The bartender was pouring before he'd even finished his gesture. He looked back at Janice, who appeared to be keenly waiting for an answer. He tried.

"We...we here in Highland, we had something strange...very strange, happen a couple of years ago."

"You mean all that business over on Devonshire?" she asked quickly.

"Well, yes," he answered. He was surprised that she knew. "It was before your time. Before you were hired, Janice."

"And that Jon, Jon what's his name. He wrote a book about it. Yeah, I heard about that. I know that. Haven't read it. Mostly a fairy tale, right?" She asked with brows knitted in concern. "Are you telling me that this is related to...? Should I read the book? Is that what you're saying?"

Darrin smiled a little and held up his hand to slow her down. The bartender put the new beer in front of him. He waited for the guy to leave.

"I don't think anything that's happened could be related to that case," he stated frankly, "And believe me, it's crossed my mind. Nothing has happened, at least not yet, on Devonshire. I should know. I live there. But...that "flash" thing happened there, just like everywhere else. My friend Jon told me, as the matter of fact."

"You didn't feel it? The flash thing?"

"No. I was out of town."

"Then why did you bring up the Devonshire thing?"

The gal is smart all right, but she thinks almost too fast, Darrin thought. "Because I'm trying to make a point about, maybe, the way we have to think about what's happening in a different way. That's what I did back then." She looked puzzled. Clear as mud again. "Let me try to explain," he began.

"I've got to read that book. Tonight!" she said.

★　　　★　　　★

Joanie had cooked a wonderful pot roast dinner, and her husband Rodney was hardly touching it. Instead, the distracted Police Chief was spending most of his time pushing the food around his plate; his mind the proverbial "million miles away."

Joanie knew he was upset, knew he wanted to get back to work, and as usual, only knew some of the reasons why. She'd seen this many times before. Even before he was Police Chief, unresolved cases that he was working on, office politics, and even seemingly minor run-ins with various Highland citizens (who, for example, may have vehemently disagreed with the supposed extent of their speeding) would all get to Rodney. And he brought it home. He tried very hard to never show how sensitive a guy he was, but Joanie sure knew.

And she knew that tonight he had every reason to be withdrawn and upset. Like everyone else in town, along with (by now) the entire metro-east St. Louis area, she knew what had happened to poor Bart Melville. She knew the fear and panic that it would cause in Highland, and she knew that her husband wouldn't rest until the killer was caught and the case was solved. As she looked across the table at her frowning, silent husband she was aware of all of that. She'd done the drill before.

But what was different this time was that Joanie was very nervous herself. She had some bad news to give him. It wasn't earthshaking news; certainly not even close to being on the scale of murder in a small town. But it was upsetting, and she had to tell him, and she didn't know how.

Her opening came unexpectedly. He raised his head up and actually looked at her, as if he was about to say something. She seized the moment.

"Rodney, you need to know that Mitzi is dead," she blurted out. She took a deep breath. "There," she thought. "Done."

Rodney stared at her. He blinked several times. He put his fork down, carefully, on his plate. "What?" he finally asked.

Joanie felt tears welling up and fought against them. She looked down at her own uneaten food while answering. "She must have gotten hit by a car," she said as quickly and clearly as she could. "I let her out after work, like I always do. Then I got busy with other things. It was 20 minutes before I even thought to check..." she paused here to swallow hard. She knew was going to cry. She couldn't help it. "I found her in the yard," she continued, her voice higher now. "Whoever hit her must of put her up there... and then just... left."

Joanie brought both of her hands up to her eyes and she began to cry softly.

Rodney sat stunned. He watched her cry for almost half a minute without moving, then gathered himself enough to get up, walk around the table and put an arm around his wife. She leaned into him and began to cry harder.

It would be a while before he could ask any more questions.

★　　★　　★

They had just finished watching an episode of "Law and Order," and Darrin had just clicked off the television so that he and Marilyn could happily go to bed when the doorbell rang.

It startled them both.

Darrin went immediately and angrily to the door. He swung it wide open. It was his neighbor, Jon Parker.

"What the hell, Jon! It's 10 o'clock, man!" Darrin exclaimed before Jon could open his mouth.

Jon had been startled himself by the violence with which the door swung open, and took a step back reflexively. He looked up at Darrin. He was pale and appeared to be very frightened; more frightened than a person should be just from having a door open.

"What's wrong, Jon?" Darrin asked. His voice had gone from angry to concerned in about two seconds.

Jon tried to look over the taller Darrin's shoulder from where he stood. He was trying to see if Marilyn was around. He quickly gave up when Darrin didn't move. "I, I need to talk to you," he said. He took another step back.

Darrin looked hard at his friend, and was alarmed by what he saw. There was unmistakable fear in his blue eyes. Something was very wrong.

Darrin looked at him a moment longer, then back over his shoulder at Marilyn, who gave him a look of concern. Beautiful. Damn.

"I'm going to talk to Jon for a minute, honey," he said reluctantly. "I'll just be a minute."

With that he half closed the door, kissed her, then opened it, stepped resolutely out into the chilly night air and closed it behind him.

"What's up?" he asked Jon. The impatience was back in his voice.

Jon looked away from Darrin and toward his house. "Oh, Jesus," he said, half under his breath. He looked back at Darrin, directly into his eyes. "You need to come back to my deck for a few minutes, Darrin." He looked away in that direction again.

Darrin suddenly felt a cold knot in his stomach. "No!" he thought, "...not again!"

Jon turned back to him again. When he spoke his voice sounded oddly emotional; almost desperate. "We could be in real trouble, man," he said.

Chapter 12
October 6th 8:17 A.M.

"By the time we got back there, out there on his deck, there wasn't anything to see," Darrin said. "But I believe Jon," he added hastily, "We've...we've been through too much together, for me not to believe him."

Darrin stopped there. He leaned back in his chair, folded his hands behind his head and looked out the window at the light, cold rain that was coming down. The beautiful autumn days were slowly, depressingly, coming to an end now, he thought.

Janice Granger, who was sitting next to Darrin, stared at him in wonder. Chief Thomas, simply stared at his own outstretched hands as they rested on his desk. None of the three said anything for a while.

Darrin had filled the Chief (who was back at the office making calls) in on the basics by phone the night before. Darrin had expected his boss to challenge him, to question the credibility of Jon's story, even to be dismissive - but he hadn't. He had just listened, and when Darrin was finished, the Chief merely thanked him and told him to come in early the next morning. Now, after asking Darrin to give the report again, with all the details added in, Rodney Thomas had merely listened, again. He didn't scoff, roll his eyes, or even lean back in his chair like he usually did.

He just listened, and it frankly unnerved Darrin.

The City Manager was a different story. Janice listened to him with such intense ferocity that it was palpable. When he told them what Jon claimed to have seen in the pasture behind his house the night before-a tall figure dressed all in white leading a small group of children into the woods, and how he could hear their laughter, long after they'd disappeared from view-she looked like a little kid hearing a ghost story around the campfire for the first time. Even after Darrin had finished the story she didn't move her eyes off of him. It was obvious that she wanted to hear more. "Is that all?" she finally asked after a full minute of silence.

Darrin didn't answer. The Chief said nothing.

Janice looked hard at Darrin, and then Chief Thomas. Then back again. One studied the window, the other his own hands. Both seemed lost in thought. The only sound in the room came from the raindrops hitting the small window.

When Chief Thomas broke the silence, it startled the other two. "How many kids..." he stopped to clear his throat, "...how many children, exactly, did Jon say he saw walking into the woods, Darrin?" he asked without looking up.

"I asked him that," Darrin said after turning toward the Chief, and after a moment's hesitation. "He wasn't sure. 'At least three or four,' he said."

Janice looked from one to the other again. "I'm sorry," she said, "but what would children be doing at 10:00 at night walking around in woods? I mean...do you guys both believe that?"

Chief Thomas glanced up at Janice, then quickly down again. "We've got three kids missing as of this morning...four, if you count that crazy Meachum kid who escaped from the hospital."

"You're kidding!" Darrin said, even though he was, somehow, unsurprised. "What kids? What ages?" He leaned forward toward his boss and rested his elbows on his knees. He looked intently at the Chief.

The Chief sighed, then for the first time that morning leaned back in his chair. "Well, besides the little Crawford girl from that farm outside of town...and the Meachum kid, we've got a 5th grade boy and a sophomore girl gone. Both from town here. We got the calls in the middle of the night. Parents were frantic. Not even officially 'missing' yet, but..."

"Why aren't you searching the woods behind that Jon guy's house then? I don't understand!" the frustrated City Manager blurted out. Her voice was a few octaves higher than the men's had been..

The Chief looked at her, then Darrin, then back at her again. Then he put his feet up on the desk, his hands behind his head and looked up at his much-studied ceiling. "Based on what you told me last night,I sent three men out to search those woods this morning," he said almost casually, like it was a bit of a bother. He looked at Darrin again. "...even though I'm betting they don't find anything. I've got two others interviewing the families, trying to trace down where the kids might have traipsed off to. And we've got a whole team working on the Melleville murder, along with some outside help." He looked down at Janice with what could have been interpreted as slightly peevish face. "I got no men left to do anything else," he told her.

And then it got quiet again. Janice and Darrin's minds were left racing, albeit in very different directions, and the Chief just leaned back and studied his ceiling, with what appeared to be sorrowful resignation, as the raindrops continued, hitting the window harder and harder.

★   ★   ★

Officers Ben Christopher, Joel Banks and Bill Stephens had been assigned to search the infamous woods behind the Devonshire cul-de-sac that rainy morning, and they weren't happy about it. Ben had expected to be on the murder case, and the other two had been on routine traffic patrol on the sunny day before (and many days before that), and now, well, they felt they had definitely drawn the short straws.

All three would have killed (not literally, of course) to be assigned to the Melleville murder team. Officer Christopher had, after all, arrived first at the grisly scene, and so had a particularly strong case to make on that one. It was where the action was, and where they wanted to be. Barring that, all would have preferred being sent up north to help in the search for the missing sheriff, or even being assigned to fill in for some sick or tardy crossing guard helping grade-schoolers safely cross the street-anything, but this-a search in the rain for kids that were obviously not going to be there; that were probably staying overnight with friends somewhere.

"God, this is going to suck," Officer Banks said, stating the obvious as he and the others put on their rain ponchos as they stood in the street at the end of the Devonshire cul-de-sac.

The other two didn't respond. There wasn't much to say..

After a quick equipment check, the three of them started off, walking through Jonathon Parker's front yard, around his house and to the fence that separated his back yard from the hilly pasture and the woods beyond. There, by silent consensus, they stopped as one before climbing the fence and the first grassy hill lying before them.

The cold rain, as if mocking them, started coming down harder. The drops made loud popping sounds as it hit their ponchos.

"I repeat: this is going to suck," Officer Banks said.

"You got that right," Officer Stephens seconded.

Officer Ben Christopher didn't say anything. His eyes were focused instead on the woods in the distance, at how still and ominous they were. He found himself beginning to feel unaccountably queasy.

"You guys...you guys know the history, about those woods, don't you?" he found himself asking just as Officer Banks had taken the lead in 'getting it over with', and who already had one foot over the fence.

Banks stopped and turned, one foot still on the fence, and looked at Officer Christopher. "What are you talking about?" he asked irritably.

"He means about the cops that died out there a couple of years ago," Stephens said. "Don't you read anything, dip shit?"

Officer Banks held his awkward position. "I wasn't anywhere near Highland a couple of years ago," he said. He brought his foot back down to the ground, and looked up at Officer Christopher. "What happened?" he asked simply.

"Oh shit," Stephens said sarcastically.

"Like he said, two cops got killed," Christopher said. Stephen's sarcasm made him want to explain quickly, and to get going. Get it over with.

"And...?" Banks asked.

"And...well, they never caught the killer," Officer Christopher said reluctantly. For some reason, this was embarrassing for him.

"And...?" Banks repeated.

"And they say...some people say its haunted." Christopher said. He looked at Stephens defensively. Stephens was wearing a mocking smile. "It's all in the book that guy wrote. That teacher. 'A Haunting in Highland,' or something like that."

Stephens had had enough. "OK, pussies," he snarled. "You two can stand here in the frigging rain all day and tell ghost stories if you want. I'm gonna go do the job." With that he walked over, put two hands on the top of the fence, neatly vaulted over it, but lost his balance upon landing and dropped heavily, and comically, onto the soaked ground. "Shit!" he yelled out, before scrambling up and beginning to walk toward the woods as though nothing had happened.

Officers Banks and Christopher looked at each other and grinned, then both turned and began climbing the fence to follow.

★   ★   ★

Less than ten miles away the beleaguered Deputy Sheriff Harvey Milton was also braving the rain, and also staring at a patch of woods-but he was alone. The search for his boss (and more importantly, his best friend) had been postponed for at least the first half of the day because of the downpour. And he couldn't stand it.

It was a search that had been completely fruitless up to now. There had been, essentially, no clues found; no tracks, sightings, pieces of clothing-nothing. The only *very* strange "clue" so far had been reported by Harvey himself: the call that he later dutifully reported; a call from Sheriff Blanton's cell phone to his, with nothing but kids giggling on the other end. It had been quickly dismissed as some sort of electronic anomaly by the bosses though, and ultimately Harvey decided that he couldn't disagree with them. It was crazy, after all.

It was all so discouraging...and with the possible exception of Sheriff Blanton's splintered family, to Harvey most of all.

So when the almost sleepless Deputy Sheriff heard about the search postponement while drinking his first cup of coffee that dismal morning, his gut reaction was predictable: "Well, I'm going out there, God damn it!" he'd said to his wife.

But standing there in the rain (when he could have much more comfortably been sitting in his office, or even in the car) at the now abandoned spot where the Sheriff's car had been found gave him no comfort at all. In fact, it exacerbated the feeling of abandonment and frustration that was eating away at him.

He just didn't know what more he could do...but he kept thinking there must be something.

It was raining hard, but he stood there steadily, if uselessly, watching the woods. His vision was almost constantly blurred by the raindrops dripping off the brim of his hat. "Everybody willing to help on a sunny day, when its still fun," he thought bitterly. Then "What the hell happened out here, Joe?" this time out loud, and in anguish, a few moments later.

For another fifteen minutes, he stood there sulking in misery. Common sense began returning only gradually, and in direct proportion to the degree of the cold soaking that he was absorbing. As the minutes passed an occasional shiver ran through him, and eventually his teeth began to chatter. His thoughts grew even more embittered. "No one gives a damn," he mumbled once.

He heard the voice at the exact moment that he had finally willed himself to get back into his car to at least warm up. He was in fact half-turned, and had his hand on the door handle when it heard it.

"Harvey! I knew you'd be out here, old buddy!"

It was the Sheriff! He knew it immediately. It was the voice he knew so well, and it was coming from right behind him! Harvey whirled in wonder with an instantly wildly beating heart.

He saw only the road, the half flooded ditch beside it, and the yawning, empty woods. The rain was coming down hard enough to cause a mini-flood to pour off the brim of his hat. He whipped it off, then frantically looked to his left, and then right.

Nothing.

Then a deep chuckling, followed by the light, tinny laughter of a child. Very close. But where? Harvey looked around desperately.

"Up here Harvey. Up here!" Sheriff Joe's voice said.

Harvey looked up and saw him immediately. There, not 50 feet away and directly across from where he stood, was the Sheriff, sitting on a branch about fifteen feet up a giant oak tree, his legs lightly kicking and dangling in the air as he smiled from ear to ear like a little boy who had put one over on his parents.

Harvey was too shocked to react, or to move. What he was seeing was too strange, too unexpected... too wrong, to immediately respond to. "He looks like a little boy..." went through his confused mind, and little else.

Then the child's laughter again. There was a flash of white to the Sheriff's right. Or was it?

Harvey reluctantly moved his eyes off his friend and in that direction. It felt like the hardest thing he had ever done. But he saw her there, almost immediately. A little girl, sitting on her own branch just to the right and slightly above his Joe, dangling her legs and smiling at him.

Then a low, growling laugh, if you could call it that, was coming from below. Harvey, now close to mental and physical collapse from confusion and shock, slowly moved his glance back down toward the ground. A young man, maybe a teen-aged boy, stood below the tree where there had been no one just a few seconds before. He wasn't smiling, and after holding Deputy Sheriff's stare for a few long seconds, he began to walk slowly, but purposefully, toward Harvey.

Harvey watched him, completely mesmerized; frozen into place. He watched the boy cross the ditch and then come up onto the road without taking his eyes off of him.

He walked slowly closer. Yellow eyes. Now he began to smile.

Harvey?...Harvey?" the Sheriff's voice called. "Harvey...?"

With all the strength he had left, Harvey willed himself to look up.

★   ★   ★

"It's a god damned cow skull! That's what it is," Officer Bill Stephens cried.

The three soaked and dispirited Highland Police Officers were now deep into the legendary woods behind Devonshire. They had found, up until now, absolutely nothing of any interest, which was what they had truthfully expected, but which soured their moods nonetheless, all the more.

Joel Banks was the one who had "discovered" the skull. He had accomplished this by tripping over it and falling flat on his face in a puddle just a few moments before. "Yeah, well now we've found something. I say we go back and tell the damned Chief," he said sarcastically while actually trying to wring water out of one of his sleeves.

"Suits me," Officer Stephens affirmed quickly.

The two of them then looked anxiously at Officer Christopher for final affirmation, but he had wandered about 30 feet away, and wasn't listening. He appeared to be studying the ground.

"What do ya say, Ben? We're thinking we should head in now, OK?" Bill yelled out impatiently.

Officer Christopher, still looking down, disappeared behind a tree, then came out again. He looked over at the other two. "Come over here and look at this," he said.

"Shit," Bill said.

"God damn it!" Joel mumbled.

But they began walking over, with Joel wringing out his other sleeve as they went.

"Look at this," Ben said when they got within a few feet.

They looked down at what appeared to be a large femur-type of bone, along with some other scattered smaller ones.

"More cow bones," Bill said disgustedly after a few moments. "So what?"

"Can we go home now, Daddy?" Joel asked.

Officer Christopher looked up at the two of them disgustedly. "There's still meat, and blood on some of these," he said after looking down again. "And they're scattered...all over. What's that tell us?"

"That the coyotes weren't done yet," Joel said dryly. His teeth were beginning to chatter.

Ben looked at him seriously. "Maybe," he said. "But here's the important thing, guys: nobody has cattle anywhere near here. This isn't exactly Clinton County, you know. And besides, nobody steals cows to eat them raw. How in God's name does a cow..."

The sharp cracking sound frightened all three of them as much as a rifle shot would have. All three jumped involuntarily as a large tree branch fell a few seconds later, not fifty feet away from them. As soon as it had fallen there was another crack, closer and even more ear-splitting, and then another huge branch crashed down not fifteen feet away.

The three looked from the closer branch to each other, with eyes widened.

The rain had suddenly stopped. There was no breeze There had been no lightening. Nothing. It was very still, the way its always said to be before...something happens.

The air felt suddenly warmer.

"I think maybe you guys are right," Ben Christopher said a few moments later. He looked quickly around, briefly at the other two, and then behind him, as if he was expecting something else to happen. And soon. "We need to get out of here," he said. "Right now."

Chapter 13
October 6th 4:14 P.M.

Darrin and Janice were waiting in her office, this time nervously, for Police Chief Thomas to arrive. He was almost half-an-hour late. There wasn't much to do but pace, look out the window at the rapidly clearing Autumn afternoon, and make small talk.

Darrin did the pacing while Janice sat at her desk looking, at least outwardly, calm and in control. Darrin provided most of the small talk too. "Generally, he's not this late," he said as he stood by the window looking out. "But in truth, he averages about 15 minutes and 37 seconds beyond the assigned time." He looked at his watch for effect. "He's not late, technically, if he's within that amount of time. So that makes him a little less than 15 minutes late this time, which is not bad at all. No problem!"

Darrin turned to see Janice's reaction, expecting a grudging smile at his boyish charm, at least. But she appeared not to have heard him. She was instead looking thoughtfully, lips pursed, at the conference table across the room; the table that they had been working on for most of the past four hours. Her usually fluttery slender hands formed a still and perfect temple on the desk before her. She was lost in her thoughts.

When Chief Thomas finally came through the door exactly one minute and three seconds later, he was exactly the Chief

Thomas that they didn't want to see. His forehead was creased, his eyes narrowed and challenging, and his posture was well, the "to hell with all of you and the horse you rode in on" posture.

He didn't even apologize, as he always did, for being late. Instead, after swinging the door open and giving each of them "the look," he silently and purposefully strode over to the conference table, pulled a chair out and sat down hard, then looked at all the drawings and paper piled before him.

After a silent moment he shot a menacing glance toward Darrin, who was still standing by the window. "What the hell is all this stuff?" he demanded.

Darrin looked at his boss, then at Janice (who now seemed to be studying her fingernails to avoid looking at either of them), then back at the Chief again. "Good afternoon!" Darrin smiled.

But Chief Thomas didn't. He kept his expressionless glare on Darrin, and didn't move a muscle otherwise. "The man could intimidate the damned Pope," Darrin thought as he struggled to meet the Chief's eyes.

What happened next could not have surprised Darrin more. Or the Police Chief, for that matter.

"That *stuff*," Janice said, "is what we've been working on all afternoon, Chief Thomas. We asked to see you because we think some of it may be important." Darrin looked at her in amazement. She was looking directly at Chief Thomas, and spoke with a direct, commanding voice. "You are half-an-hour late," she continued, "and you are obviously upset about something. My suggestion would be that before we share our information with you, you tell us why; why you're late, and what it is that's got your shorts in a bunch."

Darrin whirled his head back toward his boss so fast that he hurt his neck. As he had anticipated, the Chief's glare was now directed fully upon the City Manager. If anything, his glare seemed even more terrible. For the next few long moments, Darrin looked quickly back and forth at the two of them, as though he was watching a fascinating psychological tennis match. Which he was.

Then the second impossible thing happened. Chief Thomas looked down, sighed heavily, and said "I'm sorry, guys."

"Definitely the Twilight Zone," Darrin thought as he looked at the still demanding, confident demeanor of Janice. She was looking at the Chief hard, and waiting for him to go on, like a mother waiting for an apology.

"Somebody dug my dog up," the Chief said as he studied his lap. "Somebody stole his body. I had to go home for a while." He looked up at Janice, the strain now plainly showing on his face. "Who would do such a thing?" he asked pleadingly.

Darrin listened, and watched, with his mouth hung open.

He decided he needed to sit down.

★　　　★　　　★

Not a half-mile away, Amanda Meachum was carrying a basket of clothes outside to hang on her clothesline. It was windy and very chilly outside with the reluctant sun only occasionally peeking out from behind dark gray clouds, but it least the rains had moved on, and Amanda needed desperately to stay busy.

In fact, she had needed to stay busy, to bury herself in work, for a long time now. True-it was worse, much worse, since Bobby had been bitten and horribly mangled by the dog, then gotten sick and disappeared from the hospital after the awful attack on Dr. Bledsoe. She didn't want to even think of all that, and had re-doubled her self-assigned tasks since then. But her compulsion to work in order not to face things had been there, and had been steadily building, for years. As Bobby grew wilder and as her husband grew more distant, it had just grown.

Her dryer was working fine. There was no need at all for this, she knew. But it was busy work. Blessed busy work.

The wind gusts made it hard. She kept dropping clothes, which immediately got even wetter and even grass-stained from lying even momentarily on the saturated lawn. Her tennis-shoed feet began to absorb moisture and make her uncomfortable. Her hands were getting numb, and she kept dropping clothespins. A gust of wind blew so hard that it tipped her basket up and almost over, and a pair of her husband's underwear escaped onto the ground.

"Damn it!' she cried out loud, then immediately looked up at her nosy next-door neighbor's windows to make sure no one was watching. No one was. She paused, dropped her arms. She suddenly felt like crying.

"Hi, Mom," her son Bobby said.

He was standing by the fence, about twenty feet away. He was smiling, in a strangely knowing, confident, unnatural way. In a way he never did before. His lips were pulled way back. Almost all of his teeth were showing.

Just then, the sun came out. Bobby looked up at it, and as he did so, his mother caught a glimpse, in a lightening-like flash, of his solid yellow eyes.

Amanda couldn't breathe. She took a step back. Then another. Her son still looked up in wonder at the sun. She heard a low, seemingly appreciative growling coming from him.

She took several more steps back toward the house, away from him, more rapidly now.

He began to slowly lower his head. She turned and ran. She got to the door in seven more steps, fumbled with it, opened it, went in and then slammed behind her. She locked it with shaking hands, then sank to the floor, sobbing, and trembling. She was more afraid than she'd ever been in her life.

It took minutes for her to gain a semblance of composure. All the while she tried to listen, tried not to breathe too hard, tried to get a hold of herself...but occasionally it would hit her, and then she would sob loudly, and would have to fight to keep from losing herself altogether.

Eventually, after several failed attempts, she gathered enough courage to shakily get to her feet, to practically crawl up the door, and finally, to look out the window.

She saw the all yellow eyes first, then the tiny black pupils. It took her a moment to understand. Bobby's pale, distorted face was pressed against the glass. And he was smiling at her.

★   ★   ★

"...so there's been no progress, on anything, really. Nothing yet on the Melleville killing, except that it was definitely cat hair that was floating all over the place, if you can believe it," Chief Thomas said. Darrin and Janice exchanged a look. "Nothing, absolutely nothing on the missing kids," he continued, "and that's going to blow up big time if something doesn't give pretty damned soon. News media is already interviewing the parents. They're all over it." The Sheriff leaned back and took a breath. The stress he was under was incredible, and very obvious just from looking at his face, now that Janice had managed to deflate, or at least re-channel his anger.

"Nothing on the Sheriff either, I'm guessing?" Darrin ventured.

"Not really," Chief Thomas answered after a pause. "There is one thing kind of new. Seems that old Harvey Milton...you know, the guy we ran into out there?" the Chief asked as he looked Darrin's way.

Darrin nodded.

"Well, seems he went out searching this morning when the others were waiting for the rain to quit. On his own. Well, now they can't find him either. Isn't that wonderful?"

"Probably wandering around the woods. Hopefully, not lost," Darrin said.

"Probably. Probably that's it," the Chief answered. He wanted desperately to put his feet up on the table and lean back in his chair, but was afraid to in someone else's place. "But they found some blood on the road. By his car. Looked fresh, they said, but..."

"There was so much blood from that torn up cow," Darrin interjected. "How could they tell..."

"Tests, my boy. That's why they run tests," Chief Thomas interrupted. He leaned back in his chair and ran his hand through his thinning hair once again, but he did not put his feet up. "It's so damned frustrating," he said. He looked over at Darrin. "Kind of like it was back then, isn't it?" he asked, his voice sounding oddly vulnerable.

Darrin nodded, but did not answer. He looked over at Janice, who nodded firmly toward him. It was time. He took a deep breath and began: "Chief, Janice and I have been working on something. Now I know, with everything going on, that you could say that, maybe I should have been out there working in the field this afternoon," he said a little too defensively, "but, well...I feel, we feel, that maybe somebody ought to be looking at the bigger picture here. Do you know what I mean?"

Chief Thomas sat with hands folded on the top of his head, staring glumly at Darrin.

Darrin didn't continue. Instead he looked away, toward Janice. They had listened to the Chief's update (from the horrible personal story of his dog to the total lack of progress on everything else) for the last 10 minutes. It was their turn now. That's why they'd asked him here.

But... how to start?

"We made a map," Janice said flatly. And again, unexpectedly. At least by Darrin. "We took all the police reports, all the 'unofficial' things we knew about...that we heard from doctors, vets..."

"And Priests," Darrin added.

"Right, right," Janice said quickly, "and we put in the houses where the kids are missing, where the County Sheriff disappeared... everything we had."

She stopped here and looked at Darrin, hoping he would pick it up there. He didn't get it, until she nodded.

"Oh, uh... yeah," he finally began. "Uh... I want you to look at this map thing we made, Chief." He stood and moved papers around until he found the map. Then he turned it the right direction and laid it in front of his boss.

Chief Thomas glanced at both of them while reaching into his pocket for a pair of reading glasses; glasses that Darrin had rarely see him use. The expression on his face was a cynical one though. He put on his glasses, bent forward, and studied the map of the Highland area that had been put before him.

For about five seconds. "Looks like some retarded kid tried to draw a circle on your map," he said peevishly as he leaned back in his chair. "...and he did a horrible job."

"That's not the point!" Janice snapped. "We plotted out the exact point where every , uh, strange thing happened since that... that flash thing happened. Then we drew a line to connect them all...to see if there was a pattern, or, or a limit, of some kind..." She was stumbling. Too angry. She looked over at Darrin for help.

He was ready this time. "Chief, this stuff that's happening in Highland, and around Highland; it isn't happening anywhere else. We know that. You know that. And before you say it, yes, it might be that everything, all these events... are totally unconnected. We know that. But I, we...don't see anything wrong with working with a different assumption here, just for the hell of it. Suppose it's all connected? Suppose that this map shows us, in some way, where its all coming from...where the center of it is?"

The Chief's face didn't really show it but Darrin could tell, from experience, that he was at least trying to listen.

The Chief looked at Darrin for a few seconds, sighed, then leaned over to look at the map again. This time he studied it for half a minute before leaning back, taking off his glasses, and tiredly rubbing his eyes. "OK, I see your point," he said unenthusiastically. He looked at his watch. "Got another meeting to go to." He looked at Darrin. "It's with those three I sent into the woods behind Devonshire. Wanna come?"

Darrin glanced over at Janice before answering. She looked very disappointed. "Did they find anything?" he asked the Chief?

"No, as far as I know, but they wanted to talk to me after their shift was over." He looked at his watch again. "And that's about now."

Darrin shrugged his shoulders. "Yeah," he said, "I'll be along in a minute."

Chief Thomas got up and left the room without another word. The door closed and the room was silent, with neither Darrin nor Janice said anything. There really wasn't anything to say.

After a moment, Darrin got up and walked over to the window. The sun was momentarily out, the wind was blowing hard and in gusts, and he could hear the distant sound of an ambulance headed somewhere, again, in the little town of Highland.

Chapter 14
October 6th 7:57 P.M.

The "party" was Darrin's idea. Fortunately, his friend Jon was all for it. That part was important, because the party was to be at Jon's house.

He had gotten the idea on the way home after listening to the three young cops describe their experience in the woods in Chief Thomas' office. What he'd heard from them was familiar... and chilling. Nothing had really happened (bedsides the bizarre discovery of cow remains), yet the experience had clearly gotten to all three of them; especially their spokesman, the sharpest of the three, Ben Christopher. The kid was careful with his words but, Darrin could tell, he knew something wasn't right out there. Something large.

And the Chief knew it too. Darrin could see it in his face, though the boss wouldn't so much as look at him the whole time Officer Christopher was talking.

So inevitably, when he finally got behind the wheel to head out of there after a long, frustrating day, Darrin's thoughts were on the infamous woods, what had happened there two years ago, and what Jon had seen out there just the night before. The map that Janice and he had made (if it was worth anything at all) showed the woods behind Devonshire to be on the outer, southern perimeter of all that had happened. But there was nothing but more woods and endless fields south of those woods. Maybe it was actually the center of the "flash"? It was worth a thought, at least.

All this made him realize he wanted to be on Jon's deck that night. He wanted to see what Jon had seen, even if a repeat was unlikely. But he was married now. Happily. And it was Friday night. Going out night. Couldn't just go traipsing off to a buddy's house. Unless??

It was easy to get Jon to host a party. There were two good reasons: the previous night had shook him up, and he loved the idea of having company around should anything happen again, and secondly, Darrin had had the wherewithal to promise that Marilyn would invite a few single women. Jon hooked. Easy.

The second part was harder. Marilyn had wanted to do nothing more than go out for a quiet dinner (...we still can, honey!!), and she felt awkward about inviting her friends to a last minute party. Darrin told her to "tell them we're going to see ghosts," and "... this is the guy that wrote the scary book!"

She eventually, if reluctantly, agreed.

With that completed, Darrin decided to invite two people himself: Ben Christopher and Janice Granger. Ben was understandably tired, but was flattered because it was Darrin asking, and so readily accepted. Janice demurred at first, but in the end her own curiosity won her over. She had at least begun reading Jon Parker's "A Haunting in Highland," was fascinated with the story of what Jon had supposedly seen the night before and, well, frankly, she didn't have anything better to do that night. " "I mean, I could sit around listening for my dead cat, or..." she'd thought.

"I'd be glad to come," she'd said.

So Darrin and Marilyn were the first to arrive, walking next door at a few minutes before 8:00 with a bottle of wine and a 12-pack of beer. Jon greeted them wearing a big smile and a white shirt and tie, which amused Darrin, but he didn't say anything about it. The mere prospect of a woman on the horizon could make a man do strange things, he knew.

Darrin's immediate interest was to check out the deck. It was chilly and still a bit breezy out, and he wanted to make sure it was comfortable, even inviting out there. It wasn't. Jon had been so busy trying to clean up his house and himself in the previous few hours that he'd done nothing for what Darrin considered to be the main attraction. Who the hell would want to stay indoors making small talk all night?

So Darrin went to work. He brought up Jon's fire pit, cleaned it out, fetched some fire wood from the pile down by the fence, built an inviting fire and cleaned off the lawn chairs. In no time, the deck was the warm, cozy party-escape place. he'd envisioned. Perfect.

By the time he had finished and came in to wash his now filthy hands several of the others had arrived, and the kitchen was filled with amiable small talk. Besides Jon and Marilyn and the just arrived Officer Ben Christopher, there were three people that Darrin didn't know. Two gals, one of whom Jon was awkwardly trying to talk to, and a guy who looked like some actor Darrin knew but couldn't think of the name of. He looked like he was already bored, and Darrin guessed that he was with the other new girl; the one who kept looking worriedly at him.

After washing up and grabbing a beer out of the cooler (and getting a rather dirty look from his new wife, for some reason) Darrin was quickly cornered by the nervous looking Officer Christopher. It was easy to understand why. Darrin was the only person there that he knew.

"Hell of a day, wasn't it?" young Ben asked.

"Hell of a week," Darrin answered, thinking about how, inevitably, people go to a party or out for a drink to get away from work, and then talk about work.

"Yep, it was," Ben replied. He didn't know what else to say. He looked nervous to Darrin. He saw Ben's eyes wander out toward the deck. "Can we go out there?" he asked, pointing his beer bottle in that direction.

"Sure," Darrin answered. "Go on out. I'll join you in a minute."

And though he wanted nothing more than to do so, it was a full half-an hour before Darrin would join his fellow officer outdoors. There were introductions, handshakes and much small talk to make. And there was an intricate, sensitive verbal dance with Marilyn that had to be done, which would end with a charming confession, an effusive declaration of love, and then grudging, if predictable, forgiveness (somehow, and it was a mystery to him as to how, she had figured out his true intentions behind planning this "party").

It was only when Janice Granger arrived, nervously clutching a bottle of wine that was far too expensive for the caliber of the gathering, and only because she looked like she desperately needed a place to retreat before she had even taken her coat off, that Darrin remembered the forlorn Ben Christopher waiting for him on the deck.

But it took almost another ten minutes for Darrin to steer Janice out there. Besides mandatory introductions ("... and she's the City Manager!"), Darrin was interrupted by a phone call from Chief Thomas, which caused an almost five minute retreat into Jon's study.

"Ben Christopher, this is Janice Granger. She's the City Manager, and a good friend," Darrin said by way of introduction as he, Marilyn and Janice moved to their seats by the fire.

Ben had been sound asleep, and was now blushing heavily as he jumped up and reached to shake Janice's hand. It was dark enough on the deck, even with the low fire, that no one could tell that he was blushing. In fact, no one knew he had been sleeping either, but he didn't know that. "Sorry about that," he said sheepishly, "It's been a long day."

Janice was confused, and assumed that he must be apologizing for his handshake, or something. She smiled, said nothing, and sat down.

"That was Chief Thomas on the phone," Darrin said immediately to Janice. "That ambulance we heard this afternoon? It was for that Meachum kid's Mom. You know, the one that bit Dr. Bledsoe's hand off? She had a heart attack and died this afternoon."

Darrin was obviously not yet at the stage in his young marriage where he would keep certain professional information from the ears of his wife. The idea had yet to even cross his mind. But his stark relating of the brutal facts made both Janice and Ben visibly uneasy. They both stole glances over at Marilyn, who was merely smiling as patiently as she would if her husband was discussing football.

"Heart attack?" Ben ventured to ask after an uncomfortable moment. It was a mistake.

"Yep. And get this: the Chief said she had this frozen look of, like, terror on her face, like somebody scared her to death. And there was blood all down the front of her because she had bitten her own lip half..."

"All right Darrin! We get the picture!" Janice interrupted forcefully. She looked over at Marilyn, who was still smiling, but looking less comfortable. "It has been a long week," she added in a much softer voice, "maybe we should talk about something else."

The ensuing silence was broken quickly. The glass door leading out to the deck opened, and Jon came out, leading the cute little blond that he had been spending all his time talking to indoors. Both were smiling happily. As soon as the door closed it opened again and the remaining two partiers - Marilyn's other friend Mary and the tall, aloof guy named Jim, the guy who looked like that actor Darrin couldn't think of - came out. There were more people than lawn chairs now, but most of the guys stood, and no one seemed to care.

It was a crisp, beautiful fall night; still a bit windy but perfect temperature wise, with the fire. The mostly cloudy skies made it very dark most of the time, but occasionally the almost full moon would break through dramatically above them, which always caused at least one person in the group to interrupt whatever conversation was taking place to call everyone else's attention to the wonder of it. In general though the weather, the atmosphere and the alcohol made it increasingly easy for everyone to talk, laugh, and enjoy themselves. The next hour passed in this way; general, convivial conversation interrupted only by quick individual trips inside to fetch drinks or to use the bathroom-or by sudden moon appearances.

A good time, it seemed, at this improbable, impromptu party, was being had by all.

But, as the saying goes, it only takes one.

Tall, sullen Jim was unusually quiet, though only his date Mary seemed to notice (and she paid it less and less attention). He spent most of that increasingly jovial hour standing by the railing of the deck, his back to the fire and the conversation, staring moodily out into the blackness that was Jon's back yard, with the pasture, and the woods beyond. The view he had was basically non existent, except for the times when the moon made a dramatic appearance, and even then he saw only indefinable shadows. Still, he stood, and watched, and sulked...and waited.

"So this is supposedly where it all happened, huh?" he said suddenly in a loud voice, right at one of those rare, always odd moments that happen at a gathering when three or four conversations stop, for some reason, in unison.

And it worked. They all stopped and turned to look at him. Jim waited, his back still facing them, for a few long moments. Then he turned and looked directly at Jon. "Am I right?" he asked in an unmistakably mocking tone. "Isn't this where all the ghosts come out and get you?"

Mary was immediately embarrassed, and the rest were confused and uncomfortable. No one was prepared for sarcasm directed at the host; or a mean drunk.

Jon looked at his new friend Belinda, who's hand he had just gotten up enough nerve to tentatively hold, and then over at Darrin. Darrin was looking at Jim. Everyone else was doing the same.

"Yeah, I read your book!" Jim said; again, in a voice much louder than necessary. "Pretty good...pretty good. But you don't expect anybody to buy all that shit, do you?" he sneered as he tried to turn so that he was completely facing Jon. He hit his foot on a chair and almost stumbled, but grabbed onto the railing in time to steady himself.

Jon squeezed the hand he was holding harder, but didn't respond.

Darrin did. "It happened, dude," he said calmly, then: "What's your point, anyway?"

Jim turned slightly to look at Darrin. He looked for a moment like he was about to fire something back, but then changed his mind. Instead he grinned, turned unsteadily back toward the darkness, and said "Why don't we go out there right now? See how scary it is. Huh?" He turned back again to the now silent group. "Who's got the guts to go with me? Huh? Who's not chicken?"

All the others either shifted uncomfortably or just plain looked away at this point. There was a long silence.

"I wouldn't go out there, if I were you," Ben Christopher said, surprising everyone.

"Why not?...Shicken?" Jim slurred.

"It was soaking wet this morning, and I'm sure its soaking wet now," Ben said.

A sudden, very strong gust of wind swept the deck. Jim had to hold hard onto the rail to keep from toppling over, several of the men who were standing had to shift their feet for balance, and the fire was all but blown out, with a single weak flame licking up when it was over.

"Yes," Ben Christopher added shortly afterwards, "... to tell you the truth, I'm chicken."

Chapter 15
October 6th 10:33 P.M.

"Hell of a way to end a hell of a week," Darrin said as the four of them finally got to their seats around the dying fire.

It had taken over 45 minutes in all to: talk Jim down from his drunken insults and threats, convince him that it was time to go home, convince him (Darrin had to resort to threatening arrest) that he was in no shape to drive, and finally, to get him loaded into the back seat of his own car, put his seat belt on, and wish the luckless Mary luck as she drove him away.

Belinda, who seemed to be as initially smitten with Jon as he was with her, had reluctantly agreed to ride shotgun for Mary, and Marilyn had feigned a headache and walked home next door at the conclusion of the excitement (not a good sign for the rest of Darrin's night, the rest of them could see, but again, he seemed totally oblivious to it, and went happily back to his beer on the deck).

So then there were four. Darrin and a disappointed Jon were the old hands on (the) deck, literally, having spent many an evening there in the not too recent past. Janice and Ben were new and had to be asked repeatedly to stay, which they did after many "...the evening is still young!" type pleadings. After all, they had both been having a good time, they both needed to get away from the center of the storm they had been in, and truthfully, they both wanted to talk some more.

The fire was fed and soon re-enlivened, Jon fetched a blanket that the chilled Janice covered up with, fresh drinks were provided to all, and soon the four were comfortable in the invigorating autumn air. There was no thought of going inside, or being anywhere else but where they were, there on Jon's deck, for at least a little while longer.

"Were you kidding when you told him that you were "chicken" to go out there?" Janice asked Ben as they settled down.

Officer Christopher had just met her, and he wasn't sure why, but he found Janice to be a bit intimidating. There was something about her eyes, and that "in charge" voice that made her seem a little smarter than whoever she was talking to. He knew it was silly, but he had avoided eye-contact with her when he could. He had the same problem with Chief Thomas, and at first, even with Darrin. He knew it was something he had to get over.

But not tonight. Before answering her he half-turned around in his chair and, looking pensively into the direction of the black woods, said "Not really, I guess, although I'd hate to go out there now. It was pretty creepy out there, though. I'll admit that."

"You don't know the half of it, dude," Darrin said flatly. He shook his head and looked at the can of beer that he was holding in his lap.

Jon cleared his throat, rather theatrically right then. It was an effort, Ben thought, to get Darrin's attention. It didn't work.

"Jon could tell you, but he won't," Darrin continued suddenly. He looked briefly up at Jon, but not long enough to see him shaking his head no. "Jon's book is called fiction, but most of it isn't. Those woods are haunted." He looked up and made eye contact with Janice, then Ben. "I know that sounds nuts, but its true." he said firmly.

"Come on, Darrin! Cut it out!" Jon snapped. He was obviously uncomfortable with where Darrin was taking the conversation.

But Darrin just smiled and looked down. Jon stood up, then sat right back down again. Ben could see the tension in their host, even if Darrin was oblivious.

Then, unexpectedly, Janice came to the rescue. At least in a sense. "I'm more interested in what you saw last night," she said to Jon, "and trying to understand what's happening now." She looked from Jon to the other two. "Aren't you guys?" she asked. "I mean, we all know that something...happened. And I think we all know that, whatever it is, it's, it's all related, or tied together, somehow. But we all act like its not. Like everything's normal... and it's not."

With that she sat back, took a sip of her wine, and waited.

But whatever dialogue she had hoped to start by this stating of the obvious, didn't materialize. No one said anything. Ben was interested, but felt like he was the least informed about everything (he had no idea, for instance, what Jon had "seen" the night before), and so waited reticently and said nothing. Darrin had suddenly gone silent, and seemed content to just stare glumly at the fire. Jon still appeared to be angry about something, and either didn't hear Janice's question, or didn't care to answer it.

So they sat in a silence that seemed to feed on itself, with each passing moment not only sustaining, but seeming to call for more of the same. The wind still blew in gusts, though not as hard. The air grew chillier by the minute. The clouds had completely, depressingly covered up any semblance of the moon, and the foursome gradually surrendered to just quietly nursing their drinks and morosely staring into the still hearty fire.

It was Janice, who had inadvertently ushered in the time of silent reflection, who some long minutes later broke it. "Like Darrin said, 'its been a hell of a week.' I think I'm headed home, guys. A good night's sleep would do us all..."

The cat's piercing cry stopped her. It came from the darkness just off the deck behind Janice. Darrin, who was looking directly past the fire and at Janice's shadowy face as she spoke, suffered the uncanny optical illusion that the wailing was coming from her mouth. Jon would say later that, in those first few, panicked moments that that was his first impression too.

Ben was stretching and beginning to yawn when it happened, and had no such illusion. The only question in his mind as he jumped to his feet was whether it was a cat...or something bigger.

It was (mainly) the sound heard on a thousand summer nights-a mating or battling cat, yet, there with something more to it, that made it twice as chilling. Jon, the writer and English teacher, would later describe it as "a lion's deep, throaty gurgle," and though the three others readily agreed with that there would still be a feeling that it really wasn't quite right.

It was beyond description. It was horrifying to them all, perhaps especially so because it had followed a long period of silence. And because it was right in the yard, right next to the deck, and right next to them.

By the time they had all leaped to their feet, it had stopped. All four froze. Ben looked out and down at the ground off the deck behind Janice, but could see nothing in the inky blackness. The other three looked at each other. All held their collective breath.

Then it came again, now from the other side of the deck. Piercingly loud and overwhelmingly menacing. Especially because they couldn't see it.

By the time all four had jump-turned in the direction of the cry, it stopped again. No sound could be heard then but the leaves rattling in distant trees with the wind and the crackle and licking flames of the fire right.

"Get the hell in the house," Darrin said in a low, calm voice a few moments later. "Right now."

Jon was closest to the door. He scrambled to it, opened it, and waved frantically for the others to run in.

The wild cat scream came again, this time loud enough to make Ben grind his teeth, right before ran inside the door.

Chapter 16
October 7th 9:33 A.M.

"I don't care how late you were up, or how bad your hangover is. Get your ass in here!" is the stark way Chief Thomas had put it.

So Darrin did, and now found himself sitting and waiting, as usual, outside of the Chief's office. His headache was enormous, partially because the aspirin he'd gulped hadn't had time to work yet - but mostly because he'd kept drinking long after the others had gone to coffee (which was right after they'd all scrambled inside). He'd kept it up 'til 4:00 in the morning, knowing that he had the day off to sleep in. And now??...well, sometimes the best laid plans...

"Good morning, Darrin!" a smiling Chief Thomas seemed to scream as he turned the corner in surprise.

Darrin spilled some of the soda he was nursing onto his shirt. "Damn it!" he cried. The scare made his head start throbbing even harder.

Chief Thomas walked right past him and into his office. "Come on in as soon as you've got it together there, missy," he shouted happily over his shoulder.

Darrin put his soda down, his hands up to his head, and took a deep breath. "What a prick," he mumbled.

A minute later he was sitting on the other side of the Chief's desk. He had every reason to be in a foul mood, but really wasn't. He was more interested in trying to survive the hangover. Despite whatever Chief Thomas wanted, or what kind of games he played, he had bigger problems to solve. Number one of course, was not throwing up. But the fact that his new wife wouldn't speak to him that morning was even bigger. And of course there was the fact that he couldn't remember how he got home from his friend's house next door...

"I wanted you down here because Nancy Melleville called me, and she's coming in to talk in about a half-an-hour," the Chief said as he put his feet up on his desk.

Darrin squinted at the Chief, who was spinning slowly, and tried to think. Nancy Melleville? Oh yeah, the wife of the murdered guy. Half-an-hour? I could have slept for another half-an-hour??

"She didn't go into much detail, but I got the impression that she wants to tell me something new...something that she hasn't told any of the detectives about yet."

Darrin looked down. The floor wasn't spinning, but it seemed to be slowly receding. He burped, then said "Why do you need me for that?"

Chief Thomas looked down from the ceiling and over at Darrin. He wrinkled his nose. "Gee whiz! You smell like a brewery, you know that?"

Darrin didn't answer or look up. A receding floor was better than a spinning Chief.

"Because I want you here, that's all. Two brains are better than one," The Chief said affirmatively. He rubbed his feet together in order to take care of an itch on the top of his left foot. To Darrin, this sounded like thunder. And he didn't respond this time either. He was trying to think coherently, and not get sick. At the moment that was all he could do.

"Nothing happened last night, thank God," Chief Thomas continued. He obviously didn't care about or was oblivious to

Darrin's current physical state. "'Course, we didn't find the missing kids, or the Sheriff or nothin," he turned to look at the top of Darrin's head, "...but nobody got killed, anyway."

Darrin took a breath, then slowly, painfully turned his head to look up at the clock on the wall. Twenty minutes 'til Mrs. Melleville.

"What the hell is happening here, Darrin? What the hell are we gonna do?" the Chief asked suddenly.

Chief Thomas' question caused Darrin to look up at him, even though he didn't want to. The Chief wasn't looking at him. He was looking back up at the ceiling. The bizarrely spinning ceiling.

"I have to go to the bathroom," Darrin said.

And he raced out.

★   ★   ★

Janice had slept all of two hours, but she was already up and working and feeling more energized than she had in recent memory.

She sat in her robe at her kitchen table. And on that table, beside her cup of coffee, lay the spread out "Incidents Map" that she and Darrin had worked on the day before, her just finished copy of Jonathon Parker's "A Haunting in Highland," and a yellow legal pad that she had been wildly scribbling notes on for the last half-an-hour. And she was thinking of things to write down far faster than her aching hand could handle.

Finally, despite the fact that much of what her mind was moving toward was illogical; even impossible, she felt like she was (maybe) on to something.

For Janice, the long night before had turned, in a flash, from a mostly pleasant get-away from a monstrous week-to a riveting, if terrifying, epiphany.

After the screaming cat, or whatever it was, incident (which took a long time for them to come down from) the four had sat around Jon's kitchen table and talked and talked-well into the night. At first, it was mostly Darrin. But he kept drinking and gradually became more incoherent and then, finally, quiet. Ben told them, in detail, about the morning search, the cow bones, and the mysterious tree limbs breaking from no apparent cause.

And eventually, Jon started talking. It took only a couple of strategic, careful questions from Janice to get him going, but the mad cat was probably the real impetus. Once he started he didn't stop-for almost an hour. It was as horrifying as it was captivating, and she and Ben had listened for most of that time in rapt wonder. Darrin had listened for a while too, but his familiarity with the story along with his continued alcohol consumption soon had him fighting to stay awake.

Between what Jon said, finishing his book and the implausible thoughts scurrying madly through her own mind - Janice was on a high that she'd seldom felt before.

She was on to something. She could feel it. But what?

She sat back, took a sip of coffee, then leaned forward to read her own notes for the first time. It wasn't easy. It was haphazard, stream-of-consciousness stuff at best:

"cats by the deck...cat fur at murder scene...Socks dead but-calling in the night

...missing cows...dead cows found-two places...dog attacks...dead dog missing...animals infected? somehow?

Could flash moment cause insanity?...dreams of children dead, but not

...children missing -also "infected"?? unsolved murders - animals and people - two years ago...woods haunted - no one, nothing caught-still there??

Are we trying 'logic' when this is not 'logical'??"

And that was just the beginning of them. Her scribbling went on for two pages. She felt fevered with excitement; but frightened and a bit frustrated too. All of it seemed linked, but mysteriously so. Wildly so-inexplicably so. She couldn't quite see it, or understand exactly what she was even looking for. It was a crazy, and probably a total waste of energy to do this, but...

But there was something there! Had to be!

Janice read through all her notes, all her random thoughts, once again. Then she deliberately sat back, looked away from the table and out the window at the sunny Saturday morning. She tried to think clearly; to breathe and think clearly.

"Whatever was out there then...is back now. But its worse than before. I can feel it, and it's worse," Jon had said to them, dramatically, in the wee hours of the morning.

There was something there. Something out there.

And she knew it too. In her bones, she knew it.

★   ★   ★

Darrin walked back into the office 15 minutes later. Nancy Melleville was already there.

"Come on in Darrin. We're just about to start."

As Chief Thomas said this, Mrs. Melleville turned around to see who he was talking to. Darrin saw two things at once: Nancy Melleville's red, hopelessly sad eyes...and the very dirty look the Chief gave him when he knew she wasn't looking.

Darrin steeled himself, then walked over to sit next to the stricken widow. He barely had time to offer his condolences before the Chief started the interview.

"Mrs. Melleville, I've asked Detective Crandle to come in and listen to what you have to say. I hope you don't mind. He's one of the best we've got, Mrs. Melleville," he added, "...and he's trustworthy."

"You can call me Nancy," Nancy said. She then looked from Chief Thomas over briefly to Darrin, and then to the Chief again. "OK," she said, "can I start now?"

Chief Thomas nodded. Nancy leaned back in her chair and took a deep breath. Then she looked away from the Chief again.

She seemed to focus on one of the few pictures he had in the office. It was the picture of his dead (and now missing) dog.

"I just thought you should know..." she began in a hesitant, wavery voice, "that, that I saw something...I saw something when I found Bart." She sobbed slightly and brought the handkerchief she had in her shaking hand up to dab at her eyes. Darrin thought that the Chief needed to say something reassuring here, but he didn't.

"I...I didn't say anything to, to the other policemen, because it seemed so...unimportant, so unbelievable that I, I thought it was because I was in shock, you know...because I had already found my husband, and..."

She stopped, and started crying. Hard. Darrin looked at Chief Thomas, who didn't move. So he reached a hand over and patted the poor woman on the arm. "Its OK. Its OK now," he said as gently as he could.

Nancy looked at Darrin, and tried a smile. It was a weak one. "Thank you," she managed to eke out.

"What did you see?" Chief Thomas demanded. Darrin gave him a peeved look. Chief Thomas didn't see it, or didn't care.

"When...when I looked out back, in the back yard, I mean... because the door was open," she stopped and had a sharp intake of breath; stifling a sob. Darrin wasn't sure she was going to make it. "I saw this big cat," she said suddenly, "...this horrible cat...just looking at me. And...over by the fence, right by the fence, there was a man, or maybe a boy, I guess, I don't know...he was coming for the cat. Maybe?...I don't know..."

Then she started to cry again. She tried to fight it, but couldn't, and eventually covered her face, and sobbed.

Darrin started to comfort her again, but thought better of it. Let her cry it out. He looked at Chief Thomas. He was staring intently at the widow, studying her. And there was no sign of sympathy on his face. Darrin knew him well enough to know why. In the Chief's mind, she had withheld information. Obstruction of justice-pure and simple. That's the way he saw things.

"Why were they in your yard?" the Chief demanded a moment later. "What were they doing there? Where did they go, Nancy? And why didn't you tell us before?"

"He's mad alright," Darrin thought. The poor woman didn't have a chance, now.

But to his surprise, Nancy seemed to be shaken out of her hysteria, if only for a few moments, by the harshness of the Chief's questions. He saw her look up pleadingly at Chief Thomas as she struggled to compose herself.

"I...I didn't see them again. I mean I saw them, then knelt down by my husband,,,and when I looked up again...they were gone. They disappeared!" She paused, struggling to keep from breaking down again. "I thought...I thought I must have imagined it...because they disappeared!"

Chapter 17

It was, after all, the weekend. And weekends are the goal, the ultimate respite for all who work hard, all who pretend to, and all who don't even try. Time to do something different. Time to work, if work was necessary, for yourself-not someone else. Time to play. Or do nothing.

For Janice (Maker of Lists), what was normally a time of relaxation and trivial, leisurely task-making, was quickly becoming a Saturday of high anxiety and intense frustration. By late morning she had arrived at a state where she needed to talk-right now-with one of two people - Darrin, or Jon. Her ideas were on high boil, and she was desperate for an outlet.

And so, putting aside all of her normal reticence, she finally called them both. The results were predictable. It was the weekend, after all.

Darrin was on his way home from the Nancy Melleville interview. Though he listened politely, and showed some obvious interest and curiosity, he just wanted to go home. It was obvious. First, he was still suffering from a terrible hangover (which he told her about, directly) and he was carrying all the physical and mental burdens that came with it. Secondly, and not unrelated, he was buried deep in the marital doghouse, a deeply depressing place that he was visiting for the first time, and he needed to concentrate all his energies on finding a way out.

And even Darrin knew, instinctively, that going over to Janice's house to talk for an hour or two would not be helpful for his cause.

Jon's reaction reminded her of a guy who had gone out on a date the night before that he thoroughly regretted in the light of the next day's sun. He was polite and cold. While he had "really enjoyed the talk last night," he was "all tied up today." And "sorry about that..."

Janice wondered after hanging up if the poor boy thought she was making a play for him. It was probably a silly thought, but made her blush anyway.

But she didn't give up. After briefly considering, then rejecting the idea of giving a ring to the young Officer Ben Christopher, she called Police Chief Rodney Thomas instead.

He answered on the first ring. He told her he was talking to the F.B.I., and would call her back.

Janice hung up, sighed, then went back to her notes.

★   ★   ★

Jon went out to clean up his deck as soon as he had gotten off the phone with Janice. Three empty beer cans, another almost full one, and a broken wine glass. Not too bad.

He picked the stuff up, moved the fire pit off the deck (heavier than he thought), and grabbed his broom to start sweeping off the ashes and leaves off into his yard.

He thought about two phone calls as he swept: the date for that night that he had made with Belinda a half-an-hour before, and the awkward conversation with Janice Granger just a few minutes ago. In a way, the two put together were a perfect symbol for where his mind was now: anticipation, even excitement at the prospects of a new start with the first one, and an undeniable sense of dread as to what unpredictable, ominous events were on the horizon with the other. He wanted the normalcy of the first one desperately, and he dreaded the second... because his gut told him that second one was coming, whether he was ready for it or not.

Nothing against Janice, though. He had liked her. She was clever, attractive, and very smart. She was also sweet, in a way. Good company, and even though the subject matter of the long night's conversation was mostly serious, he had basically enjoyed it.

He just didn't want to go there again. That night or ever again, if possible. If he could help it...

When the sweeping was done he took a walk around the deck to look for any signs of the big tomcat that had spooked them the night before. He found one more beer can, but no sign or smell of cat.

He went back up, stood on his deck and looked out toward the woods for a minute before going back in. It was good to have the sun out, and good to have the wind finally dying out a bit. Though the temperature was still cool it felt good, almost too warm to be standing there in his flannel shirt. It made him feel a bit tired, and he stretched his arms out and yawned.

He saw it suddenly, in the middle of his yawn, which he abruptly cut off. It was way out by the woods, but not in the direction he was absently staring at the moment before. He saw it out of the corner of his eye, to his right. He closed his mouth, turned his head that way and looked.

Even in the fraction of a second it took him to move his head and focus, he prayed that it was a deer. It wasn't. It was not one but two children. Even from a quarter mile away he could tell that. They were standing at the edge of the woods, dressed in what looked like flowing white gowns or nightshirts of some kind. They didn't move, even though their gowns were flapping in the wind. They just stood there staring, it appeared, directly at him.

★　　　★　　　★

It hit him out of nowhere, right as he was waking from his nap.

And it made Darrin sit up immediately and squint his eyes to adjust to the sunshine pouring into the living room and onto the couch where he'd been sleeping. It took a few seconds to get his bearings, to remember exactly where he was and why. But even in temporary confusion, the thought was still racing through him.

Nancy Melleville had said something as she was leaving the office that morning that was important. Maybe very important. And he had been too sick with his hangover, and the Chief had been too focused on being mad, to really hear it. Or to follow up.

"It was just like in his dream," she had said, trying to explain why the cat and boy she had seen in her yard may have been a hallucination, "I was probably thinking about the dream."

The dream. Neither Chief Thomas nor he had even remotely thought about asking "What dream?" or, "What did he dream about?" They had been concerned with only what was real; about whether or not there really was a damned cat and kid (possible witnesses?) in the friggin' back yard.

Darrin looked down at his lap. No wonder he was sweating. Someone (Marilyn, obviously) had covered him up with a blanket as he slept off his hangover. What a useless piece of garbage he was.

"Marilyn? Honey?" he called out limply. His mouth felt like it had a dirty sock in it. Disgusting.

There was no answer.

He tossed aside the blanket and got to his feet. Headache better, but why was he sore?. He needed a shower and a new start.

He walked stiffly over to the door that led the garage, opened it and confirmed for himself that Marilyn was indeed gone. Then he walked over to the kitchen counter, poured and drank a glass of cold water, then picked up the Highland phone book. He looked up the number of Bart and Nancy Melleville, pulled his cell out of his pocket, and dialed it.

★   ★   ★

"Say that again Bill?" Chief Thomas said. He had actually heard Bill Bellicheck, the funeral director, very clearly. It was just that he desperately didn't want to hear it; desperately wanted it to be a bad joke (which Bill was very capable of) or a hearing problem on his part. Anything else would do..

He was in the process of driving home to spend the rest of his Saturday quietly with his wife. He didn't need to hear what he had just heard. He needed some semblance of normalcy instead. A break of some kind. Because he felt like he was going nuts.

The interview with Nancy Melleville was maddening and frustrating, but the F.B.I. guys were even worse. They had been called in because of the missing kids; the *possible* kidnappings. They called it a "preliminary fact-finding mission," whatever the hell that was. They were rude, and treated him like a rube. He'd pretty much known that they would, and they did.

Now, he just wanted to go home to Joanie, if just for a little while...at least until something else blew up.

"I said the body is missing!" Bill Bellicheck yelled into the phone. "Stolen! I said someone got in here and stole Bart Melleville's remains last night! Can you believe it?" he asked the Chief of Police.

Chapter 18
October 7th 5:17 P.M.

"Janice is on her way, and Chief Thomas might be coming over here too," Darrin said as soon as Jon had opened the door.

Jon opened his mouth to make some kind of objection but Darrin walked right in and past him. Jon was temporarily left standing there holding the door open, looking helplessly out at his front yard and the end of the Devonshire cul-de-sac just beyond.

"Tell me what you saw again, man. Or better yet, come out and show me," Darrin said from behind him.

By the time Jon finally got himself together enough to turn around and answer, Darrin was out of the living room and headed for the deck. "Uh...come on in," he said sarcastically to the empty room.

There was nothing to do but close the door and follow Darrin out back. So after looking once more up the street to see if any more of his other "guests" were turning into the cul-de-sac (they weren't), that's what he did.

"I've got a date in about an hour and a half," Jon said as he opened the door to the deck.

Darrin was at the rail looking out purposefully toward the pasture and woods, and didn't answer. To his dismay, Jon saw that he was keyed up. He hadn't seen that in a long while, and knew that anything could happen now.

"You're the one that called me," Darrin said as he turned from the rail. This was true enough, and stumped Jon for a moment. "Now come here and tell me what you saw, and where you saw it," he added. There was still at least an hour before the sunset, but Darrin was acting like a man with no time. He was on a mission.

Jon walked over to where Darrin was standing and pointed out and to their right. "Over there," he said quietly. "Like I told you, it was two kids. They just stood out there, not moving. Looking this way. The trees were right behind them."

"Girls or boys?"

"Too far away to tell. Definitely kids though. Kids acting, uh, well, strangely," Jon said. Thinking about it again made him shiver. He'd gotten pretty good at blocking things out, but this stuff was starting to get to him. Again. "I should have moved two years ago, Darrin," he said, "you know it?"

"You told me you tried to take their picture?" Darrin asked, ignoring Jon's question.

Jon sighed. "Yeah. I ran in and got the damned camera, but they were gone when I came out, of course." Jon felt it welling up in him then. All of it. The horror from two summers before that he thought was long gone, the dread, the gnawing *knowing* that had almost overcome him when the sudden "flash" happened, the sightings-both the other night and just a little while ago...the stuff that he had tried so hard to bury...

"What's happening Darrin?" he asked. His voice was shaky; on the edge.

The doorbell rang just as Darrin turned to look at his suddenly unhinged friend. Jon was now breathing very hard.

"Someone's at the door," Darrin said quietly. Jon didn't move, so Darrin went to answer it.

★   ★   ★

Bill Bellicheck was waiting for Chief Thomas on the front steps of his funeral home. Even as he pulled his police car up, Rodney could see the hand-wringing anxiety in the demeanor of his old friend. Bill was always the picture of ultimate cool. Nothing ever got to him. He was a funeral director, after all.

Bill walked down the steps, across the grass and quickly to the curb to meet the Police Chief before he could even get fully out of his car.

"Come on in and see for yourself, Rodney. Unbelievable! I can't imagine! I mean I just can't imagine such a thing," Bill babbled as Chief Thomas shut the door of the squad car and walked calmly over to where he was standing. The funeral director's face was puffy and flushed.

"OK, now Bill," the Chief soothed. "The guy's already dead, remember? Take it easy. We've got some pretty sick vandals out there...doing stuff like this. Just calm down and let's go see, OK?"

"What do you mean?" Bill asked immediately, and without moving. "There's been other bodies taken?"

There was no mistaking the look on the funeral director's face. He was actually hopeful. "Well, sort of," Rodney answered uncomfortably. "Mostly animals, but..."

"Well, come on then," Bill snapped as he turned toward his building. If there weren't other dead people missing, he apparently wasn't interested. "I'll show you this thing. Its unbelievable!"

Bill walked away rapidly and Rodney was already several steps behind when he turned and said, "The thing is, nobody could have gotten in, Rodney. You'll see. Someone had to have been hiding in there. I swear!"

★   ★   ★

It was a very revved-up Janice who met Darrin at the door. She had done virtually nothing all day but write, think, drink coffee and then write some more. All day. The cat screams, late-night conversation, and (especially) finishing Jon's book had all combined to animate her already creative mind. She was in overdrive. She was full of intriguing theories, and half theories... and they needed an outlet.

They met Jon, who to Darrin's relief looked better, in the kitchen. First there were awkward apologies from Darrin, then Jon, for brushing off Janice earlier in the day. Janice politely waved them off. Even with so much to talk about, they were all initially quiet. Jon eventually broke it by offering drinks to his guests. Darrin and Janice both had tea. Jon grabbed a beer.

All three were soon sitting reasonably comfortably but still quietly around the kitchen table sipping their drinks when Darrin (who was the one who, after all, had called the hasty meeting) took a long sip of his tea, put his glass down hard, then began: "Janice was right," he said. "No matter how much we try to deny it, something very strange, and very bad, I think, is happening here. And it's happening fast. And we need to admit that to ourselves."

He stopped there for a moment and studied them both. Janice's wide eyes were fixed on him, Jon was looking out the kitchen window, as though he was distracted by something. But Darrin knew he was listening.

"Stuff's happening faster all the time," he continued. "and all of it came after that "flash" thing that you guys, and everybody else around here went through. Just today, just a little while ago, you saw those kids out by the woods again." Janice shot her eyes toward Jon, who reddened and closed his. "Chester's woods, Jon."

It was if a taboo had been broken, at least for one of them. Jon immediately pushed his chair back, got up and walked away from the table. He walked out of the kitchen, through the living room and out of sight.

"Chester," Darrin thought. That's all it took. An old-fashioned name that had the power to stop his friend in his tracks.

A minute went by without a word between Janice and Darrin, and without Jon's return.

"Quit acting like a hurt little boy, Jon!" Darrin yelled from the kitchen. "We need to talk about this! Get it in the open!"

He was sure Jon could hear him, but there was no answer.

There was a long, long silence. Then Darrin yelled again: "Jon? Are you on the crapper or something?"

Janice giggled, and a few moments later they heard what sounded like a short chuckle coming from somewhere in the back of the house.

And less than a minute later Jon came back in and sat down in the chair he had abandoned. His face was red, and his blue eyes still seemed to seethe with anger. Janice looked away, but Darrin looked directly at him. Jon met his gaze for a moment, then he too looked away.

"I didn't hear the toilet flush," Darrin said.

Janice almost choked.

Jon's head snapped back and his eyes blazed at his friend. There was a tense silence, then: "You know I never flush," he said.

★   ★   ★

It was almost dark. He knew he would have to head home soon. And he dreaded it. Dreaded it almost as much as his heart ached.

But a couple of minutes later, Jim Ray Crawford turned his pick-up truck around on the lonely country road he was searching, and started driving back.

His little Marsha had been missing for almost exactly two whole days now; easily the two longest, most emotional and terribly frustrating days of his life.

They had determined that yes: she had ridden the bus, and yes, she had gotten off where she was supposed to. And yes-the police and neighbors, in fact the whole community, had responded terrifically, even though she wasn't "officially" yet missing, and even though many folks were already busy looking for their missing Sheriff. He had no complaints about any of that.

But his heart was slowly breaking, and he felt more dread, heavy dread, as each painful minute went by; wondering, wondering, wondering...where she could be.

It was terrible for him out here in the country alone, like he was now, but it was worse...far worse at home. Watching his wife cry, and occasionally go into a fit of helpless, wailing grief was horrible enough. Going by Little Marsha's room was bad enough. But the endless parade of phone calls, visits from the well-meaning neighbors and their pastor, interviews with the police-and today-an actual FBI agent-made for an environment that he couldn't stand.

Jim Ray was a proud, independent man who felt totally helpless; almost emasculated staying at home. Not with the jewel of his life having been taken from him.

So for most of the two days he had simply gone out looking. He drove every road, paved or not, through the whole countryside around his farm. Some of them over and over again. He knew, increasingly, that it was probably useless. But it was all he could do. All he knew to do.

When his cell phone rang it startled him. Still a good twenty minutes from home, he had just turned the truck's lights on to meet the rapidly falling darkness, and it was as if that act alone had caused the ringing. He jumped a little, then pulled up the phone, and saw right away that it was Brenda. Brenda again. She called him constantly, the last one not half-an-hour ago.

He opened the phone, brought it up to his ear and said "Yeah honey?"

"She's home!! Marsha's home!! She's home! Oh my God!! Jim... SHE'S HOME!!"

Jim Ray was so overcome that he immediately hit the brakes and shakily pulled the truck over to the side of the road. He had very nearly lost control of it. He couldn't talk or even think straight for a minute, and the tears that he'd worked so hard at holding back now seemed to be coming out of nowhere, cascading down his unshaven cheeks.

With the truck safely pulled over he laid his head on the steering wheel and sobbed hugely in relief. He tried to thank God aloud, but couldn't catch his breath, so he prayed silently.

It took him a while to gather himself. Even while crying, he could hear his wife's voice saying something. It was coming from the phone that he'd laid on the passenger seat when he'd pulled the truck over to stop.

Finally, he picked it up. She was still on the line.

"Honey," he said, voice cracking with emotion, "that's wonderful! Thank God!"

She didn't answer.

"Honey? You there? Is Marsha there?"

"She's right here, smiling at me," Brenda said. There was joy in her voice, but it was more restrained now. Oddly so. More sober, somehow. Shock?

"Who found her honey?" Jim Ray asked. "Where did they find her?" There was something about his wife's voice...

There was a long pause before she answered. "The Sheriff. Sheriff Blanton is here. He brought her home, and..."

She stopped there. Jim Ray waited a few seconds for her to continue. She didn't.

"Did you say Sheriff Blanton, Brenda?...Brenda?"

There was no answer.

Jim Ray closed his cell, put the truck in drive and quickly peeled out, headed for home.

Chapter 19
October 7th 6:46 P.M.

"I talked with Nancy Melleville today," Darrin said. "She's the wife of Bart Melleville, the guy that got murdered," he added for Jon's sake. "Two things jumped out. First, she said she saw a kid and a cat in their yard, right after she found her husband's body. And she said they disappeared, just like that." He snapped his fingers for emphasis. "And the second thing...and I just found this out a little while ago... she said her husband had a dream, 'a horrible nightmare,' she said, about dead animals and children. Almost cracked him up. Had to see a doctor. That's why he was home when he got whacked. His dream sounded just like yours, Janice."

Janice had been looking at and listening intently to Darrin the whole time, and with his last words she grew pale. Jon kept his expressionless eyes focused on the middle of his kitchen table, as he had during the entire narration.

In addition to what he had just said, Darrin had told them about Amanda Meachum, the missing Bobby Meachum's mother. She had appeared to have been an otherwise healthy woman when, apparently, according to at least one doctor, something had "frightened her to death." He told them about reported "sightings" of Highland's missing children; and how they were similar (children always seen at a distance, not moving naturally, often dressed in white or in nightclothes, unresponsive, etc.). And he told them again about the reports of strange, violent behavior of pets and other animals around Highland, and about the fact that not only a sheriff but his deputy sheriff had gone missing. Finally, to lead into his story about Nancy Melleville, he told them that he had learned when he'd called Chief Thomas (to try to get him to come over, a little more than an hour before): the funeral home was reporting that Bart Melleville's remains were missing.

It was a lot to absorb. The two listeners, with so much laid out in front of them at once were, obviously, a bit overwhelmed. Understandably so. Both Jon and Janice already knew some of what Darrin told them, but some of it was new - and put together - it was numbing. Even Darrin, who had meticulously rattled it all off, seemed affected. Everything that had happened seemed undeniably related. Especially when bunched together in one monologue.

"Could this mean...I mean... could I be in danger here?" Janice asked hesitently.

"I think we could all be in danger, because its getting worse, and its all happening faster now. I mean...its picking up speed." Darrin said soberly.

Jon glanced up at Darrin for the first time in a long while. "I think that's being a little overly dramatic there Darrin. Come on now..."

"No," Janice interrupted, "I think he's right." She was looking at her hands on the table when she said it, and looked up at Jon now. "And you know he's right, don't you. Don't you Jon?"

★　　　★　　　★

Jim Ray could see that the living room lights and the kitchen lights were on. He could also see that there were no cars at the house. He'd expected a bunch.

He pulled the truck into his long driveway going too fast and his back tires skidded out. He fought to get it under control, did, then hit the gas hard again. He screeched to a stop when he got even with the house, put the truck in park, then bolted out of it, leaving the engine running, the lights still on and the driver's side door swung wide open. He didn't care. He sprinted for his front door.

When he got there, he actually hesitated. The porch light wasn't on, which was strange, and he stood in the last new night's darkness and tried to catch his breath. It felt as though his heart was beating through his chest. He was sweating, even in the cool autumn night. His mouth was dry, and his hand was shaking a few moments later as he raised it to turn the knob.

He opened the door. Every light in the living room and attached dining room was on, and the brightness that poured out made him blink for a moment. He stood there, beyond anxious, but oddly hesitant. It was so quiet. He had a feeling, a strange, uneasy feeling...

"Marsha?" he yelled, loud enough for anyone in the house to hear. His own voice sounded odd to him.

He listened, still standing in the doorway. He didn't hear anything. Not anything at all. "Marsha? Brenda?" he yelled out again.

Everything was so bright. So still, so quiet. It was as though the house itself was holding it's breath.

Jim Ray took a few steps into the living room. His own footsteps sounded, felt...heavy; as though to move was to intrude. He started to call out again, but thought better of it.

Then suddenly-a loud ticking sound. He looked up at the clock on the wall centered above the couch; the clock that you could always here ticking, steadily on and on when the house was quiet. Why was he hearing it, and so profoundly and suddenly, now, and not when he first walked in? Had it stopped, and started again?

He looked at his own watch to compare times. The living room clock was 10 minutes slow. He felt an icy chill run through him. Did it, somehow, stop and then start again? But it was plugged in. It was electric.

A short, low growl, or what sounded like a growl, came from off to his right, toward the kitchen. Jim Ray whipped his head in that direction and then froze, listening.

He heard only the ticking of the clock.

"Brenda? Marsha?"

The kitchen light went out.

"Brenda?"

Jim Ray felt a small, cool breeze, like the kind felt when someone opens and then closes an outside door in the dead of winter. It hit him and then stopped. He involuntarily shivered. The kitchen light switched back on.

"Brenda?" he called. Now he resolutely walked that way.

He was two steps onto the tiled floor when he heard the low growl, louder this time, coming from behind the island counter at the far end of the kitchen. He saw something briefly stick out from behind it at floor level, then quickly jerk back again-out of his sight.

A small shoe? A rat?

Jim Ray jerked back reflexively at the sight of it, but just as quickly gathered himself, cursed under his breath, and strode over there to see. "Marsha?" he called as he walked.

He got to the counter, then a step around it before looking down.

Little Marsha looked up at him and growled. Jim Ray saw the yellow, angry flashing eyes, and the rich red blood flowing out of and dripping from the slowly chewing mouth of his little girl. She was on her knees over her mother. Brenda's face had the look of a woman who was lying there in a deep, peaceful sleep, but with another second's look Jim Ray also saw what remained of her intestines, scattered haphazardly and in pieces, across the kitchen floor around her.

Jim Ray stared, dumbly, paralyzed...but not for long. A strong hand gripped his shoulder before he could really even think, and turned him instantly around.

"Hello Jim Ray," the smiling Sheriff said.

★　　　★　　　★

"We could be jumping to conclusions, ya know. Maybe we're getting way ahead of ourselves," Jon said in exasperation. "That's all I'm saying, guys."

Darrin gave his friend a long, frowning look. "Facts are facts, Jon." he said. "Haven't you been listening?" He was getting frustrated. "We're just trying to find a way to deal with it, OK?"

Jon scowled but said nothing that was decipherable. Darrin sat back and glanced looked up at Jon's kitchen clock. A quarter after 8:00. "You're going to be late for your date, by the way," he added.

"Not meeting her 'til 9:00." Jon snapped. "I called her a half an hour ago."

"You did? I thought you finally went to the bathroom?" Darrin smiled.

"Nope," Jon answered breezily, "Called her and told her I had some guests I couldn't get rid of."

Darrin looked bemused, Janice looked horrified. She quickly rose from her seat.

"I am so sorry!" she apologized. "I've been talking up a storm and didn't even have the courtesy to realize that you had..."

"Sit down, sit down," Darrin said while gesturing with his arm for her to do just that. He then, ironically, got up himself, but only to go look in Jon's frig for a beer. "Jon's just being bitchy," he said dismissively with his back to the other two. He found a beer and popped it open as he walked back to his seat at the table. "If anyone should be worried about the time, its me," he added. "My wife is already mad, and she'll have my ass over this." He sat down, took a long sip, then looked up at the still standing Janice. "But

I figure...what the hell? We're just trying to save civilization here, right?" He smiled and shifted his glance back to Jon. "Although, I guess I'm 'exaggerating' again, right?"

Jon sighed and looked up at Janice. "He's right," he said, "in his usual twisted kind of way. I'm sorry Janice. Just having a hard time with it. I...I just don't know. I mean, sometimes I think 'what does it have to do with me,' if you know what I mean? Feeling sorry for myself. But hey, sit down for Pete's sake. And tell us the rest of what you've got. OK?"

Janice had held the floor for the 20 minutes or so before Jon had interrupted with his plea for reasonable doubt. She had painstakingly read through the notes she had been making since early that morning, had brought out and explained the map that Darrin and she had made (mostly for Jon's sake), and had begun to talk about what she referred to as the "commonalities" of the events that were known to have taken place. It had been thorough, somewhat confusing-and for Jon-a bit of a stretch.

"The reason it involves you is because of your own book, Jon," Janice said. She still hadn't sat down. "I read the rest of it last night. That, along with the things you told Officer Christopher and me last night...makes you vital to this, this thing that we're doing."

Jon looked up into her eyes. He seemed to consider what she had said for a moment, but then shook his head and said "That doesn't make sense. What are you talking about? And what are *we* doing?"

Now she sat down. "Because your own book shows how two guys solved a mystery," she said passionately. "Two guys who weren't supposed to. A transcendent mystery. One that defied logic, as we know it. And the reason they did is simple. They were the smartest guys! The smartest people out there."

"What does "transcendent" mean?" Darrin asked.

Janice ignored him, and kept her bright eyes fixed on Jon (who seemed to be having trouble looking away, Darrin noticed). "And now we have something happening that's even bigger; even more horrible. We know that. In our guts, we know that. Who knows what's happening out there tonight, even while we're sitting here talking?" She waved an arm for emphasis. Jon watched her closely, seemingly spellbound. "I don't know if this has anything to do with your...your 'boy spirit' out there, Chester...but I know this; and I know it from you: we've got to be the smartest people in the room now. We've got to try to figure this out, because..."

The doorbell rang, stopping Janice cold as well as badly startling all three of them.

After a few moments, highlighted by Darrin's pantomime of a heart attack, he got up to answer it.

★   ★   ★

Chief Thomas appearing at Jon's front door after dark on a Saturday night surprised all three of them. Even Darrin, who had earlier asked the Chief to come over by phone, and had mentioned to the others several times that he might be dropping by, was more than a little stunned to see the man himself standing there frowning on the front porch.

And besides temporarily immobilizing them, it immediately did two other things to the group dynamic. It introduced an even higher level of seriousness (if this guy was willing to leave his easy chair to come and see them on a Saturday night...just how much shit were they really in?), and it made them start their information-sharing and discussion all over again-from scratch.

A fourth chair was found and placed around the crowded kitchen table for two (when he'd purchased it, years before, Jon had never imagined that he'd ever need any more room), Jon put on a pot of his notoriously hot coffee, and then left the room to call Belinda and tell her he would be even later. Within 10 minutes the four of them were seated, somewhat awkwardly, around the paper-strewn little table.

It can best be said that at the outset Darrin was excited, Jon glum, Janice nervous, and Chief Thomas troubled. Those initial frames of mind determined how the opening cards were played.

Darrin went first, repeating what he had learned that afternoon from Nancy Melleville, along with the other information he'd shared with his "non-uniformed" friends an hour before (some of this seemed to irritate the Chief, but he let it pass). Janice, at Darrin's repeated urging, went next. She went through her whole presentation again. It was smoother this time, and she only stumbled a bit when (again, at Darrin's insistence) she was urged to go into her rationale as to why they, the people sitting around the table ("...tell him how we're the smartest ones" Darrin had urged) should be the ones who should solve whatever was happening. She got through it all right though. And overall, impressively.

Jon went next; again prompted by Darrin. He repeated, reluctantly, his sightings of the mysterious children by the woods. His report was short, factual and dry; as though he was a man in a hurry to finish and go somewhere else. Which he was.

Chief Rodney Thomas listened to it all with what, for him, was remarkable calm. Even the bit that Janice brought up about "Chester," the controversial ghost (or demon) from the past, left him unmoved...at least on the surface.

And after he'd heard them all, and after getting up in the ensuing silence to get himself another cup of coffee, and then, after stopping to take a sip and putting the cup down on the kitchen counter where he'd stopped, it was his turn to speak.

"As hard as it is for me to say this...to admit this," he said, obviously being very careful with his words, "I think we've got something going like we had two years ago. Only, maybe, worse." He looked down at the counter that he was already resting both hands on; as though he were trying to keep his balance. The other three stared up at him. "Jon, I never read that book of yours. I admit it. I...I just couldn't. No offense or anything, but after what we went through then," he looked up and directly at Jon,

"...what we went through that night..." The Chief shook his head and looked down at the counter again. "It was something I never wanted to ever happen again, or think about again, and I couldn't go reading about it."

"I understand," Jon said. Janice and Darrin gave a simultaneous quick look of surprise to Jon, then swiveled their heads back towards the Chief.

"Well, I'm thinking you guys are right. About some of it anyway. I can feel it. And it scares me, just like the last time, because it's bigger than us, and I don't understand it, and it feels like its going to get worse...and I'm afraid of it," he said. He stopped there and looked at them. His blue eyes were misty.

The other three remained frozen in place. This kind of thing; this vulnerability, really, being expressed by the chief law enforcement officer and symbol of order and strength to all of them-was both welcome and unnerving. Mostly unnerving.

So they waited in silence, not knowing what else to do.

"There's a lot to talk about," Chief Thomas finally said. He looked at each of them, but kept his last look on Darrin. "There certainly is. And I...I respect the work, and the thinking you've all done, but, guys, we've got somebody stealing dead bodies now. First animals, and now people. We've got something absolutely horrible going on. And its getting worse, all the time."

The Chief's eyes looked as if they were almost pleading. He took a step back, as if to re-gather his thoughts. He looked at the three, then his watch. He sighed. He was obviously very tired. "Janice, you've done some good work here," he said. His voice was lower; patient. "And Jon, I know about the work you did with Darrin the, uh, the last time. And I appreciate, believe me, any help you can give us."

He grabbed his coffee cup and walked toward his seat at the kitchen table. "But you know what?" he asked, "whether its Darrin and I, or our department, or you guys, or the damned F.B.I. or anybody else who figures this out...its not going to be enough. We've got to not just find out what's causing this, guys, we've got to be ready to do something else," he said as he sat down. He looked at each of their three faces again before finishing, "...we've got to be ready to kill the bastards responsible."

Chapter 20
October 8th - Sunday morning

It was sunny, crisp and exhilarating. Perfect, if rare, St. Louis area weather. It was the kind of early autumn morning that inevitably engenders a kind of reckless, almost illogical enthusiasm to any who stepped outside to pick up the morning paper and took their first breath of the amazingly fresh air. Instant enthusiasm to do, well, *something* (triggered by some mysterious biochemical mechanism buried deep in all of us) was instantaneously called for. It might call for football, raking leaves, a long walk, going to church, cleaning the gutters, riding a bicycle, a drive through the country, or even...just reading the paper (but this time, on the porch). What action would be taken to meet the day would depend on the person, their degree of motivation, and their agenda, but it was impossible not to be affected.

Jonathon Parker went out to his driveway to get his St. Louis Post-Dispatch early. He had barely slept. The reason was simple: his Saturday night had been spent almost equally divided (physically and emotionally) between looking into an abyss of horror, and then being in the arms of a new and passionate lover. The psychic roller coaster he had been on, that he had put himself through just a few hours before, was not for weak-or the sleepy.

It had been overwhelming, and as Jon, just after dawn in robe and slippers, picked up the paper and took his first full, deep breath of the perfect, perfumed fall air-he allowed himself a moment to just stand there in the middle of his sloped driveway at the end of the cul-de-sac, squint at the rising orange-yellow sun, and just think about it all for a moment. "Life couldn't be anything but wonderful," he thought, "on a day like this."

Chief Thomas, Janice and Darrin had stayed in his kitchen for another hour and a half. It was an enlightening, frightening, but ultimately frustrating 90 minutes. The two policemen, and even Janice (with her connection to City Hall and her avid interest) knew much, much more than he, and as the various events and tidbits of the horrible week were casually discussed he had gotten a fuller, scarier picture of the overall scenario. Jon played the polite and quiet host, because there wasn't any other role to play. He had listened (sometimes intently), made and poured coffee, and went to the refrigerator from time to time for beer, soda or tea.

What he heard was depressing, and to his mind, a dreadful confirmation. There was, simply, no escaping it. The horror that he had tried so hard to put behind him was still there, and wasn't going away. It was undeniable. The story that he had written so that he could psychically expunge it from his mind, wasn't gone. Not by a long shot. As hard as it was to admit to himself, it seemed now that it had just been hiding out there...waiting. And what was equally depressing was that the trained minds sitting around his table had no idea what to do about it.

And then, when they finally left, he had taken his troubled mind over to see Belinda...and like a miracle, she had made it all go away. It was like a miracle.

He looked away from the bright morning sun, took another deep breath of morning air, and began walking back into his house, smiling, and thinking of her, despite everything else.

Jon's next door neighbor, Detective Darrin Crandle, came out to pick up his morning paper an hour later-feeling at least to some measure the same mix of dread and exhilaration that Jon had. His previous night too had been one of emotional extremes, and he too paused in his driveway to note how perfect the new day was.

Darrin had been the most affected by the appearance, words, and overall gloom of the Chief of Police the night before. The fact that he showed up at all was one thing, but the near desperation in his boss' face and voice had shaken him. More than he had shown. What did it mean when the big man, the rock himself, began showing signs of panic?

And it only got worse. And by the minute, because as the discussion went on it became progressively more and more clear that they, all of them, didn't have a clue as to what to do. Whatever was out there, whatever was going on was still largely invisible to them. To logic itself. "...It'd be easier to fight an army," the Chief had said in despair. "At least then we'd know what we're up against."

But when he'd finally gone home, to his surprise, Marilyn was waiting for him. And they looked into each other's eyes, and soon all the whole haunting, danger-filled world melted away.

Darrin too looked up at the now higher bright yellow sun. It was impossible not to love this day, and impossible not to smile, he thought.

City Manager Janice Granger didn't subscribe to a newspaper (excepting the weekly edition of the "Highland Newsleader," which she read every word of, religiously, every week). Janice preferred getting her news on-line. So her first exposure to that remarkable Sunday morning was when she took her coffee out onto the patio in her backyard. Unlike Jon and Darrin, she had had nothing wonderful or miraculous happen to mitigate the disturbing conversation and its implications from the night before. In fact, it was quite the opposite, and she had slept hardly at all.

Not that she hadn't tried. She was near exhaustion when she had finally turned out the light and crawled into bed, even though her mind was still teeming with what she had heard, and for that matter what she herself had said in Jon's cramped kitchen. Even with a growing fear gnawing at her every thought, her body was telling her to stop; to rest.

But then, soon after she had closed her eyes, there was a cat. Again. An unnaturally loud, pleading meowing. It wasn't at all like the crazed mating or fighting (or both) sound that they'd all heard right off of Jon's deck. It was just insistent, dreadful meowing, and it was just as terrifying to her as the other cat had been. Maybe more so.

Because this time, she was alone.

She just laid there and listened at first; eyes wide open and staring at a ceiling she could not see in the dark. It meowed in fits and starts, and with various degrees of urgency. And it seemed to be coming from her kitchen area, perhaps just outside the door that led out to the patio.

It was Socks. She knew it had to be. Her dead Socks. She tried to reason with herself, tried to minimize, even banish the thought, but she knew it in her heart.

She didn't get out of bed until it stopped; had stopped for a long time. Until she knew it was gone. Then she rose, turned on the lamp, then the bedroom light, then the hall light, then the living room light-and then walked around, and looked and listened.

There was, of course, nothing. She eventually went to bed again, but had trouble keeping her eyes closed. And an hour later it came again. This time it was louder, and even more plaintive and insistent. This time it came from right outside her bedroom window (as if it knew where she was!).

Janice didn't get up that time, or the next time it came, right before dawn. She laid there and tried not to move.

And now, exhausted beyond measure, sliding back the glass patio door with coffee in hand, she quickly surveyed the back yard, every inch of it, before sitting down at her table. She didn't much notice the beautiful day, but a part of her was glad for the sun. She had no thought of all the wonderful, invigorating things that she could do on a day such as this.

She knew she would be sleeping.

Six blocks away Police Chief Rodney Thomas was in his back yard too. And unfortunately, he too could give no thought to the beauty surrounding him on that Sunday morning. And he wasn't drinking coffee, and hadn't read the paper. Instead, he was on his hands and knees in the very corner of his property, studying the empty hole he had dug that abutted his tall wooden privacy fence. It was the hole he had buried his dog in.

There was nothing to see. Not only the dog but the bag he was buried in was gone. He reached in the hole and moved the dirt around. He wasn't sure what he was looking for, but he did it anyway. "Why?" he thought, "Why would anyone dig up and take a dead dog? The person who hit the dog? Why? And why get out of the car, drag it up into the yard in the first place if he was going to come back and dig it up? How would he know where it was buried? Was someone...watching?"

He sat up on his knees. He looked around him. The yard was completely fenced in. A person couldn't see through it.

Still on his knees, he looked up, squinting in the sun, at the second stories of the houses on either side of his. Someone could have seen from there. But he knew them. Good people. Wouldn't do that. No way.

He sighed, stood up slowly, and brushed the dirt off his hands and the knees of his jeans, then started walking toward the house. He knew he should go to work, but he just wanted to sleep. And to have a peaceful Sunday.

Out in the country seven miles away from where Chief Thomas was walking into his house, Burt and Molly Hester were pulling their Chevy Cordova into the Crawfords' driveway. During their visit the afternoon before, the stricken Brenda had promised their best friends that she would meet them in church the next morning, and that she would try to bring Jim Ray with her. Not only had she not shown up, she wasn't answering Molly's repeated phone calls either. So at Molly's insistence, she and Burt had left the service early to check on their friends. Molly just knew something was wrong. She could feel it in her bones.

The sight of Jim Ray's truck parked in the driveway at a funny angle, and with the driver's side door swung open, did nothing to mollify Molly's suspicions. "Oh no!" she cried out immediately.

Burt was concentrating on driving correctly up the narrow driveway, and Molly's cry nearly made him veer off. He braked to a stop, looked over at his excitable wife, saw that she was covering her mouth in alarm with one hand and pointing ahead with the other, and then turned and squinted up the driveway (he'd forgotten his glasses) to have a look for himself. After a moment he saw what she saw, but thought he must be missing whatever was so alarming.

"What?" he said, still peering ahead. "The truck?"

Molly didn't answer.

"Jim Ray probably forgot something," Burt ventured, "if that's what you're worried about. He's probably in the house gettin' his phone or something." Then he turned and looked at his wife, frankly expecting to be corrected.

But he wasn't. "There's something wrong," was all Molly said, but much more calmly than Burt had expected. She had brought her hands down to her lap, and was making no effort to get out of the car. "Maybe they're fighting," she added a moment later, "or maybe there's been some news about poor Marsha."

Burt watched his wife tear up, once again. He looked away from her and back toward the truck, and then the house. There was no sign of Jim Ray yet. Molly started crying softly. He didn't know what to do. After 36 years of marriage, he thought, it was amazing to him how many times he didn't know what to do.

She cried for a full minute before he offered: "Why don't I go up to the house and make sure everything's OK?" She blew and wiped her nose, but didn't answer. "That's what I'll do," he said decisively. "You stay here, because you don't want to upset Brenda, beings that you're cryin' and all." She reached out her hand for

Burt's handkerchief. He gave it to her. She still didn't, or couldn't, say anything. "That's what I'll do then. Be right back!"

Burt was frankly relieved to get out of the car, and away from the scene his wife was putting on. As he walked toward the front door he took a deep breath of the perfect country air, and he found himself wishing that the house he was walking towards was further away. Maybe a mile away. It was such a beautiful Sunday morning. A wonderful morning for a walk.

Exactly 90 seconds later, as Burt Hester knocked on the Crawfords' front door for the second time (this time much more insistently), Nancy Melleville woke with a start and quickly sat up in her bed back in Highland. She had heard someone knocking on the door, or something similar to that, even in her deep sleep. She was sure of it.

She sat there frozen in sitting position, and listened. She held her breath, and waited. Hearing nothing for at least half-a minute, she finally made a decision and pulled the covers back and swung her feet to the side of the bed. She heard another sound right as her feet reached the floor. She froze again, and felt a deep grieving pain suddenly tearing at her from deep within. It took her a moment for her to realize what it was, even though her body seemed to already know. It was a voice. She had heard a voice. It was her husband's voice.

She couldn't move at first. The shock of it; so real, and so close-and coming in the very first moments of consciousness after a tortured, grieving sleep...was too much. She sat there looking down at her own legs, tried to breathe deeply, and somehow make sense of it.

Then there was another knocking sound. The front door?

Then nothing for a long while. No knocking, no voice... nothing.

She stood up. Listened. Nothing.

With shaking, fumbling hands she managed to get her robe on, and stopped still to listen afterwards. Nothing. She took a step, then another, then felt faint and quickly stopped to hold onto the side of her bed for support.

"...a beautiful morning!" Bart Melleville's voice said. It had said more, but those were the only words she could clearly understand. It had come from the kitchen. Clearly, from the kitchen, in a conversational voice, as though he was addressing someone else. Someone who was with him there.

"Impossible!" Nancy whispered aloud in a voice she didn't recognize as her own. The blood pounded in her temples. She drew a quick breath, then another, and held onto the bed with both hands to keep from passing out. She heard more words being spoken, but couldn't make them out. Her heart was pounding through her ears so hard that she couldn't have heard someone talking right next to her. She struggled for composure; any kind of composure. It took her a while.

It was minutes later when she finally got steady enough to get to her bedroom door. She opened it, listened, heard nothing, and so walked out into the hallway. She stood for a few moments looking down the hall, into the living room and the kitchen beyond. All looked normal. All was quiet. She walked, slowly, down the hall and stopped at the beginning of her living room. She looked around. She listened. She heard nothing. She walked, more resolutely now, across the living room and toward the kitchen.

"Good morning, darling!" his voice said when she was but two steps away.

She stopped, had a sharp intake of breath, and held it. Her wide eyes blinked in confusion and shock. She waited for a moment. When she heard nothing more she took the final steps.

"There you are!" the yellow-grey smiling head sitting squarely in the center of her kitchen table said. "It's going to be a beautiful day, huh Nancy?"

Nancy couldn't breathe. Another movement caused her to look up slightly, at the smiling man sitting in the kitchen chair right behind her husband's head. He nodded, seeming to affirm that yes, this was going to be a beautiful day.

Chapter 21
October 9th 6:33 A.M.

"I've got a name for our group," Janice said brightly. "We'll be the 'Clueless Club.' What do you think?"

Darrin looked over his menu and directly into Janice's smiling, always energized face. Her enthusiasm at this time of the morning was a bit much for him. And he wasn't into naming things. "Fine," he said dryly, and then dropped his eyes down to resume the search for the perfect breakfast omelet.

The four of them, the newly christened "Clueless Club" (so named because the word clueless, or some derivation of it - "... let's face it, we don't have a clue!" - had been used so often in their far-ranging, frustrating conversation on Saturday night), had agreed to meet at the "8th Street Cafe" for breakfast at 6:15 Monday morning. But now, at just past 6:30, it appeared that Darrin and Janice were the only club members to show. Darrin wasn't surprised and Janice was disappointed. But she was trying (pretty lamely, Darrin thought) to make the best of things.

"Do you think we should order?" she asked a few moments later. "Or maybe we should wait. Maybe they got held up. What do you think?"

Darrin patiently put his menu down, took a sip of his coffee, and looked up at her pretty, anxious eyes. He found it hard to talk much this early in the morning before he'd eaten, but she didn't give a guy much of a choice.

"Let's order," he said. "Jon's not coming, I can tell you that. I didn't see any of his lights on when I pulled out of the driveway. I think he only agreed to come to breakfast so that he could get us out of there faster. Wanted to go meet his new little honey, remember? And the Chief? Who knows? Probably forgot. Or he's way late, like always."

"OK," Janice answered. But she looked at Darrin for a long moment before dropping her eyes to the menu lying on the table before her. "I think I'll just have toast," she said.

Darrin looked up and out the window at the cold, rainy morning. "The exact opposite of yesterday," he thought. Sunday had been so bright, beautiful, and optimistic. Marilyn and he had had the best day ever. A day away from everything else. And now this. St. Louis weather. Again.

"I'm thinking of putting an ad in the paper," Janice said suddenly. Darrin looked at her again. She was still looking at the menu. "I decided last night, after sleeping all day because of that cat."

"What cat?" Darrin asked.

"The cat that keeps crying outside my house," she said. She looked up. "It sounds just like Socks. My cat. The one that died."

Darrin just looked at her.

"Sounds crazy, doesn't it?" she asked. "But between that and the dream-I've had the dream twice now-I got to thinking about that other woman, the one whose husband got killed?"

"Nancy Melleville?"

"Yeah, her. You told me her husband had the same, or almost the same dream," she leaned forward and put her elbows on the table. "...the same dream that I had. And there was a cat in his yard. She said she saw it, right after she found him dead and..."

"You're going to put an ad in the paper to try to find the cat?" Darrin smiled.

"No, no..." Janice frowned, "I'm going to see if there are other people out there. Other people who have had the dream. Maybe we could meet, or something. Maybe it would give us, you know, a clue about this."

"But we're 'clueless'?"

"Oh come on Darrin! Stop it!" Janice tried to look angry, but Darrin's pleased with himself look made it hard. "I'm running the idea by you, that's all. I need to know what you think."

Darrin sat back in his chair, teasing smile still in place. "I think you're going to get fired. That's what I think. You're the City Manager, for Chrisakes. You're supposed to be promoting Highland. Now you're going to run an ad in the paper to see who all is having bad dreams?" Janice reddened slightly, looked down, but said nothing. "Give me a break, Janice." he added for emphasis.

The waitress came and they gave their orders. In the ensuing silence after she left, Darrin let his eyes drift around the restaurant. From their table he could barely see into the adjoining room. He could see a couple of guys at the end of the big table looking to their right, listening intently to someone spouting off somewhere toward its center. It was the table where all the big shots came for breakfast, Darrin knew. All men, all opinionated as hell, all there every morning.

"We have to think outside the box," Janice said.

Darrin turned back toward her. She was looking down again. "I hate that phrase," he said.

"You're the one who said it," she snapped her eyes up. "You're the one who said to think creatively. You've done it before you know. Magnificently."

Darrin sighed. "Jon exaggerated in that book," he said. "We didn't know what the hell we were doing. We got a little lucky, sure, but it didn't solve the problem, did it?"

Janice let that ride for a few minutes. In fact, she didn't speak again until the food arrived and the waitress had walked away. "I'll tell you another thing we should do," she said as she passed the pepper, "We should go into those woods. We should try to find out if it's coming from there...if it's the center, again. We need to find your ghost...your Chester. See if he's still there."

Darrin couldn't tell if she was serious or not, but didn't get the chance to answer anyway. Chief Rodney Thomas was suddenly there, standing at the side of their table. It seemed to Darrin (who had his back to the door) that he'd appeared out of nowhere.

This time the Chief didn't apologize to the "guys" for being late. He just looked at the two of them for a moment with an obviously distraught face and then spoke to them in a low voice, without sitting down. "We've got more trouble. A lot more." He looked around and then in the direction of the room with all the male busybodies. Sure enough, a couple of them were looking right back at him. "The Crawford woman. The one out in the country, by Alhambra, or where ever... the one with the missing little girl. They found her dead in her own kitchen yesterday. Mutilated. Half...half eaten, looks like"

Darrin put his fork down. Janice stopped chewing her toast. Both stared up at the Chief.

"What about her husband?" Darrin asked, in just above a whisper.

Chief Thomas shook his head, "No where around. His truck is still there, but they haven't found him."

"Sweet Jesus," Janice exclaimed.

"That's not all," the Chief said. "Bart Melleville's wife, Nancy. She's missing." He glanced again at the busybody room. Walter Stenger, who owned the drugstore, was looking right at the Chief. He'd gotten to his feet and was now headed their way. "She's, she's gone. Neighbor heard a scream, but get this-they didn't call the cops for a couple of hours." He looked up and smiled at the approaching Walt Stenger. "Anyway, she's gone."

"The woman whose husband got killed? Janice asked belatedly.

"Why good morning Walt!" the Chief cried happily as he reached out to shake hands.

Chapter 22
October 9th 8:45 A.M.

"And they didn't find a trace of her? No sign at all?"

"No, Darrin. I told you, there was nothing there." Chief Thomas said.

There was a knock, a hesitant one, on the Police Chief's office door. They both looked up to see who was there (the door had a window, which Chief Thomas had been meaning to board up forever now), but no one was looking in. "Come in!" Rodney Thomas yelled irritably.

The door opened and stuttering Lance Bradley, who was assigned to the front desk as usual, peeked his head around the corner. "Miss, Ms. Mrs. G-Granger is h-h-here, sir."

Chief Thomas gave Darrin a quick, questioning look, but said "Send her in, Lance."

Janice had been tied up in a meeting with the Mayor and a couple of businessmen who were potential investors in Highland's "Downtown Square Reinvestment" project. It was a so-so meeting because her mind had been elsewhere.

"Anything new?" she asked as she came into the office. Her usual smile gone, she quickly moved to the open seat by Darrin, across the desk from Chief Thomas.

"The Chief here was just giving me a heads up," Darrin said. Chief Thomas frowned and Janice sat down.

"The only thing new is that we're about to face a media storm," the Chief said as he leaned back in his chair, "...and that's worse than the F.B.I. or anybody else crawling around here trying to stick their noses where they don't belong. The papers and radio stations are finally smelling a big story. T.V. won't be far behind." He put his feet up to their customary position on top of his desk and looked directly at Janice. "And that ain't good for Highland," he added soberly.

Janice looked away from him and toward the light tapping sound on the office's only outside window. The rain was coming from the north now. It was turning miserable outside.

"Maybe..." she said dreamily, "...maybe that's exactly what we need." She turned her head back hopefully to look at the frowning Chief, then Darrin. "Maybe we need for people to read about all of this, or hear about it on television. Maybe people would, uh, come forward then. Give us the whole picture." She paused to look at both of them again. Neither of them looked particularly excited about what she was saying, but they were listening. She kept going. "I mean, we've had a bunch of weird things, and some horrible things, happen in the last week. But we don't know what's related to what. We don't know, for sure, what's random...or if there's a pattern. Maybe we tell the press everything we know, Rodney. Not just the gruesome stuff. Everything. Then we sit back, and we see what comes out of the woodwork."

She stopped and leaned back in her chair, and waited. Darrin and Chief Thomas exchanged a glance, but neither said anything. The rain seemed to pelt the window a little harder.

"Well, what do you think?" she asked anxiously a few moments later.

"I think the idea has some merit," Darrin said. He had leaned forward to rest his elbows on his knees. He seemed to be studying the floor. "We've got a couple of murders, some missing kids and..." he glanced sideways and up at Janice, "...and dead cats and stuff. But, we really don't have any idea if what we know is...is all of it, do we? I mean most people wouldn't report some of the stuff we've seen. They wouldn't associate a dog being dug up with, uh, with some woman out in the country being chopped up or..."

"Who says they're related?" Chief Thomas snapped.

"Exactly!" Janice interjected immediately. "We don't. But what if they are, Chief? You know you've thought about it. We all have. Jeez, that's all we talked about just the other night! Why not get it out there? Maybe we'll learn something? Maybe somebody can tie it all together for us. I mean, we don't have a clue now, do we?"

"Yeah. We're 'clueless,' get it?" Darrin smiled.

But the other two apparently didn't get it, and it got quiet enough to listen to the rain again.

★　　★　　★

Joanie Thomas had slept in. She'd been up late Sunday night to try to keep Rodney company, even though she knew it wouldn't go any good.

And it didn't. He was on the phone constantly (as he had been so much of the time in the last week), and when he wasn't taking or making a call he would aimlessly pace, or sit momentarily with her in front of the television that didn't work very well (with the cable still out, Rodney had tried hooking up a pair of rabbit ears. The result was one weak, snowy channel) with his mind obviously a million miles away. Or he would go over to the living room window that looked out to their back yard and stare out into the dark night for minutes at a time. To say that he was "distracted" would have been the grossest of understatements. He wasn't even there, really.

Joanie had given up at 10:30. She told him goodnight, kissed him on the cheek, and he had absently kissed her back without a word, not taking his eyes off the back yard during the whole exchange. She woke at midnight, and then at 12:45. He was not in bed, and she heard the gentle murmur of television snow in the living room, both times.

She woke again at 5:30 in the morning. It was still dark, and she didn't hear the television. She reached over to his side of the bed. He wasn't there. She sighed, then went back to sleep.

At 8:59 her eyes snapped open. She stared, suddenly wide awake, at the bedside clock; long enough for it to turn to 9:00. Something had woken her, she knew, but she had no idea what. She lay there, listening. She heard rain on the bedroom window. That could have been it. Or was it?

She sat up in bed. She stayed in that position for another full minute, listening, and trying to clear her head.

And finally, there it was: the sound that must have woken her. It was a...scratching. A scratching, coming from down the hallway and into the living room. There was definitely a scratching at the front door.

She got up, put on her robe and hurried out of the bedroom and toward the source of the noise. It wasn't until she was almost there, until she had actually started to reach her hand out for the door handle as she took the last few steps, that the fog her deep sleep completely wore off and she realized what she was hearing.

It made her stop abruptly. The scratching continued. It was on the lower side of the door, now a foot away from her. The same insistent, almost rhythmic scratching that a dog, her dog, had made hundreds of times before.

It was raining outside, and her dog wanted in.

She waited, trying to make sense of it. More scratching. Then a low, heartbreaking whine. She took the final step, unlocked the door and pulled it wide open.

"Mitzi!" she cried a moment later.

★　　　★　　　★

"I'm going to play the devil's advocate here," Chief Thomas said. Darrin grimaced. "...because that's what I do."

He glanced at Janice. Her eyes were wide with enthusiasm. Finally! she thought. "If we put all this crap out there," the Chief said, "even the, uh, small stuff, we're going to look like idiots to the uh, outside world. People go nuts with, what do ya call 'em... conspiracy theories. We'll be inundated with nuts. Nuts telling us stories, telling us things they imagined up. And your town, Janice... well, people will think twice before coming to Highland."

"You might be right, in the short run," Janice shot back. She was disappointed in the direction he was going, but was prepared for this. "I've thought about that. But you know, both of you guys know...I mean you said it yourself! We're in trouble. And right now it doesn't matter how much 'outside help' we get. We need to get it all out there, don't you think?" She looked at Darrin for support, but at least at the moment he was bent over studying the floor again. The Chief seemed to be listening, but was in his characteristic pose of studying the ceiling.

"Great," she thought. "Just great."

★   ★   ★

Beatrice Milton was once again trying to keep as busy as possible so that she wouldn't have to think. But even as she put another half load of wash in that could have waited, even as she re-washed some already clean dishes, and even as she mopped the kitchen floor for the second time in 24 hours-she kept an eye out, and her ears open, for the return of her husband, Harvey.

She just knew it would happen, and soon. The love of her life hadn't been seen or heard from since that rainy morning when he'd gone searching on his own for his best friend and boss, Sheriff Blanton. But Bea knew her Harvey. No one, from years of hunting and policing, knew the country around eastern Madison County better than Harvey. No one. Harvey knew his way home.

And it was this knowledge that gave her both hope, and, in weak or unguarded moments, almost unbridled fear.

If he knew his way in the woods, why hadn't he come out of them?

Why hadn't he called?

Why was it still called a search for the Sheriff, and not the Deputy Sheriff?

Bea's mind had gone into a kind of primitive survival mode quickly. Almost as quickly as Harvey had disappeared. She thought only positive thoughts. She avoided talking to anyone whenever possible; even her own grown children at times. She stopped answering the phone (after checking to see who was calling, of course). And she worked. And worked.

But she went to the front window, and looked out the back door-every few minutes, all day long. She knew, in the part of her mind that she hadn't purposefully closed down, that Harvey would be home. Any minute now.

At 10:00 A.M. on that rainy Monday morning she turned on the radio news while scrubbing a seldom used roasting pan. She did so on a whim. She hadn't heard a voice other than her own in two days. The radio was going in and out. Mostly out. But she heard the news announcer say the word "murder" once. She dried off her hands, then turned it off. Then before returning to the pan, she walked to the back door to look out at the yard and woods in back.

She took a quick glance, and had just started her automatic turn back toward the kitchen sink when she realized that she had actually seen something. A person.

With heart suddenly fluttering, she whirled to look again. She was way out there, by the woods. A little girl, dressed in a nightgown, it seemed, standing very still in the soft rain, looking her way.

Bea felt confusion, as well as disappointment. She rubbed her hand on the glass to get a clearer view and looked again.

What she saw stunned her; disoriented her, even more. Now there was a boy standing in the yard. He was smiling broadly at her. He was close enough for her to see. His smile showed his twisted, discolored teeth. And he was just standing there…right there in the yard.

Bea looked past him quickly to find the girl. She was still out there, still wasn't moving, but appeared to be much closer. She was all the way up to the edge of the yard. But she was standing still. She wasn't moving. How…?

Bea could feel her heart beating faster. She looked away from them and down, on purpose, and blinked several times. Was she hallucinating? How in the world…?

She looked up again, and there he was. Harvey! She looked down, took a deep breath, closed her eyes, then opened them, looked up…and yes! It was Harvey! He was standing next to the boy. And the little girl was now, somehow, right on the other side of the door. She was looking up at Bea. Her lips were moving. She was saying something, but Bea could not hear her voice.

She looked out at Harvey again. He was closer. He was smiling. He had raised his arm up. He was waving for her to come out…but stiffly, awkwardly.

But when Bea saw him gesture she felt a sudden, overwhelming joy that wiped out all the confusion. She opened the door. She tried to run out to him, but something stopped her progress immediately. Something was tugging on her. Something that was indescribably painful. She didn't want to look away from Harvey, but…

Bea looked down at the child… the beautiful child, right there, pressed against her stomach. She didn't understand.

★　　　★　　　★

"There's a c-c-call for you, sir. From the ha-ha-hospi…from a doctor."

All three of them jumped a little. Officer Bradley had merely leaned into the open office to notify the Chief (Janice had not closed it behind her when she'd come in earlier). It startled them all.

"Jesus, Lance!" Darrin said. He had somehow hurt his elbow while jerking back up to a normal sitting position. "Don't you ever knock?"

"S-S-Sorry," Lance replied.

"Doctor who?" Chief Thomas asked as he swung his feet to the floor.

Fortunately, Lance had written it down. He held it up, Chief Thomas nodded and Lance hurriedly walked in and handed it to him.

"Dr. Harbough," the Chief read aloud. "Isn't he that new doctor you guys brought in?" he asked Janice.

"Yes," she said. "Quite a catch for us. What does he want?" Janice asked.

"Well, I don't know," Chief Thomas said as he looked up at Lance. "Is he on the phone now?"

"N-N-No. The number's right th-th-there. He said you sh-sh-should call r-r-right away." With that Lance stepped back, appearing exhausted, and asked by signaling with his hands for permission to go back to his desk.

Chief Thomas nodded his assent and pulled out his cell phone. "I better see what's up," he told the other two. First Janice and then Darrin got up to leave the room, but the Chief waved them back down before dialing.

So they sat down quietly while the Chief got a hold of and then listened to his caller. Before Lance had burst in the discussion had veered from how to handle the coming storm from the press (Chief Thomas had finally, grudgingly consented to the strategy of "getting it all out there" that was being pushed by the other two), to a discussion of the "flash" moment the Monday evening before. Darrin had led the discussion by asking lawyer-type questions. Being that he was in Mexico at the end of his honeymoon at the time, and being that it looked more and more every day that the flash was (possibly?) some kind of trigger for the bizarre events that kept happening-it was an easy, natural thing for the three to get caught up in. Darin's questions, from "...Exactly what do you remember about that moment?" to "...What was the first thing you noticed was wrong after it happened?," caused the other two to really think through it again; every detail-hoping that something would be revealed-something clarified. Somehow.

And as the Chief listened, Janice and Darrin looked dreamily away, still riding in the train of the previous discussion.

"OK, be right there," Chief Thomas said suddenly. Then he snapped his phone shut and stood up. Darrin and Janice came to attention. "Gotta go," he said. The other two looked puzzled. "To the hospital," the Chief added as he walked around his desk and toward the door.

"What's wrong?" Darrin asked.

Chief Thomas stopped abruptly and looked back at his questioner. "You better come too, come to think of it." he said. then he glanced at Janice, paused, then said "You might as well come along Janice...that is, if you want to. Maybe you should see this."

"See what?" she asked. She was still sitting.

"I'm not sure, exactly," he said after a moment. He suddenly looked upset, "but I think it might be important."

Chapter 23
October 9th 11:24 A.M.

Jon Parker was anxious to get to the teachers' lounge (or Teacher Workroom, as the Highland school administrators insisted upon calling it). In fact, he had never been so anxious. He had been dying to get there since mid-morning.

The teaching schedule that he'd been assigned for that year was not his favorite. He started with two 84 minute "Block" classes of junior English, then another Block of Greek Mythology (which he didn't particularly like) that was broken up by a lunch period, which he was now on. From the start of the school day until lunch, then, he felt like he was "teaching his ass off." Easy afternoons didn't make up for it. He wasn't a morning person.

He walked straight to the lounge without getting his lunch first. It was a place he usually avoided. It was gossip central, and the juicy tidbits dropped usually centered around students and administrators. He found it depressing. But today was different.

He wasn't even hungry. He just wanted to talk.

But almost no one was there. There was only Barbara Kingsley, from the special education department, sitting there glumly at the table stabbing half-heartedly with her fork at something on her tray that could have been mashed potatoes.

"Where is everybody?" Jon asked after a few moments of being ignored. He stood just a foot inside the doorway, ready to turn and go where ever "everybody" was.

"Oh, hi Jon," Barbara said as she looked up, pretending she didn't already know he was there. She looked quickly back down at her food. "Half of them are absent, and their subs probably don't know where the lounge is. Poor people are probably eating with the kids," she said. Then she appeared to smile at her mashed potatoes.

Jon stood looking at her. He wasn't sure if he should say anything. He didn't know her very well. Then again, hell-she was the only one there.

He gave it a shot: "Barb, have you noticed that the kids, some of the kids are acting, well...strangely today?"

Awkward, and a huge understatement, but he didn't know how else to put it. First, at least a third of the kids were absent, which was unheard of at Highland unless the flu was going around. It wasn't. Second, the ones that were there, most of them anyway, were acting as if they were...well, drugged. Vacant faces, a seeming inability to understand the simplest instructions, and eerily, no apparent memory function. At all. They were just blank.

And finally, and worst of all, he had had three students (two girls and a boy), one first Block and two in the second-just get up and leave the room. Just like that. He had tried to stop all three, verbally (physical restraint was for trained administrators only, which was fine with him). All three acted as if they couldn't hear him, all three took their time walking away, as if they were doing it in their sleep-and all three had the same goofy, but also eerie grin on their faces when they left. Like they knew something that he didn't.

By third block he felt like he was going nuts. He felt as though something huge, and organized was happening, but he had no idea what. Some kind of mass sickness? A huge practical joke? ...And, most of all, he feared that it was somehow related to well, the flash...

Actually, he knew it was.

"Not any more than usual, " Barb said casually. She played with her mashed potatoes. He realized he hadn't seen her take a bite yet. She looked up at him quickly and gave him a big, vacant smile. He recognized it. It was the same one that they kids had worn when they left his room. "But my kids are all a little 'unusual' anyway...aren't they, Jon?" she asked.

*　　*　　*

Dr. Harbough was down waiting to meet the Police Chief at the entrance to St. Joseph's Hospital. He was alternately standing and nervously rubbing his hands together or pacing aimlessly there, watching anxiously as the three waited for traffic to pass so that they could cross the street from the parking lot. From where they stood they could see that the doctor was agitated and nervous looking-even from 75 feet away.

"What's this about, anyway?" Darrin asked nervously as he stood watching the doctor pace.

Chief Thomas held his hand up instead of answering. He had his phone up to his ear. He was trying to get a hold of his wife for the third time since leaving the office. For the third time, there was no answer. He had just wanted to tell her he wouldn't be home for lunch.

"He wants us to see something," the Chief said casually after snapping his phone shut. The last car passed and they stepped in unison off the curb. "We're going to see a baby. A sick baby."

Darrin and Janice exchanged looks on that one. But there was no time to ask anything else. A few seconds later they were there. The doctor himself held the door open for them. "Hi. At least it quit raining, huh?" he said awkwardly in greeting them.

There were quick introductions. The doctor nodded and shook hands at the appropriate times, but Darrin had the impression that he wasn't really listening to the names, or anything else. He was a short, dark-featured, handsome young man-who looked like ha had something inside him that was eating him alive; which was just the case.

"Please, just follow me," he said as soon as he'd shaken Darrin's hand. Then he whirled and headed down the hall going double time, with his white gown flapping.

They went all the way down a hall, up a flight of stairs, then half-way down another hall. The circuitous route confused even Chief Thomas, who knew the hospital pretty well. It was almost as though they were *sneaking* to their destination. But it took all they had just to keep up with the young doctor, and no one had the breath for any questions.

It was only when they got there; the door to the room he wanted them to go into, that Dr. Harbough stopped. He turned and waited for the three to catch up (Janice was last, as she was wearing heels). When they were all there and had had a few moments to catch their breath, he spoke: "This three month-old child was brought in late yesterday afternoon," he said. "The parent-she's a single mother-said that they were outside enjoying the weather when her baby was attacked by a stray cat."

Janice felt her stomach clench.

"She said the cat came out of nowhere, and scratched and bit the child as she lay on her blanket in the yard. She said she was able to chase the cat away, but not before being bitten herself. We treated them both, but determined that the baby should stay the night for observation. We reported all this to the police, and animal control, of course," the Dr. said, looking directly at Chief Thomas. "I...I wanted you to see this while the mother was away. She called us this morning to say that she's too sick to come in, which worries me too...but..."

Janice could see sweat on the man's furrowed brow. She also saw that his hands were shaking slightly.

"Just... just look at this," the doctor said decisively as he pushed open the door.

After the ominous build-up they had just listened to, none of the three exactly rushed into the hospital room. They edged their way in; Chief Thomas right behind the doctor, the other two behind the Police Chief. But a few moments later they were there at the crib. To their collective relief they saw only a baby lying on her back with eyes closed, sleeping peacefully.

"Awww!" Janice mewled in a whisper. She couldn't help it. Darrin and the Chief looked on in silence. Their instinct was to be quiet, protective. The doctor moved to the opposite side of the crib from his three guests.

"I want you to look at this," he said (not whispering). He raised the covers up and off the baby's legs. The sudden move surprised them and their three heads moved back together in unison, blanching in advance from what they expected to be a horrible sight. But they saw only a baby girl's legs with light red marks on them. "Do you see those marks?" the Dr. asked insistently.

They all looked closer. Unremarkable, hardly distinguishable red marks.

Chief Thomas looked up at Dr. Harbough. "What about them?"

"They were wounds yesterday afternoon. Deep ugly wounds," he said without taking his eyes off the child. "And this!" he reached down and turned the baby so that they could see a spot on her upper thigh. Another dull red spot, with a feint brown mark running across its middle. They all three looked at what his finger pointed to, then up at him. "That was a vicious bite. She lost a lot of skin there. It took nine stitches!"

Janice looked from the baby to the doctor's face, and then to the faces of her partners. She saw that Darrin and the Chief looked as shocked and confused as she was. Either they were seeing something remarkable, even impossible...or this new Doctor was nuts.

Darrin leaned down for a closer look, then looked back up at the doctor. "You can't be serious," he said, but in a whisper, perhaps because it seemed wrong not to do so. This was a sleeping baby, after all. "Are you telling us that this kid healed in less than

24 hours?" he asked. The whispering hurt his throat, so he said the '24 hours' part out loud.

Dr. Harbough gave Darrin a steely-serious look as the baby began to stir. "I'm telling you it was less than that," he said evenly.

The baby stretched its little arms up above her head and her legs started to move. She was waking up. The doctor looked down at her for a moment, then said "And watch this," very calmly. He reached down and shook the baby to wake her. And not very gently, at that. All three of them noticed that, and Janice almost said something. But he was a doctor.

"You may want to step back," Dr. Harbough said calmly. Then he did so himself.

They didn't though. This was a little baby, after all. A baby that had its covers taken away and now had been rudely shaken awake. The collective sympathy in the room was not with the doctor.

But they watched intently. The baby's face puckered up as though she was about to cry, but she didn't. Then her face seemed to relax, with its little mouth forming a perfect 0. Her eyes blinked open for a second, closed, then blinked open again. They looked jaundiced, and had black enlarged pupils. They didn't look right. Not at all. Not like a baby's eyes. The baby stared straight up at the ceiling without appearing to blink. At all.

Then, very suddenly, noiselessly, the baby flipped over onto her stomach and in the same quick and effortless motion raised up onto her hands and knees. She stopped there and held very still for a few seconds. Then she made a gurgling noise that seemed to Janice to be an impossible noise for a baby to make. It was deep and phlegm-filled; like an old man trying to clear his throat.

Chief Thomas and Darrin both took an involuntary step back. Janice stood frozen; fascinated and horrified.

"Jesus," the Chief muttered.

"Can babies do that?" Darrin asked.

No one answered. The baby was very still. She seemed frozen in position there on her hands and knees, as if not sure what to do next.

Janice found her voice: "How...how in the world can..."

As if activated by the voice, the baby suddenly snapped her head to the side, toward Janice. She seemed to almost smile for a moment, then crawled, lightening fast, to the side of the crib. She got there and pulled herself up to her feet and put her tiny face within an inch of Janice's before any of them could react.

Janice screamed, Darrin lunged to try to pull her back, and the Chief pushed at the crib with his foot to try to slide it away-all in the next few seconds.

The baby just stood there holding the bars of the crib, head bent slightly down so that her yellow and black eyes could see through them, and calmly watched them all.

★　　　★　　　★

"That was NOT a baby in there, Doctor." Darrin said as he paced rapidly back and forth. "What the hell? What in God's name...!"

Fifteen minutes had elapsed since their party had left the baby's room, and only the "mute" stage of their shock had begun to pass. And only after they had been sitting in absolute, stunned silence for ten of those minutes in the windowless conference room had any words been exchanged at all.

The Chief had finally broken through by asking the doctor a couple of quiet, innocuous detail-oriented questions. The doctor had, just as quietly, answered them. That was all until now.

Darrin was ready to burst. The very sound of his boss' calm voice asking about the mother's wounds (or whatever), made his shock turn into rage. Now he paced while the other three sat mutely around the conference table. He wanted answers. And he wanted to drop all the pretending.

"I DON'T KNOW!" the doctor shouted back. It was loud and unexpected enough to stop Darrin in mid-step. The two of them made eye contact. "That's why I called you here," he added, this time with his indoors voice. "I've never seen anything like it." He looked away from Darrin and down at his own hands spread out on the table in front of him. "Obviously."

Darrin started pacing again. "Well, I think we get an expert, a whole team of them in here," he said. "Whatever's happening, and I don't think we can deny this shit anymore...whatever is going on here, we've got...we've got one of 'em right here. Trapped in a crib. To study. Am I right?"

"We've got one of what, exactly?" Chief Thomas asked irritably.

"Hell, I don't know! One of...one of the things! One of the infected things!" Darrin sputtered. "I mean, we all know it, right!"

Chief Thomas turned around in his seat at this (Darrin had been pacing behind him). "Darrin, we've got a sick baby up there," he said very deliberately, "and I admit that it's very strange but..."

The door to the conference room opened right as Darrin was walking by it. It startled him enough to jump away and momentarily reach for his weapon. A woman in a nurse's hat on peeked in. "Oh, sorry," she said to Darrin. Then she located the doctor. "Doctor? May I see you for a minute?"

Dr. Harbough got up quickly, as though he was relieved to have an excuse to leave the room, which he undoubtedly was. He quickly disappeared into the hallway.

Chief Thomas turned back around from his face-off with Darrin. The room grew quiet, until the Dr. hurriedly entered again.

He got right to the point. "Chief Thomas, I'm afraid they're bringing your wife to the emergency room. She's been hurt. Please come with me."

Chapter 24
October 9th 4:37 P.M.

"She's in serious condition. She's going to lose a leg, it looks like. The dog, or dogs that attacked her..." Darrin was telling Jon.

"I thought they didn't know that for sure," Janice interrupted, "...about the leg, I mean."

Darrin gave her an irritated look. "Hell, you tell it then. I've talked enough."

But she ignored the comment and reached for her purse instead. Sharon, the owner, bartender and cook there at the Cypress was bringing the drinks to their table. Janice wanted to buy. It would be something normal, trivial- but good to do.

Everything felt like it had changed. In one day. Two especially implausible events had seen to that. The three that were meeting for "a drink or two" after work were fundamentally different than they had been when they had gotten up for work that morning. Things were different now. As bad as it had been before, now it was worse. It felt like their world was collapsing.

Seeing that baby and then seeing the Chief's wife after an inexplicable mauling had done it for Janice and Darrin. Seeing Highland High School disintegrate into numbed chaos before his eyes had done it for Jon.

What had been an ominous, but still vague dread before had now turned into cold (if still inexplicable) reality.

"Here you go!" Sharon said brightly as she placed the two beers in front of the men and the gin and tonic in front of Janice.

"Is this enough?" Janice asked, holding up a $10. The two men were late to the draw and were fumbling for their wallets. "I'll get this one, OK?" she added.

"That'll cover it," Sharon answered. She smiled, started to leave, then hesitated. She seemed undecided for a moment, then settled it by abruptly sitting down in the fourth chair set around the table, surprising all three of them. "I'll get your change in a minute, but..." she looked directly at, and leaned a little toward, Darrin. "Can I ask you something first?"

Darrin took a quick swig of beer without taking his eyes off of her. "Sure," he said. He was trying to be pleasant, trying to fight back the overwhelming feeling that, well, there was simply no time for any of this anymore. Questions, small talk... any of it.

"Things are, uh, crazy around here, and getting crazier. Anybody can see that. Is something going on that you can tell me about? Something that we should know? All the rest us...the ones who are still OK? Is there?" she asked.

Darrin looked at the worry lines around Sharon's pretty face. She was scared, he realized. Like everybody was who had half a brain, and could add it all up. And she was smart, he knew. Not one to take any bull. Cops were always supposed to be careful, very careful, when answering questions like this. Loose lips could cause a panic. With somebody like Sharon, though...well, you couldn't insult her, or insult her intelligence (the food at the Cypress was too good for one thing, right?). You had to balance on the line between the whole truth, and the kind of outright lie that politician's specialize in. She had watched people. Customers. She did that for a living. She could see the changes in some of them. Probably more of them every day. He knew that.

Darrin looked directly into her eyes and started to speak, stopped, then leaned back and sighed. "Sharon, I don't know. I really don't. A lot of weird stuff has happened in the last week, since that thing happened."

"You mean the "flash," right?" She asked quietly. Then she looked up at the clock at the bar. "Almost a week ago. 5:34, last Monday night."

Her preciseness surprised them. It shouldn't have, by now. The "flash" had happened to everybody. Or almost everybody, Darrin thought.

"Where were you when it happened?" Jon asked her.

"I was home," she answered quickly. "We're closed on Mondays. We're having a special birthday party here in a little while or you guys would be drinking somewhere else right now, as the matter of fact. Cause its Monday, honey." She seemed a little irritated to be thrown off her quest to get information from Darrin, and turned her body toward him again.

"What was it like for you? The flash, I mean?" Jon asked sincerely. He either refused to take her hint, or was oblivious to it.

Sharon sighed and looked back at Jon. She scooted her chair back a bit, and for a moment it looked as though she might give up, get up, and go back to work. But after hesitating, she answered. "It was like...nothing, but it was the worst thing ever, in a way." She looked from Jon over to Janice. "It's funny. I was at home, but I was still at the stove, like I would've been here. It was like everything, well...kind of left for a second. Not even a second. And then it was back. But nothing was the same anymore, it felt like. I'm starting to wonder if it ever will be." Sharon looked past Janice and up towards the bar. A customer had just walked in and had called out her name in greeting, but she didn't answer. Her eyes had a dreamy far-away quality to them. "My dog started howling, like he was hurt, right afterwards. And I...I felt like crying, but I didn't know why."

Yeah, I'll have a beer!" the customer yelled out jovially. He was sitting at the bar, looking back at Sharon.

"OK, OK," Sharon finally answered. She scooted her chair back, and without another word got up to go back to work.

"Well, that was dramatic," Darrin said as soon as she was out of earshot.

Jon gave him a dirty look. "You had to go through it to know," he said.

Darrin looked at his friend for a moment, sighed again and leaned back in his chair. "I know," he said. "I don't know why I said that. Stupid. It's just that...I mean, do we have time? I mean we already know, don't we?"

★   ★   ★

Police Chief Rodney Thomas was a wreck. He was pacing around a rough circle, over and over again, in the waiting room they had told him to stay in (*warned* him to stay in, actually), feeling about ready to bust open. From the moment he had seen his poor Joanie, lying unconscious on that stretcher when the paramedics wheeled her in, he had been close to uncontrollable.

Darrin and Janice had tried to calm him first. That had ended with him physically pushing Darrin away and telling Janice to go to hell. Then there was a tense scene with Officer Christopher and a couple of paramedics, and finally a heated "conversation" with Dr. Harbough himself. It took a full half-an-hour after Joanie's arrival by ambulance for the man known for his self-control and cool dispassionate judgment to regain a semblance of it.

He was far better now, on the outside, but still at full boil internally. His family had been attacked. The love of his life was fighting for hers. And somehow, somehow...somehow, it felt like it was his fault. His brain teemed and raged with aberrant, violent thoughts...and with his guilt.

This is war! But with who? This wasn't just dogs! I don't believe that for a second. But who? Who? Who! They knew who she was, who I am! Monsters! Damned monsters. I'll kill...And that poor baby!... Monsters!!

"Mr. Thomas?"

Rodney whirled around as if ready to fight. It was Dr. Harbough. With a sober look on his face. And Officer Ben Christopher, standing nervously right behind him. Bodyguard?

His stomach tightened, lump in his throat, tears welled in his eyes. He clenched his hands into tight fists. He felt frozen. "Yes?" he heard himself say.

"Your wife is out of danger, for now. But she's been badly injured. I think we can save the leg. But she lost a lot of blood. She'll be here for a while. And Rodney...you may come to see her now."

From somewhere way on high, above the ceiling and the small room itself, Rodney saw himself drop to his knees. And he heard himself say "Thank God," over and over again.

★   ★   ★

"It's all out war now," Darrin said. He looked around the room. Sharon was wiping down the bar. Her only customer was drinking his second beer. People were beginning to arrive in the dining room beyond the bar for their birthday party, and their merry voices were already getting louder. "The people don't know it yet, but they're in the battle of their lives." he added. And then a few moments later: "Now if we can just figure out who the hell we're fighting."

Janice and Jon listened to Darrin's words in resigned silence. What would have been challenged as a ridiculously over-the-top statement by either of them just a few days before now had the ring of undeniable, disquieting truth.

Jon had actually called Darrin from school to ask him to meet for the drink after work. Darrin had asked the equally numbed Janice to join them. The meeting had started with Jon reporting on the alarming events and aberrant behaviors he'd witnessed that school day, then Darrin and Janice teamed up to tell the story of the baby. Darrin had related what he knew about the

185

dog attack on Joanie Thomas (after calling in for an update from Ben Christopher)...and of course, they had talked about the kids and adults disappearing at an alarmingly increasing rate, and all the rest (as well as listening to the wise bartender Sharon. Twice now.).

They were a traumatized and mystified (as ever) "Clueless Club."

"I think we should start thinking differently. I know we've said that before, but I think we need to really start doing it." Jon said out of nowhere as he looked absently at the bar's clock. It effectively broke the silence that had ruled since Darrin's aimless declaration of war.

"What do you mean, exactly?" Janice asked.

"I mean...like Darrin did, like you said, when we had the Devonshire woods thing going on."

The other two looked at him, but said nothing.

"Darrin did research back then. He found out about possible causes, even though they were, on the face of it, impossible. Illogical. And you two have started it again. With your map and everything."

"'Bout time you came around," Darrin said.

"Yeah, I guess," He looked up at the clock again. 5:28. "What I saw at school today was...I'll just come right out and say it: like possession. Like the kids, and some of the teachers, the ones that were there, were possessed. And a lot of it had to happen over the weekend. Some of the kids were like, like zombies or something. And I think that's a, uh, microcosm for what's happening all over. Because it's speeding up, right?"

"Which is it, 'The Exorcist' or 'Return of the Zombies'? Because we need to know the right weapons to use, ya know?" Darrin asked with a sardonic half smile. He couldn't resist, even under these circumstances."And what the hell is a microcosm, by the way?"

"But what do we research? How? What is there to look up?" Janice asked.

"We go to the library, look at the history of Highland, study your map thing...look for weird shit that happened...I don't know. All that stuff, I guess. Maybe we even talk to Priests or something," Jon answered. Then he looked directly at Darrin. "And we might have to go witch-hunting again. Maybe go back into those woods, man."

"I can't believe I'm hearing this," Darrin said.

"Well, we've got to do something. I mean-you talked about the National Guard maybe coming in, and the F.B.I., and whatever else you guys have talked about. But the thing is...what are they gonna do? Shoot dogs and cats? And... and kids? It's not gonna help, and you guys know it. It's not going to solve the problem, because it's bigger than that. Come on guys! We've got to get proactive, don't ya think?"

With that, Jon sat back, temporarily exhausted. The three were quiet for a minute. Then Darrin broke it. "I don't know if we have time. I really don't. Not after today."

"What do you mean?" Janice asked. "Why not..."

"Drinks on the house!" Sharon cried. None had seen her approach and they were startled. "It's almost time," she added, nodding toward the clock as she put the drinks on their table.

They all looked. It was 5:32. No, 5:33. The minute turned for them as they looked.

"One minute until the one week mark," Sharon said.

The flash moment was indeed only seconds away from being one week old. And there they were, in a bar, about to celebrate... what? Survival? It seemed like a twisted anniversary moment.

Sharon stood her ground right there and watched the clock intently. Janice, Darrin and Jon did the same found themselves doing the same. Darrin looked around, and noticed that as the seconds passed, it became increasingly impossible not to feel the growing tension in the room, and within themselves; there was an undeniable tightening of the throat at the building uncertainty of it all. Sharon had turned off the snow on the television (it was funny how most people kept their sets on-even with no hope for a picture) before coming over, and he noticed that now. Also, the party in the next room had grown eerily silent.

The man at the bar got up, looked over at them, then quietly walked out, leaving a full beer on the bar, untouched.

They waited. No one moved. No one talked. It was getting hard to breathe.

Then the clock flipped to 5:34.

Nothing happened. They waited...waited, but felt nothing, and heard only the barking of a dog somewhere in the distance. Then suddenly, there were frenzied shouts and party horns wildly blaring, all coming from the people in the next room.

"SURPRISE!" they screamed in clumsy unison.

Chapter 25
October 9th 9:46 P.M.

Chief Thomas started turning his car around from his ride home to head to Darrin Crandle's house before he had even called him. He didn't even have to think about it. He almost hit a fire hydrant trying to find his phone before the u-turn was complete. He would have kept going if he had.

"Darrin?" he said a few moments later, "I'm coming over, OK?"

Long pause. "Sure," he said finally. "Is...is Joanie all right?"

Another long pause. This time because Rodney suddenly felt like choking. Or worse. "Yeah. I mean, I think so. Nothing more to do tonight," he finally said.

Darrin heard the emotion in his voice. He didn't know how to respond, so he didn't. In the ensuing silence the Chief heard the jumble of other voices in the background.

"You got company?" he asked.

"Yeah. The others are over. We're, uh, trying to figure this out," Darrin said, then added, "We...we could use your help, Chief," even though he wasn't sure this was true.

During the next long pause Darrin could almost hear the Chief reconsidering it. But he kept quiet.

"I'm headed over," the Chief said said. Then he hung up.

The people at Darrin and Marilyn's house were Jon, Janice and Ben Christopher. Chief Thomas was only surprised by Christopher. They were all seated haphazardly around the living room, except for Marilyn, who was frantically trying to make coffee for the Chief in the kitchen. Everyone except Janice looked up when he walked into the room. She was poring over some papers she had spread out on a card table that had apparently been set up for that purpose. There was an awkward silence.

"Good to see you, boss," Officer Christopher said as he rose to his feet. The others mumbled the same.

"They found another woman dead. Did you hear that?" the Chief asked as he looked at Darrin.

Darrin looked at his boss. He was pale, very tired looking... but apparently ready to get down to business. About what you'd expect, Darrin thought. "Yeah," he answered, "and three more kids missing this afternoon. At least. Didn't come home from school. At least that's what their parents are saying. It's getting hysterical out there fast."

"I'm not surprised," Jon said as he walked over to Janice's table. He looked at what she was working on briefly, then took his cell out of his pocket to make a call. Ben, who was seemed a bit intimidated by the appearance of his boss, followed Jon over to Janice's table and at least pretended to study one of the papers there. Darrin stood by Chief Thomas and tried to think of what to say. Marilyn came to the rescue by bringing in a cup of coffee a few moments later.

The Chief thanked her and sipped at his cup with slightly trembling hands. "Very good," he said. "Not too hot, like that guy over there makes it." He tried to smile. He'd meant for Jon to hear the dig, but he was busy with his phone.

Darrin decided to take the initiative. "We're just brainstorming here Chief," he said. "Trying to come up with a plan. Janice organized it. She's pretty good at it, you know?" Chief Thomas nodded and sipped his coffee. "Anyway, there are three categories: 'Possible Cause,' 'Evidence Pattern,' and 'Solution.' She's got it all written up. We're all over the place on the first one, as you know... the cause one, and the third one depends on how the other two come out, so we're spending most of our time on 'Evidence Pattern.'"

The Chief looked at Darrin like he was trying to decide if he was crazy or not. It went through Darrin's mind that it was exactly the look he'd had on his face at Jon's house, two years ago. He'd thought they were pretty screwy then, too. "Anyway," Darrin continued quickly, "we've been adding things that happened. To the map I mean. Looking for patterns. And we're starting to see something, maybe." Darrin felt himself starting to perspire. His explanation wasn't going to well. He didn't even know if the Chief was really listening, or even wanted to hear it, come to think of it. Maybe he wasn't even here for that...and why was it so damned hard to talk to this man?

"It's like the flu," Janice said firmly from across the room. "It helps to think of it like that." She was still seated in front of her table, but she was looking over at Chief Thomas now. The small lamp on the table gave her up-tilted face a wise-looking, ethereal glow. Ben and Jon were turned and looking that way too. Everyone was listening. Janice's voice seemed to command everyone's attention.

"After the flash, it was just animals that were affected, at least as far as we can tell," she continued. "Then, slowly, it was people who...got the flu. Some of the people, you could say, appeared to get it from animals. And later, now, people are getting it from other people, as well as animals. It's like an epidemic now, and where it strikes...where this 'flu' strikes...well, we think it might be predictable, in a way."

Chief Thomas looked at her steadily, but said nothing. Janice looked down at one of the papers in front of her and read from it: "Boy bitten by dog, boy escapes from hospital, still missing, mother at same address dies mysteriously. Farm family cows stolen, daughter missing, mother killed, father missing. Man goes missing in woods, wife killed. Man murdered in home, body missing, wife missing. Two cases of missing children now have missing friends." She looked up. "It's still sketchy, but it works like the flu, doesn't it? You're more likely to get it if your pet, or family, or friends get it."

"Sort of like 'Chief's dog killled, comes back to life, tries to eat wife?" the Chief asked bitterly.

The room got still. No one moved or spoke. And it wasn't just empathy for Chief Thomas. No one had really, seriously mentally confronted the prospect of things coming back to life, either. Not really. Not way down deep.

"My cat died, Rodney," Janice said a long moment later, her voice a little different, a little more empathetic than the "in command" one she had been using, "and now...he keeps trying to get back into my house at night. I swear he does! I'm not crazy. At least not yet. I swear he does." They all looked at her. "How can that be?" she asked.

No one had an answer for that. Marilyn though, to Darrin's surprise, spoke next: "The 2nd grade class right next to my room only had five kids in it today. Miss Young, the teacher, told me that one of the girls in her class had a birthday party Saturday. She said no one who went to the party came to school today."

Darrin saw his wife's suddenly haunted face and grew immediately concerned. He hadn't heard this. He hadn't given her the time, actually. He hadn't even asked her about her day.

"Maybe it was food poisoning," Ben offered helpfully. He got several dismissive looks, and then reddened.

Chief Thomas then spoke, apparently trying to bring things back to center: "So you're saying, you guys are saying that...you know where the next thing will happen? Or you think you might know?"

"Not exactly," Jon answered, "But these incidents, they seem to circle back to the same, uh, families, or friends. So far." He looked down at Janice's map for a few moments, then back up to the Chief. "It's a start," he finally added.

Chief Thomas' coffee cup started to rattle in his hand, and he took two quick, staggering steps toward the sofa.

Darrin saw that he was about to pass out, but got there a little late, and almost landed on top of his boss before pulling up and away from him at the last second. "You all right Chief?" he asked.

★　　　★　　　★

Chief Thomas was fine (if a bit embarrassed) after eating the sandwich Marilyn made for him.

It was the first food he'd had since morning. Eating hadn't exactly been a high priority, lately.

Before long, the group was back at work. Over the next hour and a half, through discussion, argument, sometimes wild-sounding supposition, and Janice's determined leadership-they even arrived at somewhat of an agreement on several points. Though continual doubts about the effectiveness of it all continued to persist, they were finally ready for a plan of action.

First, in general, they agreed that they (and their city and township area) were in trouble and it was past time to put everything else aside to try to get a hold of the thing. It was time to be proactive, and to reach out for help if necessary (once they could identify how "the help" could help).

They agreed that the "Flash Moment" probably started it all, but that there was no use speculating on what (or who?) caused it. There was no way of knowing. The same went for the similar nightmares that some Highland residents had had (including Janice) before the killing started. No use going there. Too speculative. Too late.

They also agreed that all the evidence showed that it was a local phenomenon. They agreed that the "incidents" were somewhat predictable, when plotted on their map-although they were multiplying so fast now that it was getting harder to do so.

Still the Evidence Pattern they had created at the very least gave them some ideas.

It was time to talk Solution. Or at least a plan of action.

"After listening to all of you, and thinking and talking this thing to death-it looks like there's at least a couple of things we could do," Janice said when she had finally gotten everyone's attention. "First, and I don't know if this is possible Chief Thomas," she said deferentially, "...but could we put men-policemen-in particular spots at particular times? Where stuff might happen, instead of just on patrol?"

All eyes turned to Chief Thomas. He fidgeted uncomfortably before answering. "Well...yes, but, I don't have all that many men Janice. They're being affected too. And their families. Officers are suddenly calling in sick left and right. And who decides what spots to put them in?"

"We could work on the County guys, the State guys, maybe..." Darrin interjected.

"You can decide, if that's what it takes," Janice interrupted, ignoring Darrin, "And, excuse me for saying this, but I'll tell you one spot you should consider covering beginning tonight. Your wife's hospital room. You should have somebody watching her right now."

The air seemed to go out of the room. Except for heads turning immediately in his direction, no one moved a muscle. Chief Thomas glared at Janice and his face went from pale and tired to beet red, very quickly. He looked ready to burst. Again.

But in just moments, the Chief's demeanor changed again. He went from looking boiling mad to looking vulnerable and unsure, right before their eyes. "Do you think," he said in a quiet voice, "she might be in danger?...In danger of..."

"Changing?" Janice asked, "I don't know Rodney. But..." she stopped there and reddened a bit herself. She quickly looked down at her map and papers. After a long pause, she cleared her throat and said "When you look at these patterns...I think she could be, may be attacked again?...I don't know."

Darrin looked at his boss, who looked devastated. "We'll find a way to put them in better spots," he said. "Even if it means double shifts. What else Janice?"

Janice was still looking at Chief Thomas. It was hard for her, for everyone else in the room, to not feel empathy toward him. She coughed, cleared her throat again and said "Jon brought up being aggressive. Maybe going to the source of all this. The center of activity spots on the map, like we talked about. Investigate them. I know we can only guess about that, but what have we got to lose?"

"Just our asses," Darrin said.

"What spots?" Chief Thomas asked.

"There are really three," Janice answered. She looked down at her map. "One would be the Crawford Farm. The northern edge. The one that lost the cows, then had the daughter disappear, and the dad, then the mom getting murdered."

"The State boys, the Sheriff's Office...what's left of it, and even the F.B.I. are all over that. And it's out of our jurisdiction," the Chief said flatly. He appeared to be recovering a bit.

"So?" Janice asked.

"We can't let anything stop us. Nothing is stopping them!" Officer Christopher said. He had been silent for so long that his outburst immediately drew everyone's attention. They all looked at him and he blushed.

And no one bothered asking him who "them" was.

"Where else, Janice?" Darrin asked, centering them all again.

"Well, one would be the exact center, geographically, of all the incidents that have been reported." She looked down at her map and squinted. "That would be 802 9th Street." She looked up. "Its smack dab in the middle, and Ben...Officer Christopher here, says he's been called there twice in the last week."

"That's 'The House of Plenty'!" Chief Thomas cried. Then, for the first time all day, he smiled.

Janice looked back at her map. "It is?" she asked.

"Damn right it is!" the Chief virtually snickered. "The haunted house of Highland. You've got to be joking, right? Pulling my leg?"

"I was called there twice Chief. Both times someone claimed they spotted a couple of our missing kids there," Ben said quietly. Everyone looked his way again. This time he didn't look away. "I'm just sayin'…" he added.

"Did you find anything?" the Chief demanded.

Officer Christopher quickly shook his lowered head.

"It's the geographic center, Rodney!" Janice said impatiently. "That's all *I'm* saying."

"And the third spot, Janice?" Darrin asked. He was obviously trying to move things along. It was late. They all were looking very tired. Marilyn had already given up and gone to bed, people were getting crankier by the minute…and it was so damned late…

"The third place is the woods, guys," Janice said. "The woods behind Jon's house. Because of what happened two years ago, and because Jon has spotted kids back there. Twice." She stopped and looked from face to face. The Chief wasn't smiling now. No one was. All looked gravely serious. "And," Janice continued, "Ben and those other policemen found a cow skeleton out there. Actually, more than one. And that doesn't make any sense. It could have been…" she hesitated, as if to be careful with her wording, "…a food source, for something. We have to find out for what."

For almost half-a-minute, Janice's words seemed to hang in the silent air between her and the three men.

Then they, along with plans, doubts, and theories they'd formed over the long evening were suddenly shattered to pieces by Marilyn's piercing scream.

Chapter 26
October 9th 11:27 P.M.

It was chaos at first. A totally unexpected, horrifying woman's scream can only produce hair-raising panic in its first moments; no matter when or where it occurs. But with the time of night and the circumstances the group found themselves in, it seemed all the worse now.

Janice shot up, knocked her card table over and put her hands instinctively over her ears. Ben gasped and took an involuntary step backwards. Darrin's eyes bugged in shock, and he effectively froze in horror for the length of the scream. Then he dashed toward the bedroom and his wife. Jon flipped the paper of notes he had been holding into the air and let out a smaller, shorter scream of his own. Only Chief Thomas appeared at least outwardly cool. He stayed seated and merely turned his head sharply toward the source of the cry.

Moments later, Darrin swung open the door to the dark bedroom. He frantically reached for the light switch, missed it, then flicked it on. Marilyn was sitting on the still-made bed in her robe. Her hands were covering her eyes, and she was sobbing. She was facing the bedroom window.

Jon came in right behind Darrin and bumped into him. Ben was right behind Jon but scooted to a stop right outside the door frame. Jon's bump propelled Darrin toward his wife. A little too hard. He almost knocked her over when he got there.

It took him a long minute to calm her down enough even to get a clue from her as to what had happened. She was hyperventilating, and she was hysterical.

"Faces...in... the window," she finally got out as she clutched her husband desperately.

"God damn it!" Ben cried, and he turned and ran immediately out of the room. After a moment of indecision, Jon followed. Darrin grimaced but stayed there soothing and shushing his wife. He really had no choice. She was holding him with shaking arms, as tightly as she could.

Ben very nearly ran over Chief Thomas at the end of the hallway. "There's someone out there!" he yelled as he headed for the front door. He was taking out his gun.

"Hold on there!" the Chief commanded. His deep voice was authoritative enough to stop Jon in his tracks, and Ben a couple of steps later. "You stay here!" he said, pointing at Jon. Then he pointed at Ben, "And you come with me." He walked briskly to the front door. "And put that gun away!" he said after opening the door. "We don't want to shoot some damned kid."

"Probably a good idea," Jon said softly after the door shut. He looked over at Janice after he'd said it, but she wasn't there. Somehow, she'd slipped past them and gone back into the bedroom. He could vaguely hear her voice, and then Marilyn's as he stood there alone in the middle of the living room.

★   ★   ★

"There were two faces, pressed up against the glass. They were... kids. One was older, maybe a teenager. The other was this little girl!" Marilyn brought her hands up to her face, again. She lowered her head, sobbed deeply, then began to cry. Again.

Chief Thomas, Jon and Janice sat around the Crandle's kitchen table with her. Darrin was alternately pacing angrily or stopping directly behind his wife to sympathetically rub her shoulders and say whatever comforting words he could come up with. Ben stood because there weren't any more chairs in the kitchen.

He and the Chief had found nothing. No sign of kids, adults-anything. They had taken flashlights and studied the ground outside the bedroom window for footprints, and the window for hand or face prints. All nothing. No clue that anyone or anything had been there.

And now they and the others were, as gently as possible, trying to get as much from Marilyn as they could. It wasn't easy with an enraged, protective husband standing right behind her.

Marilyn finally pulled her hands away and laid them on the table while gulping for composure. Janice reached over and covered one of those hands with both of her own. "It's OK, honey," she cooed. "It'll be OK."

"To hell it's OK!" Darrin barked fiercely, "I'm gonna kill those bastards!"

"Be my guest," Jon said flippantly. "I could use some sleep tonight."

"That's not helping!" Janice pleaded. She glared up at Darrin but he was too busy to notice. He had begun his pacing again.

"Can you..." Chief Thomas began in as kind a voice as he could summon, "...can you tell us anything else, Marilyn? I know it's hard, but if we're going to catch these...these kids, or whatever they are..."

"They looked dead," Marilyn blurted suddenly. She was trembling, still fighting for composure, but now seemed determined. "They were white. Very white. Like dead people. And they were...smiling. Sort of smiling. I could see their teeth." She looked at the Chief with what seemed to be great effort, with red, tear-filled eyes.

"I think that's enough!" Darrin snapped. He put his hands on his wife's shoulders again and rubbed them. He bent his head down close to hers. "Honey, don't you think you need to lie down now?"

"NO!" she shouted. Under different circumstances, on a far better and peaceful day-like they all used to have about a week before- Darrin's reaction to his wife's unexpected shout would have been funny. Even now, Jon couldn't help but smile when Darrin pulled his head up so fast from the shock of her voice that he smashed his nose-hard-on the side of Marilyn's head.

"Shit! Ow!" he yelled, then "Damn it!" for good measure.

And so there was Darrin, jumping around and swearing a blue streak with a new bloody nose while Marilyn sat relatively calmly, seemingly oblivious to it all, acting as if nothing had happened.

So as Jon grinned and Janice and the Chief looked on, Ben walked over and tore off a few paper towels to help his enraged and wounded comrade.

Marilyn was still holding her tearful but brave gaze on Chief Thomas. He immediately took advantage of the newest chaos.

"Marilyn?" he asked, "What made you go over to the window in the first place?"

Marilyn seemed confused.

"The curtains were closed, right? Or did you close them after you saw the faces?"

She looked at the Chief for a long moment, then shook her head no. "No, they were closed," she said. "I pulled them back to look. I thought I heard a voice...voices, and there was a scratching sound. A scratching on the window. So I went to look..."

"Did the voices sound like, uh...children?" he asked gently. "Did you hear anything they said? Any words?"

She shook her head again. More slowly, less definitively this time. "I don't think so. It...it wasn't like kids though. The voices didn't sound like kids."

★   ★   ★

"Those faces in the window pretty much shoot your theory to hell, ya know," Chief Thomas said off-handedly. "I mean here they are, at a house where no one had the "flu," he added.

Janice gave him a perturbed look. "This time it really might have been kids, you know. It's getting close to Halloween. Maybe kids in make-up, getting some practice in."

"I don't think so," the Chief said, shaking his head. "Not on a Monday night. Late, very late on a Monday night. A school night, for God's sake."

"There's no school tomorrow. Because of the flu, or whatever this is. They can't figure it out," Jon said as he smiled at the irony of it all. "I thought I told you guys that."

Their conversation, which at first reinvigorated and reunited them after the horrible window scare, was beginning to deteriorate 45 minutes later. It was now well after midnight, and exhaustion and crankiness were seeping back in.

Marilyn had been asleep (on the living room couch) for a while now. The window episode had been discussed and theorized about ad nauseam. They were trying to wrap up now. But putting a plan together, which had seemed to hold so much promise, and had given at least a sliver of hope earlier in the evening, seemed almost useless now. The faces in the window had not only re-introduced the immediacy of the terror-it had in a way made them feel, once again, powerless. Frustrated. Helpless.

"What do you say Ben and I go to the House of Plenty and the woods tomorrow," Darrin said. "The Chief can take a drive up to the Crawford Farm and look around. Maybe take Janice along. Nobody will stop you two." Again, Darrin was obviously trying to move things along.

"I don't know," Chief Thomas said as he rubbed his eyes. "I don't know what good it'll do. And I've got Joanie to worry about. In fact, I'm going to sleep at the hospital tonight, if they'll let me."

Despite the possibility of charges of favoritism being leveled against him down the road, he had decided to post a man outside Joanie's room that night. He'd slipped away not too long after the window incident to make the call. After that, and what Janice had said, he wasn't taking any chances.

I want to go," Jon said to Darrin. "No school tomorrow." He looked at the Chief, who was yawning.

"I can't stop you," the Chief said. He looked, with bleary, bloodshot eyes at Jon, then Janice, and then up to Darrin. "Do what you want to do. All of you. I know you're all trying, but... just...just let me know, if you should find something out." he said tiredly. He got up and stretched. "Just be careful. I'm going to the hospital now."

"Thank God," Darrin mumbled to himself.

Chapter 27
October 10th 7:58 A.M.

Cold, windy and cloudy. First sunshine, then rain, now this. In three days.

Darrin stood in his underwear looking out his front window. Marilyn was still asleep on the couch. He had slept on the carpeted floor beneath her, which had led to an inadvertent scare, once again, when she woke from a nightmare in the middle of the night.

But he didn't want to think about that now. His thoughts instead were on what had happened two years before in the woods behind Jon's house, along with the deaths and other ominous events that had taken place in the last hellish week. He was thinking about how overwhelming it all was, and how helpless he felt-even in trying to protect his own wife.

And he was thinking about getting out of Highland.

It was different the first time. Jon and he had been basically on a scary, but ultimately great adventure then (although he knew Jon would vehemently disagree with that). It had been exhilarating in most ways, and if you wanted to get away from it, you just stayed out of the woods behind Jon's house. Away from Devonshire.

And he had had only himself to worry about then. Very different from now. He turned and looked at his sleeping bride, all curled up and sound asleep on the couch. There wasn't a way in the world that she deserved any of this. It was, obviously now, very dangerous here. For her, for everybody. They had been watching her last night. *Watching her!* Anything could happen now...just look what had happened to Joanie Thomas.

And everybody knew-those weren't kids out there last night. At least they weren't kids anymore. No way.

His cell phone started ringing; muffled by being buried in a pocket in his jeans, which were lying on the table by the couch. He jumped over and grabbed his pants, then sprinted out of the room so as not to wake Marilyn.

He knew it would be Jon.

★ ★ ★

Chief Rodney Thomas woke up with a terrible crick in his neck and a tight lower back. The cot they had provided him reminded him of his army days, so it was somehow appropriate that he would wake with his body feeling like it was going through the soreness of basic training.

Despite this, he got quickly to his feet and to his wife's bedside as soon as he was fully conscious enough to remember where he was. She was sleeping peacefully. He watched her, gently caressed her cheek and forehead, and listened to her deep breathing for a while. Then, after using the restroom and checking his cell for messages, he wandered out into the hospital corridor to try to find a doctor.

★ ★ ★

Father McGahee saw her coming. He remembered her. He rose from the seat he had just arrived to sit in and met her, just outside his study.

"Hello Father McGahee," Janice said as she extended her hand. "I don't know if you remember..."

"Of course I do Ms. Granger. You're the one who's not a Catholic," he smiled as they shook hands.

"Oh my," Janice blushed. "Sometimes the right words just aren't there for me, Father."

"That's fine. Don't worry about that." His smile disappeared. "I assume you want to talk to me again. Am I correct?"

She hesitated, then blinked in apparent surprise at the priest's understanding. "Things are getting serious," she said after a moment.

Father McGahee stepped to one side and waved her toward his office. "I'd say it a bit more directly than that," he said. "I'd say things are going to Hell."

★　　★　　★

"What time do you want to meet?" Ben asked.

It took Darrin a few seconds to realize that it wasn't Jon on the phone. Should have known he would sleep in. "I can be ready in half-an-hour," he finally answered. "Better make it 45 minutes. I'll probably have to wake Jon up. Are you on duty now?"

"Off. Do you really think it's a good idea? Having Jon come along, I mean?"

Darrin sighed. The truth was he'd rather have Jon with him than this rookie cop. But he couldn't say that. He also didn't want to get in a debate about what had already been decided.

"Yes," he said.

"All right then," Officer Christopher said after an awkward pause, "Where do you want to meet?"

Darrin pulled the phone away from his ear and listened. Marilyn was stirring. She was waking up.

★　　★　　★

"She should wake up any time now. We gave her some pretty powerful stuff so that she could sleep, but it'll be wearing off pretty quick. You need to be with her then, Rodney. OK?"

They were standing just outside of Marilyn's room. The corridor was early morning busy, and Chief Thomas waited for a nurse pushing a cart to pass by before answering.

"I'm not going anywhere, Doc." He looked at the busy scene going on up and down the hall. He pointed toward the room. "Do you have a minute to talk, Dr. Harbough?"

The doctor hesitated. His face looked tired and nervous, as least as much as it had the day before. He was unshaven, and his forehead had worry lines that made him look far older than he was. "Sure...sure. I got a minute," he eventually answered.

When they entered the room Dr. Harbough walked directly over to his patient, out of habit, even though he'd examined her only a few minutes before (Chief Thomas had actually caught him coming out of Marilyn's room after arriving back from his wandering). The doctor took her pulse and felt her forehead before turning back to Chief Thomas. "How can I help you, Chief Thomas?" he asked curtly.

Rodney looked down at his feet, then up at the doctor "Is she...is she going to be all right, Doctor? I mean, when she wakes up?"

Dr. Harbough looked hard at Chief Thomas for a moment, then quickly away. The Chief could see the Dr. knew exactly what he meant. And he looked like he didn't know the answer.

"I mean, I was thinking about that baby we saw," Chief Thomas continued, "and..."

"I don't know!" Dr. Harbough snapped suddenly. He said it loud, and Joanie stirred as though she was startled.

She was waking up.

★　　　★　　　★

"Something horrible is happening, Ms. Granger. That I do know."

Janice thought about asking the priest to call her Janice, but dismissed it as silly. A lot of things, little things in life, seemed silly now. She stayed quiet.

"Troubled, troubled people. And some of our most devout parishioners...staying away from the Church...not answering our calls..." Father McGahee's troubled face looked above and beyond her as he spoke, as though he was talking to someone else (which perhaps he was), or even to himself. There was a dreamy, regretful sound to his voice. "There is some kind of profound...Evil among us, Ms. Granger."

His voice trailed off. Janice thought she had better say something to bring him back to earth. "Is it...is it a spiritual evil you're talking about?"

It did the trick. He brought his eyes back down to look into hers. "Most assuredly," he said calmly. "Evil doesn't exist in a vacuum, you know." He smiled at her and brought his templed hands up to his mouth for a moment, as if thinking how best to say whatever he was going to say. "Ms. Granger, we believe that there really are things like Satan, and for that matter, possessed spirits. I believe we are seeing that now. Too many..." he paused to look up and away again, "...things have happened. Too many things beyond our power to...to understand."

He grew quiet again. Contemplative. Janice found herself fascinated in the theological sense, but frustrated with his generalities. She kept thinking of what Darrin had said-"...I don't know if we have time." She'd been thinking about those words a lot.

"Father," she began determinedly, "I'm one of a group of people that's trying to stop this...this thing, whatever's happening. We're really having a hard time, Father, because we don't know what caused it, and we don't know how to fight it; to stop it. I...I believe you about there being Evil. I really do. I've seen it!" She thought of the murder scene, Socks...the baby, "Up close, I've seen

it. But Father? ...Is there anything you can tell me that will help?
Is there anything we can do, Father?'

Father McGahee looked at her with that benign, patient smile
of his. Janice didn't like it. It made her feel like she was a child he
was trying to explain something to.

"You must know the source of the Evil before you can stop
it," he said.

"That helps," she thought sarcastically.

"And you must learn the cause, the reason that...Evil was
invited in. If you don't know the reason, well...it will only hide,
and grow, and come back stronger."

He looked at her gravely, knowingly. She waited for him to
continue, and when he didn't, she sat back in her chair, completely
mystified.

"So are we talking about exorcism here, or what?" she asked
bluntly.

★   ★   ★

Jon opened the passenger side door and immediately dropped
his cup of coffee onto the curb. The top flew off, coffee splattered
everywhere (including his right pant leg), and the now empty
paper cup rolled beneath the car-all before he could react.

"God damn it!" he screamed, which startled Darrin enough to
cause him to bump his head as he climbed out of the driver's seat.
He gritted his teeth and cursed, rubbed his head for a moment,
then got the rest of the way out.

"Nice greeting for the neighborhood, dumb ass," he mumbled
to Jon after he'd walked around to see what had happened. He
could feel a small lump on the top of his head already.

Jon was trying to rub the steaming coffee off of his pant
leg with his bare hand. "Sorry...hey you got any paper towels or
anything in the car?" he asked as he looked up.

"Yeah. Never go anywhere without them," Darrin said
sarcastically. Jon looked up at him hopefully. He didn't get it.

"No!" Darrin said as he switched his gaze to the old house in front of them. "No paper towels, man."

"Shit," Jon mumbled. He was still sitting on the car seat, rubbing away at his leg. "Where the hell is Ben, anyway?"

As if to answer a car horn honked right behind them. They both turned to see Ben smiling and waving as he pulled up in his Highland police car.

"Well, if you hadn't already spilled it, you would have just now," Darrin said.

"Pretty happy to be going to work, isn't he?" Jon asked. "Like a kid.'

"He is a kid. A kid that gets to look around a haunted house."

Jon gave up on his pant leg, stood up and closed the car door and then took a long look at The House of Plenty. It was an attractive well kept up old two-story house in an old neighborhood full of them. It had been converted into a restaurant God knows how many years ago, and the legends of ghosts roaming the place at night were almost as old as the building itself. In the cloudy early morning light it looked empty and foreboding.

Jon looked at his watch. "Hey, is this place even open yet?" he asked.

"Not to fear!" Ben answered, smiling and rattling a set of keys as he walked up. "Amazing what you can do when you say 'police business' to folks!" He walked right by Jon and Darrin and toward the steps to the front door.

Darrin and Jon exchanged a quick glance, then followed.

★   ★   ★

Joanie Thomas opened her eyes, then immediately closed them again. She squeezed them shut tightly, as though to defend herself from the light in the room.

"Joanie, honey. It's me. Its Rodney...you're going to be all right, honey. It's all over now Joanie." Chief Thomas held and rubbed her cold hand as he talked. He kept his voice low. He tried to be reassuring. Dr. Harbough, who was still in the room, quickly moved to the other side of her bed. He put his fingers on her wrist, measuring her pulse yet again. To Rodney, he looked concerned; confused.

Joanie opened her eyes again. This time very wide. Alarmingly so. She blinked slowly once, then again, then kept them open wide, staring at the ceiling. It gave her face the appearance of being horror stricken.

"What's wrong?" Rodney fiercely whispered to the Dr. .

Dr. Harbough still had his fingers on her wrist. He shook his head. "I don't know," he said as he lifted her arm up with his other hand, "I'm not getting a pulse, for some reason."

Chief Thomas was more confused than alarmed. His wife was obviously conscious, if a bit understandably disoriented. "Joanie? Can you look at me Joanie?" he asked.

Joanie turned her head very slowly, but toward the window, not her husband. Her eyes were still stretched wide. A faint, deep gurgle came from her throat.

Dr. Harbough gently, slowly put her hand back down on the bed. He stared up at Joanie's face. His own face grew pale.

"Mr. Thomas...? " he said softly without taking his eyes off of his patient, "I think you'd better step out in the hall with me for a moment."

★　　　★　　　★

"So we're in. Now what the hell do we do?" Jon asked.

It was a slightly sarcastic question, but only slightly. They were standing in the darkened, empty main dining room of The House of Plenty. It was a normal dining room in a normal looking restaurant. Nice, but nothing special. Nothing ominous, or for that matter, the least bit curious. Jon had spoken for the three of them: with everything that was happening in the real world...what the hell were they doing hanging around this joint?

Darrin was feeling especially morose. He'd left a bravely smiling but still trembling wife for this. A wild goose chase based on Janice's arbitrary map. That's all it was. "We're nuts. chasing our own tails," he thought, but didn't say it aloud.

"Well, I suppose we search it," Ben answered, taking Jon's question literally. "Where should we start?"

"The basement is where the ghosts supposedly are," Jon said. Then he turned to look at Ben. "I mean that's the legend."

Ben nodded.

"You got your flashlight?" Darrin asked Ben. "I left mine in the car. I mean, in case there's no lights down there..."

Ben did but it turned out there were. Lights. After finding the door that led to the basement, the three walked single file down the creaky wooden stairs, flicked on lights that flooded over everything, and soon found themselves standing amidst supplies, old furniture and a lot of insulated piping. Ben shined his flashlight all around them and into every corner, even though the overhead light was more than sufficient for spotting anything.

It was an ordinary looking restaurant basement.

"Maybe we should call out the ghosts," Jon joked after they'd aimlessly looked around for a minute, "like you called out old Chester? Remember?" he asked Darrin.

Darrin was having none of it. "This is bullshit," he snarled. "I don't know what the hell..."

A crashing sound coming from above them stopped him in mid-sentence. All three looked up and froze, as though they might be able to see through the two-by-fours, insulation and ancient boarding above their heads. They listened intently, but heard no other sound.

"What the hell do you 'spose that was?" Ben whispered.

"I don't know, but I don't want to get shot," Darrin said. He walked to the edge of the stairwell and cupped his hands around his mouth. "Hello up there!" he shouted. "This is the police!" He looked over at Ben, then back up the stairs. "Police business! Is anybody up there?"

After a quiet moment they heard, distinctly, footsteps. Someone was walking right above them and then away from them, instead of toward the basement door.

Then the footsteps stopped. The men listened quietly.

"We could go up and check, you know," Jon said. "I mean, you two do have guns, right?"

Darrin turned enough to give Jon a half-smile, then bounded up the stairs.

★   ★   ★

"I know you don't want to hear it Rodney...but all the signs are there. I mean, you saw her. You saw that look!"

Dr. Harbough was pacing back and forth rapidly, and looked again as though he was about to fall apart. Chief Thomas sat in one of the waiting room's chairs. He stared at the carpeting and listened to the doctor. He was absolutely resigned. Depressed. Exhausted. Terrified. But so, so tired that he appeared to be preternaturally calm. Their waiting room roles had completely flip-flopped from the day before.

"Look, I don't know as much about this as you do," the Dr. said as he walked. "I just know what I've seen here, medically. She's...she's going to be different now. I can tell." He stopped and shook his head. He put his hands up to his face in despair. "And I don't know why. I don't know why...but..." he looked over at the Sheriff, "she's going to have to be watched now, and not just by that nurse we left in there. I...I mean this could be dangerous, Chief Thomas."

"Dr. Harbough! You better come! Right away!" said the red-faced nurse who had just appeared at the waiting room entrance. "It's Mrs. Thomas!"

Dr. Harbough stared at her in momentary confusion, but only for a few seconds. He looked over at Chief Thomas, who was already on his feet. Then ran, right behind the sprinting Police Chief to Joanie Thomas' room.

The door was open, held that way by the nurse they'd left on guard. The nurse was staring, terrified, into the room. She had one foot in the hallway and one foot in the room, as though ready to run at any moment. Rodney got there first and pushed past her. A second later the doctor did the same. They both stopped dead once they got into the room.

Joanie Thomas was standing in the middle of her bed, on both legs. The right one, the one the dog (or dogs) had mangled, had the bandages off and was bleeding freely. Her arms were stretched out from her sides, as though she was preparing to ascend into the air, and she was looking up at the ceiling...and broadly smiling.

★   ★   ★

After getting up the stairs, Darrin ran into the main dining room, where he thought the heavy footsteps had come from. The other two followed right behind him. They pulled up to a stop when they got to the middle of the room. Everything looked normal. No person, footprints or upset table or cart (something had crashed over, but what?).

"Someone was up here," Darrin said as he caught his breath. "You guys heard it right?"

Jon and Ben both nodded.

"All right, let's find 'em," he said decisively, "Ben, you check the eating rooms, no *all* the rooms, upstairs. I'll take the kitchen. Jon..." he hesitated, "...just have a look outside, OK? See if any body's out there, or driving away, or whatever."

They split up and quickly went to their areas. Ben crashed up the stairs, Jon went through the front door and outside so fast that he forgot to close the door, and Darrin walked quickly into the kitchen. All three felt the sudden adrenalin of the chase. All three were ready to tackle anybody they encountered. All three had had just about enough.

Darrin saw immediately that the kitchen was empty, but he was pumped up enough to quickly start opening cabinet and pantry doors, of all sizes, just to make sure. He hesitated only once, when he heard a heavy thumping sound coming from above, but continued after hearing nothing else. He knew it was Ben up there stumbling around.

In less than three minutes Jon came back in the house and into the kitchen. Darrin was, of all things, looking into a stove when he walked in. "Pretty small ghost, to fit in there," he teased. "There's nothing out there, Darrin," he added, "But what's this?"

Darrin had to get off his knees and stand up to see what he was talking about. Jon was holding a piece of paper. "Where'd you get that?" he asked as he dusted off his knees.

"It was lying on the floor, Mr. Detective. You didn't see it? You had to step right over it."

Darrin heard another thump upstairs. He looked up.

"It says 'You Are Always Welcome Here. We've Been Waiting for You!'" Jon read. "Kind of weird, don't you think?" he asked casually as he tossed the paper to the floor.

The sound of shattering glass came from above them. It was muted a bit by the heavy oak that divided the floors...but it was unmistakable. They exchanged a quick glance of alarm, then turned to dash up the stairs.

The first room they came to was a one-time bedroom that had been converted to a small, cozy dining area. No Ben. Everything in order, except for one overturned chair.

"Ben?" Darrin yelled as they raced to the next room. There was no answer.

He was lying there on his stomach, just inside the door of the second room. They both stopped for a moment, confused and disoriented by the sight of Ben lying there, the randomly overturned furniture in the office sized room, and by the cold wind that was suddenly blowing into their faces.

Darrin moved first. He knelt down and turned Ben over. Before he was even all the way onto his back they saw his horribly ripped throat and the blood streaming from it.

"Oh shit!" Darrin cried as he drew back, "Oh my God!"

Jon felt dizzy and had to look away. He felt a strong breeze hit him as he did so. He looked up and saw the shattered window, with its red curtains flapping in the wind.

Chapter 28
October 10th 11:45 A.M.

Janice's phone was buzzing again as she pulled her Chevy Impala into the Crawford's driveway. It was the third time since she'd left Highland that someone had tried to call her, but, as was her habit since experiencing a near-accident while trying to answer a call several years before, she never tried to answer while driving.

The Crawford place appeared to be (surprisingly) abandoned. There were no police cars, no yellow tape or officers standing in the cold to keep her car from approaching; nothing. Instead, her car slowly rolled up to a nicely maintained but obviously abandoned white two story house, with only a forlorn looking old pick-up truck parked at its side to show that there had been, at least recently, life there.

Only when she had pulled up close, parked her car and stepped out into the cloudy, blustery day did she see any evidence at all of the recent tragedy and consequent investigation that had taken place there. An anemic, already weathered looking sign was taped onto the front door. "DO NOT ENTER: by order of the Madison County Sheriff's Department," it said.

Janice stood ten feet from that door. She pulled the collar of her jacket up for defense against the biting wind, and wondered just what she should do. She'd had an elaborate story prepared to try to gain entry to the scene ("I'm a Highland City Official on an information gathering mission from the Police Chief there..."), but now it was obviously unnecessary. She was hoping to extract information from investigating officers that might help them as they wrestled with the overall problem in the Highland area (or at least get some clues!), but there was no one here. It was just her standing in front of a spooky house that she dared not approach, on a cloudy, spooky kind of day.

She stood for a few moments trying to decide. Her teeth soon began to chatter. "Can't just leave," she thought. "Not yet. Got to do something. Maybe walk around a bit?"

She remembered the phone calls just as she turned to walk around to the back of the house. She fumbled in her purse and pulled her phone out. No messages, but she saw that it had been Darrin who called all three times. She closed it and put it back in her purse so she could concentrate on not tripping over the rough ground she was walking over.

She'd call him back later.

★   ★   ★

"Jon, they've had to tie down Joanie Crawford. You know, Chief Thomas' wife. She's out of control at the hospital. Hysterical. Maybe rabies, or maybe...hell, I don't know. And I still can't get a hold of Janice. I think she must have gone to the Crawford farm by herself, and that's not good." Darrin looked at his friend. "Jon? Jon are you listening to me?"

Darrin was standing by Jon, who was sitting in a chair in the main dining room of The House of Plenty. He'd been sitting there silently, pale and totally uncommunicative for the last 30 minutes.

He had run to the window while Darrin called for help seconds after they'd discovered Ben. He had leaned desperately, as far as he could, out of the sill to look down to the ground two stories below to see what, or who had fallen. He saw nothing but

217

the ground, and in the process cut his hand, but didn't realize it until much later. He'd run madly past Darrin, then down the stairs and outside to the back in his rage and panic. Finding nothing but a few shards of broken glass, he then circled the house, twice, looking for something, anything-while all the while cursing through his own tears.

He didn't give up until the first police car and an ambulance arrived and men jumped out and raced into the old building. Then he went limp, dropped to the cold ground, and sat there for a long while, until Darrin found him and gently guided him back inside.

He was sitting there at the table when they brought Ben's body down, while they questioned Darrin, and while men went up and down the stairs-seemingly over and over again, lost in a cloud of shock.

Darrin had left him alone at first, then had tried quiet reassurance (between the frantic phone calls he was making and receiving). In truth, Darrin had a lot to deal with and think through himself. For the first half-an-hour or so there was little time for Jon, no matter what condition his friend was in.

But now it was time to move, and Darrin's strategy was simple: rouse Jon to action by sharing his own sense of urgency, or if he had to, if it came to that...leave him behind.

Darrin grabbed a chair from a nearby table and put it in front of Jon. He sat down and tried to make eye-contact with him. It wasn't easy. Jon looked like a nervous breakdown waiting to happen. If he had gotten up to run, started throwing punches, or just started crying-Darrin wouldn't have been surprised.

"Jon, I can't get ahold of Janice," Darrin repeated. "This...this thing that just happened, to Ben, its happening everywhere."

Jon made eye-contact briefly, then quickly looked away.

"We've got to get off our asses, man! There's no choice! Chief Thomas, well...he's got his hands full. And Ben's gone..." Darrin choked with emotion, unexpectedly then. He looked away himself, and swallowed hard. The change in his voice caused Jon to look at him. "I'm not saying I know what to do," Darrin continued, "nobody does, but...we know Janice might be in trouble, right? I mean the least we can do now is to get in the car and go look for her. Right?"

Darrin looked down. He took a deep breath to try to keep his own emotions at bay. He thought of Marilyn, and Joanie Thomas, and Bart Melleville...the faces in the window...he wasn't sure if he believed his own words. It was getting hard to keep back the feeling that it was all so useless.

"Let's go," Darrin heard from above him. He looked up to see Jon standing there, looking down at his friend.

★   ★   ★

Seeing the empty cow pens somehow brought it all home to her. Janice had of course heard the whole story by now: a good, simple farm family's cattle disappear. One of the first strange things that occurred after the "flash," she remembered from her charts. Then their little daughter went missing, and then-the little girl's mother is brutally disemboweled, and her father is missing. In ordinary times the case might have appeared simple. Had to be the father, right? A maniac who somehow got rid of his cattle for cover, maybe molested and killed his own daughter, then finished it off by savagely murdering his wife. "It's always something sick like that, right? Just sick enough to make sense," she thought.

But not since the "flash," with missing Sheriff and Deputy, missing kids and dead wives and husbands... with all hell breaking loose. Not even close. No one suspected Jim Ray Crawford of anything. And no one could even find him.

Janice stood looking at the empty pens and feeding trough where Jim Ray Crawford, until about a week ago, used to feed his animals every day, in peace. It seemed so lonely, so tragic now. It gave her the same feeling she undoubtedly would have had if she had been able to be inside to see, for instance, the kitchen table the family used to happily sit around. Or the island counter the mother had been found behind. But standing here, alone on a cold, gray, blustery day and seeing the lifelessness of it all outside was enough. "This had all been real. There was life here," she thought.

Janice pulled her coat tighter and looked out beyond the pens to the half-harvested corn field and the rising wooded hill just beyond. Not much of a farm, but a nice one. A good, safe place to grow up, one would think.

The first thing she thought of when her eye caught the movement was that it must be a deer. It was to the left of where she was looking, and so the blur of it was caught only by the corner of her eye. She moved her head to that spot up by the woods, maybe a quarter of a mile away. She saw nothing but trees so looked further to the left, then back again.

There it was. It startled her. It wasn't a deer. It was a man standing out there, facing her way.

Janice froze in position for a few seconds. Again, under normal circumstances it wouldn't be anything to worry about, but...what was he doing way out there?

She peered harder at him, trying to make out anything that would give her a clue. Was he... was he wearing a uniform? An investigator, maybe?

Janice waved and called out "Hey there!" It was a spontaneous gesture. She was looking for reassurance of some kind. The man didn't wave back. She slowly put her hand down.

Then suddenly, he started walking. Straight toward her, and at a fairly quick pace with his head held in her direction in a very still, seemingly unnatural way.

Janice felt a new coldness inside that had nothing to do with the weather. She began to tremble as she watched him. She felt there might be danger there, but was also mesmerized. The way he held his head...

Her phone rang and she jumped, then gasped. She reached down into her pocketbook and pulled it out. It was Darrin again. She opened it, heard him say "Janice! Listen to me!" then closed it again. No time. The shock of hearing the ring had brought her back, though, and now she had an idea.

She opened the phone again and looked up. He was more than half way to her. She could see the uniform now, and his face was more clear. She knew the face....from somewhere.

She held up her I-phone, took two pictures, then turned and ran toward her car.

★   ★   ★

Janice saw the police car coming, with lights flashing as it turned around a bend on the country road, from a little less than a quarter of a mile away. She checked her rear-view mirror. For the first time, he wasn't there. She started applying her brakes while alternately looking ahead and then checking behind-to make doubly sure. She didn't see him. He was gone.

Darrin saw that it was Janice's car that was braking ahead, but he saw it late. He slammed both feet to his own brake pedal and his car went into a long, lazy-looking, squealing spin. Janice saw that the car was headed straight at her and pulled her wheel to the right and flinched backwards with the sickening expectation of an impending collision.

Seconds later, miraculously, the police car slid to a final stop just to the left of Janice's, so that the two driver's side doors were only inches from each other.

Janice, who was already nearly hysterical with fear before the near, almost certainly fatal collision, opened her eyes after a long moment and then collapsed back up into her seat. She saw Darrin there right in front of her, staring at her with a dumbfounded look as his window was going down. Looking past him she saw Jon, or the back of Jon's head anyway, hanging out the passenger side window. She put her hands on the wheel to try to steady herself. Then she laid her face on her hands. She was, truly, somewhere between laughing and crying.

"Roll down your window!" Darrin shouted at her. She peeked up at him, sat up, then checked her rear-view mirror again, just in case, as she lowered her window. She could hear Jon retching as it rolled down.

"Jon and I were just wondering if you'd like to grab a bite to eat?" Darrin asked. And then, despite everything, he smiled.

Chapter 29
October 10th 1:33 P.M.

Even McDonald's was closed.

Darrin and Jon had followed Janice's car from the Crawford farm north of Highland through Grantfork on Highway 60 to Troxler, where they turned right and drove past the closed Highland middle and high schools there and on to Mazzios Restaurant, where they'd agreed to meet.

Mazzios was closed, as was McDonald's across the street, and then Dairy Queen and Hardee's. Route 143, where so many restaurants were located and normally one of Highland's busiest thoroughfares, had only a few other cars on it. And the ones that were there looked like they were lost.

The three of them stood in the cold in the Hardee's empty parking lot trying to figure out where to go (and what to do) next.

"Maybe we better head back to the station," Darrin said bitterly. "This whole damned town's falling apart."

"Something on the square will be open," Jon said. "Maybe Marx Brothers? Or Yogi's? You like those burgers at Yogi's, don't you Darrin?"

Darrin looked at his friend. Jon had just made a suggestion, but it sure as hell didn't sound like Jon. It sounded desperate, like he was trying desperately to hold on again. He was constantly looking around, and his eyes were tearing, although that could have been from the cold.

"Look at that kid over there," Janice said with a trembling voice. She had never stopped shaking, even with her heater running full blast all the way back into town.

The "kid" she was referring to was standing in front of the bank across the street from where they stood. He was a scraggly-haired teen-aged boy standing there in just a white t-shirt and jeans staring across the street in the direction of the closed Dairy Queen. He showed no sign of being distressed by the cold and wind, despite the way he was dressed. In fact, he was holding perfectly still.

"What the hell is he doing?" Darrin mumbled.

"Oh shit," Jon said.

"He's...he's one of them," Janice stuttered in alarm.

The other two looked at Janice, then at each other, then back at the boy. He hadn't moved.

"Hey Kid! Are you one of the zombies, or what?" Darrin yelled out suddenly.

"Don't Darrin!"

It didn't stop him. This time he cupped his hands around his mouth to make sure his words would cut through the wind: "HEY KID!! WANNA COME OVER AND PLAY?"

The kid didn't move. He stared straight ahead. They watched him. A few moments later one of the few cars that was out pulled into the bank. It edged its way up to within ten feet or so of where the kid was standing, and stopped. It turned its lights on, then off. Then again. They were pointed right at the kid. The kid didn't move. The car slowly backed away, turned around, then peeled its tires as it zoomed away north on 143.

"This is too weird," Jon said, as much to himself as the others. "Let's get out of here guys."

"I agree," Janice agreed.

"Just a minute," Darrin said. He had that "to hell with you" look on his face that Jon hated. It always seemed to get them into trouble. "HEY KID!" he screamed, "WANT SOMETHING TO EAT?"

For a few moments the kid didn't move. Then, right as Jon began to say "OK, let's get out..." his head snapped over in their direction. It happened so fast that it made all three of them jump.

"Oh shit!" Jon screamed as he grabbed theatrically for his heart.

"Wow!" Darrin said.

"OK, let's g-g-go," Janice pleaded, "I'm riding with you!"

She and Jon turned to scramble away, but Darrin stood for a moment, watching. The kid's body was still facing the Dairy Queen, but his face was focused on him...on the three of them. And he was smiling. His teeth were showing. Smiling! Like he knew something secret, that they would never know.

Darrin stared back. He put his hand on his gun.

"Come on Darrin!" Jon yelled from the car.

Slowly, almost imperceptibly at first, the kid's body started to turn toward Darrin.

"Come on D-D-Darrin! Now!" Janice pleaded.

Darrin glanced irritably back at the car, then back at the kid. Somehow he had completed the turn in a split second. How had he done that?

Still smiling and staring straight ahead, the kid began to walk toward Darrin. Darrin felt cold fear grip his stomach; instantly. He tightened his grip on his gun.

"DARRIN!" Jon screamed.

"Oh, all right," Darrin said casually as the kid began to cross the street.

Then he turned and sprinted to the car.

✦   ✦   ✦

"When can I see her?" Chief Thomas asked plaintively.

The doctor looked at the bleary-eyed, almost pitiful man standing in front of him. He'd seen Chief Thomas as a clear-eyed, logical policeman, a wild-tempered, overly protective husband, and now a beaten and embittered shell of a man-all in the incredible span of the last two days. It was so sad, and it symbolized everything in a way, Dr. Harbough thought.

"I don't know if that's a good idea, Rodney," he finally said. "I really don't."

After seeing his wife being subdued, finally, by five grown men while she fought and bit at them maniacally the whole time... Chief Thomas had simply gone home. Or at least he found himself at home, because he had no memory of having driven there. He went to their bedroom when he got there. He laid down on the bed. Their bed. He stared at the ceiling. He tried to think, but soon was crying instead. He had cried for a long while, until somehow, and very unexpectedly, he fell into a deep sleep.

It was a sleep absent of nightmares, or dreams of better times. For almost two blissful hours, he was blank, and gone.

And when he finally woke, miraculously, he could feel that some of the crushing weight he had been carrying was, miraculously, gone. He sat up in bed, looked around the quiet bedroom, and knew what he had to do.

He had to go back to see his wife.

And now he was back at the hospital, pleading with the Dr. "I know what it will be like," Rodney almost whispered. "I saw it. I just need to see her, Doctor."

Dr. Harbough looked at him skeptically. He felt nothing but pity for this man, but...

"I'll just stay for a minute, Doc. I promise..."

The doctor finally made up his mind. "Come on then," he said reluctantly.

★　　　★　　　★

"The last time I looked I saw him in the mirror, before you guys came flying around the corner, he was, well, it looked like...like he was floating through the air. I swear it," she said, as though she were trying to convince herself. Janice was shaking, even now. Still shaking.

Darrin, who had been concentrating on finishing one of the grilled-cheese sandwiches that Marilyn had made for them, looked up when Janice's voice turned to a plea for understanding. "Don't worry. We believe you. I'd believe anything now," he said.

"I just don't understand...I just don't," Jon said. Like Janice, he hadn't touched the sandwich in front of him. Only Darrin seemed to have an appetite. "I mean, I feel like I'm going nuts. I..." He stopped there. Maybe because he was afraid of breaking down, Darrin thought. He looked at his friend, then Janice, and finally over at Marilyn. To Darrin, all three seemed on the edge of breaking down. He couldn't blame them, of course, but it worried him. He'd have to be careful with what he said and did for a while. For example, they still hadn't told Janice (much less Marilyn) about Ben, but it was easy to see that this wasn't the time...

As if reading his mind, Jon cleared his throat and said "I think we better tell them about..."

"You said something about the guy wearing a uniform?" Darrin loudly asked Janice while he looked at Jon sternly.

"OH MY GOD!!" Janice squealed, "I forgot! I took his picture!"

Her sudden cry startled them all. "Jesus! Can we talk with our inside voices, please?" Jon asked with both hands held over his heart.

Janice fumbled for her I-phone, got it out, dropped it, then quickly picked it back up, opened it and started looking for the pictures.

"If you find it, could you tell us calmly?" Jon asked.

"THERE HE IS!" she screamed.

Darrin scrambled around the table to have a look, but not before stuffing the last of the grilled cheese in his mouth. Marilyn and Jon stayed in their seats.

Darrin stood chewing behind Janice for a few moments, studying the image on her phone.

"I swear he looked familiar, in a way," Janice said.

"You know why?" Darrin asked quietly. "Because I think that might be the missing Sheriff. Joe Blanton. Remember him? From the meeting?"

Janice gasped and quickly put the phone down on the table, treating it as though it had something she might catch.

"Honey, we can put that picture on the laptop can't we? Or better yet, the TV?" Darrin asked Marilyn. She nodded unenthusiastically. "We need to see it close up," he added. "Could be important."

He looked over at Jon as Marilyn got up from the table. Jon made a face at him, then mouthed the words "Tell her!"

Darrin glared at him. "Jon?" he asked.

Jon fidgeted uncomfortably and Darrin kept glaring at him. "What?" he finally asked.

"Are you going to eat your sandwich?"

★　　　★　　　★

Right before reaching the door to Joanie's room Dr. Harbough reached a hand out to stop Chief Thomas. "Rodney," he said gravely, "this is not going to be pleasant. You know that, don't you?"

Chief Thomas looked from the doctor to the floor in resignation. "I know," he said simply.

The doctor looked at him for a long moment, hoping to make eye contact, and hoping to think of the right way of explaining. Neither one happened. He pulled his hand back. "All right Chief," he said. "But just for a short time."

Rodney took a step toward the door and stopped. He turned and this time looked at the doctor in the eye. "I'd like to see her alone," he said.

Dr. Harbough gave him a curious look but eventually relented with a nod. "Let me get the nurse out of there," he said.

The nurse was more than happy to oblige. She practically jumped by the two men when the doctor asked her to step out. "I'll be right down the hall if you need me," the doctor said softly as Chief Thomas walked toward the bed.

"I'll just be a few minutes," the Chief said over his shoulder right before the door closed.

Except for her hair, that soft blond hair that he loved to run his hands through, Joanie was almost unrecognizable. She was strapped down from head to toe. Even her head was restrained, to keep her from moving it from side to side. If you weren't close to her; if you didn't know what had happened already, if you were looking at the poor woman from a distance, you would have instantly felt sorry for her.

But the Chief got up close. Close enough to see her wide open yellow eyes, and the black pupils darting madly around, as if looking for an escape. And up close you could hear the low, unearthly gurgle, the deep growling sound coming from deep within her. And up close you could smell it. You could smell the unmistakable smell of death there.

Rodney Thomas could only look for a minute. Eventually, he closed his eyes. "Oh honey," he said, "Oh honey...What happened, honey?" He reached slowly into his pocket as a single tear rolled down his cheek.

★　　　★　　　★

Darrin stood in the living room with hands on hips, looking at the screen. "That's him! Sheriff Blanton! It's definitely him," he said. He looked over at Janice who was curled up on the couch with a shawl covering her that was wrapped all the way up to her neck. "'Course, they never found him," Darrin said as he turned back to the set. "But they got him. Those...things. You...we all know they did, right? But he came back didn't he? I know nobody wants to say it out loud, or think it, but he's, he's back from the dead, right?"

Janice looked from the screen up to Darrin. "I don't know, Darrin," she said meekly.

"I've got a theory," Jon said from the love seat by the front window on the other side of the room. His body was half twisted so that he could watch the TV or move the curtain back with his left hand and look outside. He had been dividing his time between the two; obviously disinterested in staring at the TV's perpetual Sheriff. Darrin twisted around to look at him. "I think there's two kinds," Jon continued. "The ones they turn into one of them, or convert...and ones that they just eat."

The room grew understandably quiet for a while, as everyone contemplated this. Darrin turned back to look again at the Sheriff. Marilyn buried her face in her hands.

"He's right, you know," Janice said softly. "Think about it. The 'missing' ones get spotted-way too many times for it to be a coincidence. And then members of their families, or friends, go 'missing.' But the ones that just get killed...I mean, we only find half of them. It's like they're food. And I was thinking out there this morning that it probably started with those cows. I mean, didn't you tell me that there was one cow found where the Sheriff went missing? And wasn't it half gone? Didn't everybody think it was coyotes, back then?"

"And how about the cow skeleton that Ben and those other cops found in the woods?" Jon interjected. He stopped there. He'd said Ben's name, which caused Darrin to turn away from the screen and glare back at him.

"That's right! Ben's cow!" Janice agreed. She pushed the shawl back and put her feet back on the floor. "That was, let's say, maybe the original food source. There's probably cow skeletons all over the Highland area! We just don't know where they are. And after they ate the cows they..."

"What about the Melleville guy?" Darrin interrupted, "When Ben found him he was all torn apart. Then his body disappears, and then his wife disappears. So is he an eater or an eaten?" he asked.

"We don't know if she was eaten."

"This is all just too much!" Marilyn cried suddenly. Her face had turned beet red, and she got up and quickly left the room.

Darrin had turned and taken a couple of steps to go after his wife when Janice's casually asked question stopped him.

"Where is Ben, anyway?" she asked.

Darrin froze in mid-step and looked over at her, then quickly to Jon. Jon's face flushed slightly but he didn't meet Darrin's glance. He was instead looking out the window (or at least pretending to).

Darrin looked down, took a deep breath and cleared his throat. With Marilyn out of the room, he was going to give it a shot. "Janice, I've got, uh...I'm afraid I've got some bad news about..."

"You might want to hold on to that thought for a minute," Jon interrupted calmly.

The other two looked over at him. He was still sitting on the loveseat, still half-twisted around, and still holding the curtain back so that he could see outside. He was, in fact, frozen there, staring out intently.

"What!" Darrin demanded. "Why?"

Jon dropped the curtain and turned around. "You know that kid we saw at the bank? The one you called a zombie?"

The other two just stared at him.

"Well...he's out there now," Jon said.

★   ★   ★

It was just over twenty minutes before Dr. Harbough remembered to check on Chief Thomas. His plan had been to give him no more than five of those minutes, but he'd been called down to the emergency room almost immediately after leaving Joanie Thomas' room. He and two orderlies had had to assist Dr, Himenaz with a hysterical out-of-control patient; the fourth one in the last 12 hours.

This time it was a nine-year-old boy with bite wounds from his throat to his abdomen...and who was in turn trying to bite Dr. Himenaz. The child was out of his head, and it had taken all four adults and a shot of a drug no nine-year-old should ever have to take to get him under control.

And the funny thing was, the shell-shocked Dr. Harbough was getting used to it. True, he felt like he was slowly losing his mind...but he was actually getting used to it.

It wasn't until minutes after that hold down, while he was looking at a chart that had just been handed to him by a shaken nurse, that it hit him.

He jerked his head up from the chart and looked into the nurse's eyes. "Aren't you supposed to be in Mrs. Thomas' room until your relief arrives?" he asked.

The nurse looked down at her feet. "You told me to step out. To leave," she said sheepishly.

Dr. Harbough slammed the chart down on the nurse's station counter, causing everyone in the area to look over. "You know better than that!" he screamed. "Do you mean to tell me that poor man is still in there with her?" he yelled as he stepped around her and headed for the room.

"No!" the nurse said to his back when he'd gotten just a few steps away. She had already turned to follow him. "He left after a few minutes! I didn't know! I'm sorry, Doctor!"

Dr. Harbough sprinted the rest of the way to the room.

Chapter 30
October 10th 4:59 P.M.

When Chief Thomas pulled into the Devonshire cul-de-sac and saw Darrin standing on the curb in front of his house waving a gun around in broad daylight, his first instinct was to screech to a stop.

And that's exactly what he did. And when Darrin responded to the unexpected noise by whirling toward the car and pointing his weapon that way, the Chief, sensibly, ducked. The car was still in drive however, so as soon as the Chief pulled his foot off the brake the car began to roll slowly down the street.

And that is how Detective Crandle found himself in the unlikely scenario of being crouched and ready to fire at an apparently empty police car that was ambling down the street on its own.

Given the traumatic events of the day and the current state of his enraged mind, Darrin was ready to fire. Only a glimpse of a hand reaching for the wheel and then a brief peek at the scrambling Chief's forehead made him hesitate. Finally, right before veering off into the Korte's yard next door the Chief popped up and the car stopped, just in time.

Darrin lowered his gun, stood looking at the odd situation for a minute, then slowly walked over to his bosses' car. When he got there he bent down as the Chief lowered the passenger side window. The two men looked at each other for a moment.

"What the HELL are you doing?" the Chief finally growled.

Darrin was about to ask him the same question but a noise coming from across the street made him jerk upright and turn around, all in one motion. He saw nothing unusual. The noise had been made by someone's escaped garbage can rolling around in the wind.

"You better come inside," he said without turning around. "I'll explain in there."

★　　★　　★

"Ben wasn't the only cop killed today," Chief Thomas said somberly. "Bill Stephens is dead. Found him on Main Street. He was lying by his car." He looked up at Janice, then over to Marilyn, perhaps worried (even now) about how much detail to give. "He was torn apart. I'll leave it at that."

This time it was Janice who got up and left the room. "I'm gonna be sick," she warned as she scurried toward the bathroom.

The others just sat there, too overwhelmed to move.

It was hard not to be. Even with a week's worth of confusing, horrifying events-what they had shared between themselves in the last half-an-hour had been too much to take, by anyone's measure. There was Ben's incomprehensible murder at the House of Plenty, Janice's story (with photographic evidence) of the Sheriff at the Crawford Farm, the seemingly possessed kid (who they all knew was, now, only one of many)-a kid who was even now probably lurking outside somewhere, and finally, the story of another murdered cop. That in addition to the whole town suddenly coming to a crippled crawl left everyone feeling a deeper sense of desperation and fear than they'd ever known was possible.

And even though it had come in stages, and steadily over the last week, they all felt that now-suddenly, inexplicably-they were in Hell.

"Your wife," Marilyn said softly from across the room after a long silence, "Is she all right, Chief Thomas?"

Chief Thomas looked at her and his face colored slightly. "She's fine," he answered. He leaned forward and looked down at the carpet as he rubbed his hands together nervously. "Joanie's fine."

Darrin studied his boss. He could read body language. Something was wrong.

"Did I miss any murders?" Janice asked brightly as she re-entered the living room. She looked pale but was wearing a brave, if forced, smile. Darrin got up and waved her to the nearest seat.

"There's something else you all need to understand," Chief Thomas said.

"Great," Jon grunted. He was in his seat by the window, looking out. Watching.

"These things...these people who have been, uh, changed, they can die. I mean, you can kill them."

Everyone stared at the Chief. Even Jon dropped the curtain and quit looking out for a moment. "Is that supposed to give us hope?" he asked sarcastically.

"How do you know this stuff, Chief?" Darrin asked. He was suspicious, and didn't like where this was going.

The Chief looked down at the carpet and didn't answer.

Once again, the room grew quiet and sullen. They heard a dog, or perhaps a coyote from the woods out back of Jon's house, howling in the distance. It seemed like the perfect, forlorn symbol for what was happening. The sun was still a half an hour or so from setting, but the cloudy, gloomy day had never provided much light, and it was already growing dark in the living room that, with the curtains closed, was only lit now by the still picture of the missing Sheriff on the television.

"Somebody should turn on a lamp," Jon said glumly. But no one did, and he went back to peeking out the front window.

★   ★   ★

"How is that possible? How is any of this stuff, possible?" the distraught Dr. Allen asked.

Dr. Harbough just shook his head. There was nothing more to add. Nothing more to say. say.

He had been briefing St. Joseph Hospital's Chief Administrator on the bizarre, hardly believable events of the day for the last twenty minutes, and it had occurred to him more than once during his presentation that what he was reporting belonged more to the realm of nightmarish science fiction than the standard, predictable goings on of a rural hospital. Hysterical, biting, clawing patients... another missing patient... a rapidly growing vicious baby, half of the hospital's staff calling in sick, or just not showing up... and now a full morgue that everyone was afraid to go into...

Their whole world was coming apart. And it was happening faster all the time.

"The, uh Thomas woman. You think her husband, the Police Chief, could have taken her?"

"I said it's possible," Dr. Harbough said. "He was seen leaving, but without her, by one of the nurses. But, well...there wasn't a sign of her when I got in there. The straps that were holding her were all, uh, chewed up. Torn up. And there was a trail of blood going to the window...and the window was shattered."

"Isn't that room on the second floor?"

"Yes, Doctor."

"Then how in the hell? Could he have...could he have come back? Come back for her? After the nurse saw him?"

"Yes sir. I suppose that's possible, but I don't see how in the world..."

"Did you call the police? Did you try to get a hold of anybody?" Dr. Allen demanded.

"Yes. I tried. I couldn't get an answer from the police department and..."

"Dialing 911?"

"Yes. It's been that way all afternoon. They're...they aren't answering. And I've tried Chief Thomas' number. Several times. He won't answer either."

Dr. Allen sighed and leaned back heavily into his chair. He tried to think clearly; not to panic. Not now. "God damn. OK... tell me about the baby again," he said.

✦   ✦   ✦

It was Janice's idea, but Jon and Marilyn were quick to endorse it.

It came to her in the depth of their gloom as they sullenly watched the darkness descend outside. There had been nothing but silent dread in the air for more than an hour when the deep vein of optimism that she'd always been able to turn to, even in the toughest of times, suddenly, improbably bubbled to the surface.

"You know what, guys? I'm getting hungry!" she said. She stood up. "What do you say we all transfer this party to my house and I'll make you all a meal you'll never forget?"

For a moment there were only four haunted, sour faces facing the one wearing a ridiculously optimistic smile. The atmosphere had been so glum for so long that no one knew what to say.

Then Jon spoke. "I'm not sure how safe it is to travel, but, why don't we have the dinner over at my house?" He smiled slightly, if briefly, then turned to the window again before adding "Surely we can make it next door. Change the scenery, anyway. And...maybe we should be where we can keep an eye on...the pasture."

The pasture and woods behind Jon's house was the one spot they hadn't "investigated" that day. They all knew without having to say it that it would have been impossible, but...

Again, there was indecisive silence, that after some time was finally broken by Marilyn. "I think that's a marvelous idea!" she said suddenly and enthusiastically. "I'd love to help! Do you have something we can cook over there Jon?"

"We could heat up the glazed doughnuts," he said dryly. He was still looking out the window, even though it was getting hard to see anything in the darkness.

"Who wants to go to the store with me?" Janice asked.

"I'll go!" from Marilyn.

"You're not going anywhere!" Darrin bellowed.

"Way too dangerous," the Chief added.

"Is it even open?" Jon asked.

"SuperValu is always open!"

And so it went for the next ten minutes. They argued planned, cajoled, unplanned, debated, planned again, and finally thrashed their way to a consensus: they were going to have their dinner, damn it. Janice's idea had at least sparked some life back into the group. They weren't quite dead yet, they'd decided.

It was simple: Darrin and Chief Thomas had the guns (though Darrin had offered Jon and Janice one an hour before. Both had refused...so far). One of the "gunmen" would be with the no guns people at all times. Darrin (after a brief argument with the Chief) would be the one to accompany the women to the store while Chief Thomas would accompany Jon over to his house. They would scout it out, walk around it, and make sure everything was safe while the others were shopping. The shoppers would come back, they'd all help with the meal-and they'd eat like starving pigs. Simple!

The very act of planning something; something positive and simple, energized them all. Even the Chief showed some enthusiasm, though half-heartedly, and with a greater degree of caution than the others.

Despite the feeling that the whole world was coming apart, that they were surrounded, and that the danger was rapidly growing to the point of overwhelming them all...dinner was on.

★　　　★　　　★

When they were finally ready, Chief Thomas and Jon walked the three shoppers out to Darrin's car. All five kept an eye out, looking around in all directions for the boy who had been seen earlier, or anything else unusual.

"You all notice anything unusual?" Chief Thomas asked as the car doors were opening. His words had the effect of freezing them in place. "No, no-don't worry," he added quickly. "It's just that its gotten dark, and nobody in the neighborhood has any lights on. There's no one...anywhere."

A quick look around by all of them confirmed it. Except for the street light at the head of the cul-de-sac and the porch light of the Crandles behind them, all was eerily black, and quiet.

"Looks like a ghost town," Jon whispered.

"Let's go," Darrin commanded as he gently guided his wife into the car.

Darrin started the car and pulled out quickly.

They saw no one on either Devonshire or Coventry as they cautiously worked their way out of the neighborhood. It was after he'd turned left on Sunflower and had gone around its first curve that they saw the first of them. It was a long-haired little girl standing almost directly in the middle of the road. Darrin slowed. She was staring at the approaching car vacantly, making no attempt to get out of the street. She was wearing a thin looking white dress that looked too big for her. It fluttered in the cold wind. Darrin put the brights on and came almost to a stop. She didn't move or react to the light. They could see that she was barefoot.

They watched her. Darrin almost honked the horn, but thought better of it. Suddenly, she started walking toward the car.

"I'm going around her," Darrin said. "Hold on!"

He gunned the engine and swung the car wide left, running over a part of the curb in the process. He made it cleanly around her though and sped up as he drove down the dark street.

"She was reaching her hands out for us as we passed," Janice said from the back seat. She was still turned around, looking. "You don't suppose she needed help, do you?"

"Help my ass!" Darrin snarled. Then he glanced in his mirror and saw Janice's distraught face as she turned back around. "We can't take the chance Janice. She...she wasn't acting right," he said.

At the stop sign at the middle of Sunflower there were four or five more. At least. One was young, but the others looked like adults. They were standing close together in the street by the stop sign. "We're not stopping!" Darrin yelled as he hit this accelerator hard. None of the people moved, even though he drove within a few feet of them.

There were no people at the next stop sign (at St. George Road), so he stopped. There were no cars coming from either direction. None of the three had ever seen that before. Especially at rush hour.

About half-way to SuperValu their car hit a dog. Or the dog hit them. Darrin had seen movement in the ditch on the right side of the road seconds before it happened. Then there was a loud thump near the back seat door where Janice was sitting. She squealed in surprise, and then unfastened her seat belt to turn around to get a look. Darrin slowed, but decided right away not to stop.

"It was a dog!" Janice yelled. "And, and it's...its OK! In fact, it's still chasing us!"

Darrin tightened his hands on the wheel and hit the gas. "Fuck the dog," he said, "We're going grocery shopping."

★   ★   ★

"This is where it all really started, isn't it Jon?" Chief Thomas mused more than asked. "We were dumb enough to think it would all just go away."

The two were standing out on Jon's deck looking out at the dark pasture and woods. The clouds that had persisted the whole day were beginning to break up, and light from the full moon occasionally splashed the view before them with an intermittent, eerie gray.

"I don't know what more we could have done," Jon replied after a moment, "It was really...well, out of our power then. Like it is now, I guess."

The two men had watched the car of grocery shoppers until it turned off Devonshire a few minutes before. Then they went right to Jon's house, turned on lights and searched the house, and as a last precaution had taken a walk around it (with Jon being careful to stay behind the gun-toting, flashlight waving Police Chief). They had ended on the deck, where, as the Chief had just observed, it may have all begun.

"But I can't help but think..." the Chief said. His voice was becoming emotional, "that if we had somehow been able to, to get that thing..."

"SSSHHH!" Jon put his hand on the Chief's arm. They both froze and listened. They heard nothing. Right then the moon came out again, and they saw the pasture and woods in the milky light. "Down by the fence!" Jon whispered. "Right in front of us!" He pointed to a spot not 20 yards in front of them.

Chief Thomas slowly, carefully raised his flashlight. Jon reached over and helped him direct it to the spot. Then he turned it on.

"Oh Jesus!" Jon cried. It was a cat. The biggest cat he'd ever seen. "Bobcat?" he wondered. It was right up against the fence that separated Jon's back yard from the rolling pasture. It had its back raised high in warning, and it was looking at and hissing at the light; at them. Its eyes were a deep yellow and its open mouth showed huge white fangs.

"Your cat?" Chief Thomas asked.

"No, but..."

The gunshot was so sudden, so unexpected, that Jon unaccountably found himself immediately down on the deck's floor. The shot had literally knocked him down in surprise. He laid there stunned, with the wind knocked out of him and his ears ringing, for a full ten seconds before he could so much as think straight.

"Probably shouldn't have done that," the Chief said calmly.

Jon looked up at the Chief, who was staring out and moving the flashlight in slow, wide circles. "WHAT THE FU...!" Jon tried to scream, but his lack of breath softened both the volume and the length of the imprecation.

Chief Thomas looked down at Jon. "You better get up and take a look at this," he said casually.

Jon's still ringing ears told him that the Chief had said something about piss, but the look on his face told a different story. He scrambled to his feet even though he was still fighting for breath.

"Look," the Chief said as he pointed his flashlight.

Between the moonlight and the flashlight they were easy to see. People. People walking slowly. Five of them...no six... walking in the pasture. Coming from all directions. Children. Adults. Walking toward the spot where they dead cat lay. Walking towards Jon's house.

What the hell!" This time, Jon got it out.

"I should have known," the Chief said as he flashed his light from one to another of them. "I saw it this afternoon. I should have known."

Jon looked, eyes racing, from one to another of them. They seemed to be multiplying right before his eyes. He felt his mouth go dry and the blood of panic race through his ears.

"You better go in," Chief Thomas said calmly. He turned off the flashlight and started walking off the deck. "I'd better do something with that damned cat....If I can find its head."

★   ★   ★

Darrin stood with Bob Jenkins, the besieged looking manager of Supervalu, as they both looked out the giant front window of the nearly empty store. They looked out at the huge parking lot that held only two cars, and deserted Broadway Street beyond. They saw no cars pass by, and only closed restaurants and shops across the street. The eyes of both of them were focused on a man across the street. He appeared from a distance to be wearing some kind of police uniform. He was just standing there, very still, in front of Sam's Pizza. He was looking in their direction.

"That's not right," Bob said as he ran a nervous hand over his almost bald head. "It's got to be one of them, I swear."

Darrin turned to look at the manager. "Bob, why are you here?" he asked directly.

Bob glanced back at Darrin, then down at his feet. "I don't know, really," he said. "It's just that its happened so fast, this thing. And there are people that depend on us, you know. Folks like you guys."

Bob had almost not let them in, in fact. He had stood at the locked entrance peering out. He'd stood there and studied them; watched all of their movements. It was only when he remembered Darrin (as the arresting officer in a shoplifting case from a couple of years before) and heard their voices and what they were saying, that he relented. He let them in, then quickly locked back up.

"There's another one," Bob said as he pointed.

Darrin looked. The man at Sam's had someone standing next to him now. A shorter person, dressed in white. They both looked in the store's direction.

"Girls! Hurry up now!" Darrin yelled. His voice echoed through the store. He turned back to look out the window.

"They say they're sending the National Guard in. Did you hear that?" Bob asked hopefully.

"Yeah. Chief Thomas told me that."

There was a long pause, then Bob looked at Darrin earnestly and asked, "Do you think it'll do any good?"

Darrin heard a shopping cart rattling down an isle right behind them. He turned and smiled when he saw his wife, who was smiling right back at him. He looked back at Bob.

"I don't know Bob. I sure hope so," he said.

Bob studied Darrin's face for a moment, then he nodded and turned back toward the parking lot and street beyond. "Now there's three of them out there," he said a moment later. "Better tell your gals to hurry."

Chapter 31
October 10th 8:17 P. M.

The garage door began opening for them right after they turned onto Devonshire. It started closing as soon as the front of their car got nosed inside. Jon had been watching for them.

"They're back," Jon said to Chief Thomas from his position at the front window. "We better go help."

It was the first time Jon had spoken to him since the Chief had come back inside. He was badly shaken, angry and his ears were still ringing. He was also more afraid for his life than he'd ever been before.

"Maybe we shouldn't spring what happened on 'em right away, OK?" Chief Thomas suggested as they headed to the door leading into the garage.

Jon didn't offer an answer.

"John Wayne here shot a cat," he said as Darrin handed him a bag of groceries a minute later.

Darrin looked over at the Chief, who was in turn giving Jon a disgusted look. Darrin shrugged his shoulders. "And I hit a dog. What the hell?"

"What did the cat look like?" Janice asked anxiously.

"Let's get the groceries in," Chief Thomas said sternly. "They'll be plenty of time to talk about..."

A loud bone-chilling howl interrupted the Chief's sentence. It seemed to come from right outside the closed garage door. It stopped all five of them cold. "At least I hope so..." the Chief added under his breath.

The howl stopped. Chief Thomas walked slowly toward the garage door while the other four remained frozen in place. Seconds passed. There was no other sound.

"Please don't shoot my garage door," Jon pleaded.

★　　　★　　　★

It was a remarkable display of the indomitable human spirit in the face of extreme adversity. Or, perhaps, an extraordinary demonstration of the incredible power of denial.

Whatever the interpretation as to why, any neutral observer would have been wholly impressed by the spirit, teamwork, enthusiasm and, yes, even humor displayed by four of the five people in Jon's house for the next hour and a half. Only Chief Thomas remained sullen and withdrawn (constantly looking out the windows, pacing from room to room) as the others assigned themselves tasks, drank wine, joked and laughed as they prepared what would become an excellent Italian dinner.

Only when another howling cry outside was heard faintly by the group during a rare lull in conversation, and when Jon told his lame joke about this being their "last supper," and when the Chief would march somberly into the kitchen with his glowering face-did they even momentarily lose their enthusiasm.

And the eating was even better. A card table was brought in to supplement Jon's small kitchen table, a clean sheet was found (by Marilyn) and used as a makeshift tablecloth, two unmatched candles were lit, and soon the lasagna, spaghetti, Italian bread, salad and dessert was being attacked mercilessly by all. Even Chief Thomas couldn't resist.

It was a respite of the best kind: great food, wine and small talk. For a little while, at least, the real world didn't matter. By silent agreement there was no talk of murder, monsters or the origin of the "flash." There was no mention of the rapidly growing specter that seemed to surround them. It was all about normal, trivial things instead. Five people at a dinner party sharing gossip, stories and opinions about real life...the wonderful, boring, real life they'd had, and taken so much for granted, just a short week before.

It ended, this spell they had willed themselves into, in an odd, inadvertent way. As he was finishing his dessert, Darrin looked at his watch and said "Hey, I think the World Series should be on. Do you think they've fixed the cable yet?"

For some reason, that stopped everything. The table grew silent. Jon looked down at his dessert and stabbed a bite of it that he didn't bother raising it to his mouth. "What do you think?" he asked sullenly.

There had been no television since the flash. And now, no radio. Everyone knew that. Some of the initial speculation that whatever had happened was electrical in nature came from that. No one knew why, or had even had much time to think about it, but TV, the reassuring boob tube, had been the first casualty of the flash.

And Darrin had brought it all back, by merely mentioning what had become one of the symbols of all the trouble.

Darrin looked from one face to the other. All but the Chief had stopped eating. The Chief, who had been oblivious to most of the light-hearted conversation, was oblivious to the silence too. His head was still down, and he was chewing away.

"Well, I'm going to go see," Darrin said decisively. He knew he'd blown it, in a way, but he was too stubborn to admit it; even to himself. He went into the living room and turned on Jon's set. A few seconds later they all heard the white noise. Then it was gone, and Darrin sheepishly returned to the room.

"Damn," he said quietly.

★   ★   ★

247

"We have to decide what we're going to do."

It had been Janice who had started the great "Dinner Distraction," and now it was she that was officially ending it (with a large, unlucky assist from Darrin). They had been sitting there in a kind of silent denial for minutes after Darrin had returned and taken his seat. It was past time, she knew, to return to dangerous reality.

"I don't know what we can do but leave," Darrin said flatly. He looked for someone to make eye-contact with, but found no takers. "Leave the Highland area. Just get out," he added for emphasis.

"We're probably going to have to fight even to do that," Chief Thomas said as he stared at his plate. It surprised everyone. He'd barely spoken a word during the whole meal, as well as the preparation time for it.

"You mean shooting, right?" Jon asked nervously.

Chief Thomas looked up at Jon. "Absolutely," he said.

Marilyn got up quickly and started nervously clearing the dishes.

"But we can't...can't just start killing!" Janice pleaded.

"I want you all to listen for a minute," Chief Thomas said as he handed his plate to Marilyn. He looked around the table. "It might be upsetting, but I think you all need to hear it." His eyes stopped on Darrin. "And with no interruptions," he added soberly. "That cat I shot tonight...I knew as soon as I did that, that it was a mistake. I knew it because I'd seen what happens before when you kill one of them."

"One of what?" Jon asked.

Chief Thomas glared at him. "I think you know, Jon. We all know. These...dead things. These monsters."

"Zombies? Can we call them zombies? Please?"

"Shut up, Jon," Darrin snapped. "Go on, Chief."

Chief Thomas leaned back in his chair. He started to speak, hesitated, and then took a deep breath before starting.

"Go on Rodney," Janice said softly.

Chief Thomas focused his eyes on hers. "It was a mistake to kill the cat so close to the house, because they come and eat what's dead. They come right away." He shifted his eyes to Jon. "Jon saw that. Didn't you?"

Jon nodded slowly then looked away.

"I had to go out and get the cat away from here, before... before they got here. I took him out to the pasture, and..." His voice drifted off. He was staring intently at the glass door that led to Jon's deck.

"But how did you know that, uh, they were coming after the cat? How did you know they would?" Darrin asked.

"You should have seen it," Jon said.

Chief Thomas finally took his eyes off the door and looked directly at Darrin. "Because that's what they did to Joanie," he said. His voice cracked as he said it, and he was suddenly teary-eyed. "That's what they did after my wife died."

"Oh, my God!" Marilyn said. Then she got up and virtually ran out of the kitchen.

Darrin and Jon exchanged looks. Janice stared straight ahead, wide-eyed at the Chief. No one knew even remotely what to say.

"You've got to shoot them in the head," the Chief said in the same unsteady voice. "It's the only way to kill them."

Janice (and the others too for that matter) even in their stunned state, knew immediately what that meant. Police Chief Rodney Thomas had killed, maybe had to kill...his own wife. He opened his mouth to say something, but nothing came out.

Janice stood up and walked slowly toward the living room. She had to clear her head, somehow. Jon leaned back in his chair, put his hands behind his head, and appeared to begin studying the ceiling. Darrin, not knowing what to say or do, got up and left the room a few moments later to go check on Marilyn.

The brutal reality of it all was back, and in spades. And it was a little too much to take.

"I've got an extra gun you could use," Chief Thomas said in a low voice.

"You already told me that," Jon said.

"Well, maybe you better start thinking about it now." With that, the Chief stood up stiffly, stretched, then walked over to the deck door to look out at the moon-lit night.

Chapter 32
October 10th 11:47 P.M.

"I want to go home now," Marilyn said.

She had come into the kitchen where the other four were squeezed around Jon's table, talking intently about something. She had been napping on the sofa in the living room, and really didn't care what they were discussing. She was exhausted, and ready to give up and go to her own bed. No matter what.

All four faces turned to look at her. "Honey," Darrin said as patiently as he could manage, "it's dangerous. Way too dangerous."

"Not if you're with me." She was determined.

Darrin squirmed uncomfortably. "We'll go in a little while. I promise."

Marilyn glared at him for a few seconds, then whirled around and returned to the living room.

"I'm guessing you'll be sleeping on the couch again?" Jon asked through a weak smile

Darrin ignored him. "Where were we?" he asked.

"I don't remember," Jon said.

"I wasn't talking to you, nimrod."

"Cut it out!" Janice commanded. "Geez! You two act like an old married couple sometimes."

"Please don't talk about that. It's just too painful," Jon said mournfully. Then he laid his head down on the table for effect.

"OK, OK," Janice said impatiently, "It was me that was talking. I was telling you that I went to see that Priest today, before I went out to the Crawford place."

"And?" the Chief prodded.

"Well, he wasn't much help. I mean he acted all...Priesty, if you know what I mean. Talking in general terms, like they do," she said. "But he did say one thing that I've been thinking about. That is, when I've had time to think."

"And what's that?" Chief Thomas asked impatiently.

"Well. he said that you have to find the source of the evil, and find out what brought it in...what invited it in. If you don't, he said it would just hide, and grow, and..."

"Janice, with all due respect, I don't see what the hell good that'll do. I mean, at this point..."

"The point is that maybe the old guy was on to something, Chief," Janice interjected firmly. "And maybe, if you think about it, we're closer to it than we think!"

The other three looked at her, now waiting for her to continue. They were perhaps confused, but they were interested, she could see.

"We went to two places where the evil was today: the House of Plenty and the Crawford farm. Evil established itself there, without a doubt, right?" No one nodded, but they were still listening. "Suppose though, that the third place, the woods right out there," she said as she pointed, "the place we didn't get to today is the *source* that the priest was talking about? Suppose all this started out there, two years ago?"

The Chief looked down and sighed. The other two just looked at her.

"I mean, you've said it yourselves, in a way, haven't you? You didn't solve the crimes back then, right? You got close, but you didn't get rid of, of that Chester kid, or ghost, or whatever. Did you?"

"So you're saying that we...that we have to go to the source," Darrin asked softly. "And then do what, exactly?"

"I don't know," Janice sighed, "but it seems like we need to do something."

"I think she's right," Jon said evenly, "but I also think it's too late. Chester, that thing out there; it's not like we could have killed him back then. It was...it's a thing, not a person. And now it's everywhere, or it's getting everywhere fast. It's too powerful. Maybe your priest should have done an exorcism or something back then," he said as he looked to Chief Thomas, "because it's not something you can shoot."

"We can damned well try!" Chief Thomas growled.

"My God! There's something clawing at the front door!" Marilyn cried.

She had appeared at the kitchen entryway without anyone hearing her approach. Darrin and Jon leaped to their feet, Chief Thomas (who was sitting with his back to her) twisted around so fast that he nearly fell out of his chair, and Janice sat frozen for a moment amidst the sudden chaos around her.

Darrin raced past his wife toward the front door with Jon right behind him. Chief Thomas got to the living room right behind them and screamed "STOP!" right as Darrin's hand reached the door knob.

Darrin whirled and cried "What?"

"Look out the window first," Chief Thomas said. He was looking at Darrin while rubbing the knee that he'd bumped, hard, on the table. "See who's out there."

Jon reacted first, practically jumping over to the window and pulling the curtain back. Darrin remained in place, with his hand outstretched.

All watched Jon, who bent at the window to try to see.

"What did you hear, exactly?" the Chief asked Marilyn.

"It was a...kind of scratching, sort of... like an animal wanting in."

"I don't see anything," Jon said as he stood up straight again. "There could be somebody out there but I can't see around the corner well enough. Maybe we should go out and check?...Or maybe you guys should..."

"Why don't I just open the damned door?" Darrin asked. He still had his hand on the knob.

"No!" Chief Thomas shouted. "That's how some of these people died, Darrin." He looked at Jon. "There's a door on the side of your garage that leads outside, right? Didn't I see that?"

Jon nodded. "It doesn't lead anywhere. You'd just be out on the west side of the house, in the yard.

It was the Chief's turn to nod. "That'll do. With the noise we heard earlier we need to check the perimeter anyway." He looked at Darrin. "I'll go out that garage door and sneak around front. While I'm doing that, you go out on the deck and check back there."

Darrin finally released the door handle. "Sounds like a plan," he said as he checked his weapon. He looked more than ready to finally do something.

The Chief looked at Jon, then Janice. "I'm going to leave a loaded gun on the kitchen counter," he said. "I'll let you two figure out who's going to use it, uh, if you have to."

"I'll do it," Jon said flatly.

"Fine, and listen," this time he looked at Marilyn first, then the other two, "don't go opening any doors...and stay away from the windows."

There was a scratching sound again, at the front door-like a pet trying to get back into the house-right as the Chief completed his sentence.

They all turned and looked at the door. "No problem with that," Jon said.

★   ★   ★

It was so dark when he stepped through the door and into the yard that he lost his bearings for a moment. The moon had temporarily hidden behind a cloud. He stood very still and considered turning on his flashlight, but heard a thrashing sound coming from the neighboring house's bushes and quickly decided it wouldn't be a good idea. So the Chief waited for his eyes to adjust to the darkness, or the moon to come back out. Or both.

At the same time Darrin stuck his head and gun outside for a quick look around, then stepped out onto the deck and quickly shut the door behind him. He saw immediately that it was going to be all but impossible to see anything with light pouring out from behind him from both the kitchen and living room. He was reluctant to use his flashlight. He opened the door, stepped back in, and closed it.

"Jon? Can you guys turn off the lights? I can't see a thing out here!"

There was a long pause, then: "You've got to be kidding!"

But the living room lamp went off a moment later, and the kitchen lights went out right after Darrin had stepped back outside. When the last light went out the full moon reappeared as if on cue, and suddenly Darrin had a magnificent view of Jon's yard, the pasture and even the edge of the woods beyond. He did a quick scan, looking in all directions while walking slowly to the deck's banister. He stopped when he got there and took a deep breath. All clear...so far.

Chief Thomas started moving as soon as the moon came out. He could see better, but still not all that clearly with the moon at his back and behind him. On his third step he kicked one of Jon's trashcans over. The clanging noise it made caused him to freeze, and his scalp to crawl. He raised his gun up quickly and strained to look in every direction while holding his breath.

"Was that you Chief?" Darrin yelled out from the back deck.

"Dumb ass!" the Chief said under his breath fiercely. He gritted his teeth and didn't answer. Instead, he took four or five deliberate steps to the west to get out and away from the shadow of the house. Now in the moonlight, he could see everything better. He crouched and started for the front of the house, double-time.

The deck door opened behind Darrin as he was leaning over the banister, trying in vain to look for the Chief around the back west corner of the house. "Jesus!" he exclaimed in surprise as he tried desperately to straighten up and confront whatever monster was right behind him.

He dropped his gun off the side of the deck in the process.

"It's just me!" Janice whispered fiercely as she ducked away from the flailing Darrin.

Darrin finally righted himself, glared at Janice for a second then looked back over the side of the deck. "Damn it!" he said, as he scrambled over the side to retrieve his weapon.

Chief Thomas could see that there was no one (human or animal) at the front door by the time he got to the middle of Jon's driveway. He slowed down but kept moving in that direction anyway, while constantly glancing all around him for any sign of, well...anything. He could see all the way up Devonshire to the beginning of the cul-de-sac in the moonlight, as well as the yards and darkened houses that lined the street. He kept checking the door that he was walking in a crouch towards, then whirling to look down the quiet street.

Something was wrong, or at least different, but he couldn't quite put his finger on it.

By the time he found the gun (he had to use the flashlight, briefly) and returned to the deck Darrin saw that both Jon and Marilyn had joined Janice outside. "Are you guys nuts!" he whispered fiercely as he rejoined them.

"Careful. I have a gun you know," Jon smirked.

Darrin squinted and saw that Jon was indeed holding the gun that the Chief had left them. He was pointing it toward his own foot. "Make sure the safety's on, man. OK?" Darrin pleaded.

"These things have a safety? I thought the purpose..."

"LOOK!" Marilyn shouted. She was standing by the railing and pointing toward the pasture. They all looked.

It was easy to see, because of the moonlight and because it was white. At first glance it looked like a bird, floating around at tree top level right at the edge of where the woods began. But when the eyes adjusted and the brain established perspective, it was quickly seen by all that it was too large to be a bird. It was swooping in ever larger circles, moving in and out of the trees as it did so. Once it flew rapidly half-way out into the pasture before swooping away toward the woods again, with robes flapping in the wind.

"Oh my God," Marilyn said softly, "This can't be happening, can it?" No one answered, and they continued to watch in awestruck wonder.

After walking up to and inspecting the front door (where there were indeed scratch marks), the Chief slowly moved toward the east side of the house, trying to watch the bushes by the house and the yards and street behind him by rapidly turning back and forth. It was during one of his pivots that he realized what was different. It was two things. The street light at the end of Devonshire was out, and there were no longer any lights coming from inside of Jon's house. But the front porch light was still on! He was confused, but knew he needed to keep moving.

After looking behind him down the darkened street one more time he turned and took the final steps around the last bush bordering the front of the house and turned the corner to walk the east side of it back to the deck. But he only took one step after making the turn.

The kid was standing there, not five feet away from where he stopped. He was easy to see in the moonlight. He was wearing a torn t-shirt. His wild looking hair was long and stringy. He was smiling a yellow-toothed smile. His eyes were almost all black, with an outline of even brighter yellow.

The Chief knew him. He'd looked at his picture two days before. The kid who bit the doctor's hand off. Chief Thomas stood struggling for a name for a moment, then remembered. "Bobby?" he asked. "Bobby Meachum?"

Bobby made a low growling sound, the very same sound Joanie had made, then took a step forward. Chief Rodney Thomas immediately raised his gun to a point right between the teenager's eyes, and fired.

Chapter 33
October 11th 12:27 A.M.

Jon shot his deck exactly one second after Chief Thomas fired his shot.

He, Janice, Marilyn and Darrin had just seen the horrifying white, ghostly object streak into the woods, and they were waiting, spellbound, to see if it would come back. When the Chief's gun fired they jumped, yelped...and Jon's tensed finger pulled the trigger.

Chief Thomas took the second shot to be an echo of the first. He bent over the body in front of him to make sure he'd hit it squarely (he had), then stepped around it and ran to the south east corner of the house. He stopped there and yelled "It's me! I'm coming around the corner!" to warn Darrin so that he wouldn't get himself shot.

He heard what sounded like crying, and several voices babbling excitedly, even angrily. Then finally, a "Come on back Chief!" from Darrin.

The confusing sounds made him a little hesitant, so he poked his head around the corner to see. Even with the help of the moonlight it wasn't clear, but it looked like several people were on the deck. It confused him, so before stepping out he yelled "Hold your fire!"

"Now he tells me!" Jon cracked immediately, but no one was laughing. Darrin was holding a nearly hysterical Marilyn and Janice was holding Jon's gun.

And she was furious. "He told you to put the safety on! Damn it, Jon!"

Right as the Chief got to the top step of the deck a loud, deep, and mournful howl echoed from the direction of the woods. It stopped the Chief in his tracks, as well as Marilyn's sobbing cries, and Janice's lecture to Jon. They all looked out over the pasture until the howl slowly died away.

"I'm not even going to ask what happened here," Chief Thomas said calmly a few moments later, after a climbing onto the deck, "because we don't have time."

The other four looked at him. He was still standing on the edge of the deck, half-turned with one foot on the top step, as though he was getting ready to leave again.

"Listen to me," he said. "Jon, give your gun to Janice..."

"No problem," Jon interrupted.

"Shut up! Janice, take the gun and you and Marilyn go inside. Lock the doors, stay away from the windows, and wait for us to come back. Darrin and Jon come with me. Now. We don't have much time."

He was so calm and authoritative, and they were so thoroughly shook that they immediately did what he ordered, without question.

Darrin kissed Marilyn and whispered something to her then guided her through the door that Jon had opened for the girls. Once they were inside the door and the lock had clicked the two men turned to follow the Chief, who was already turning the corner of the house.

★   ★   ★

Chief Thomas stopped about ten feet away from the body and turned to wait. It had occurred to him that they (at least Jon) might need a warning.

"We've got to take this body away from here," he said as they walked up.

"Body?" Jon asked.

"Yes, body!" the Chief said impatiently. "What did you think I was shooting at?"

"I guess I was hoping it was another cat..."

"It's a kid. A teen-aged kid," the Chief snapped. He looked at Darrin. "The Meachum kid."

Darrin peeked around him to glimpse the corpse they were about to encounter. "The one that bit the doctor's hand off?"

"Yeah." The Chief said. He looked back at Jon. "I had to shoot him in the head, Jon. You need to prepare yourself for that. We're going to take him out to the pasture, maybe all the way to the woods. It'll take all three of us. You're going to have to man up, Jon. You OK with that?"

Now it was Jon who was trying to peek around the Chief. He looked shaky, but he didn't say anything.

The Chief wasn't sure his message had gotten through. He stepped deliberately in front of Jon and forced him into eye-contact. "If we don't move the body, they'll all come here. Do you understand that? We'll be next Jon. And...and this is not a kid that we're going to move. You can't think of it that way, Jon."

Jon nodded He at least acted like he understood. He turned to look out at the pasture, then back toward the Chief.

The Chief had already turned around. "Take the feet, Jon. Me and Darrin will get the head."

★   ★   ★

"I'm sorry. I'm really just...so sorry," Marilyn said.

Janice looked up. She had been staring at the gun that was lying in front of her on the kitchen table. "Don't worry about it,

Marilyn. We're all scared." She looked again down at the gun. "We're all going a little nuts."

Marilyn looked out at the now empty deck. "Jon's an idiot, isn't he?" she asked.

Janice smiled. "In a way, I guess. He's scared too, you know. He just...handles it a different way. An aggravating way, sometimes."

Marilyn looked at Janice. "Why do you think they'd take him along? And, what do you think they're doing out there?" she asked. The worry was back in her voice.

Janice reached out and put her hand on the gun. Very carefully. "I'd say the Chief needs all the help he can get," she looked up again, "to move the body." Marilyn stared wide-eyed at her, and her face went even paler than before. Janice didn't want her hysterical again, but figured she needed to hear it. She was getting a little impatient with Marilyn. Things were getting tough, and she needed to, well, "woman-up." "He had to have shot one of them, Marilyn. And you know what he told us about those, those things coming after the cat he shot. He asked them to help him move the body away from us. At least I think so..."

Something hit the front picture window in the living room. Very hard. At least that's what it sounded like from where they were sitting in the kitchen. Both women were startled by it and both snapped their heads in that direction. Marilyn drew in her breath sharply but didn't squeal or scream this time. She just stood up slowly, facing the living room. Janet grabbed the gun and did the same.

"It sounded like...didn't it sound like a bird flew into it?" Marilyn whispered urgently.

Janice stepped around her and began walking slowly out of the kitchen with the gun held with both hands in front of her. "Birds don't fly into windows at night," she said. There was another loud thump. "Maybe monsters do though," she added.

★　　　★　　　★

They had to throw the body over the fence to get it into the pasture. It landed with a thump that triggered a moment from two years before, in Jon's mind, when a dog's landing had made the same sound.

"Hey Darrin, do you remember...'

"YES!" Darrin said as he began immediately climbing over the fence. "Come on!"

Both the Chief and Darrin climbed over quickly and easily. They turned and looked at Jon, who was hesitating for some reason.

"Come on! We don't have much time, damn it!" the Chief scolded.

The Jon heard, or thought he heard, something up near the deck behind him. He turned, looked, then turned back, put both hands on the fence and tried to jump it in one bound. He almost made it. His trailing left foot caught the top board and he landed hard, and partially on the dead body. Though he had knocked the wind out of himself for the second time that evening, he had no trouble scrambling to his feet quickly once he realized what was beneath him. "God damn it!' he cried as he hopped away and frantically tried to wipe off whatever he had imagined was on him.

"Over there! Look!" Darrin whispered as hard as he could. He was facing southwest and had his flashlight trained that way. The other two followed the beam. Nothing but rolling pasture, at first. Then a movement. A head appearing as a man slowly ascended a rolling grassy hill about a quarter of a mile away from them. In a moment his whole body was in the spotlight. Then suddenly, another one. Right behind him. This one was a child. A little girl who looked like she was dressed in a nightgown. They walked steadily toward them.

"Shit!" the Chief said.

"We better hurry," Darrin whispered as he turned off the light, holstered the flashlight and bent over to pick up the body.

Jon stared out at the now black space that had illuminated the people who were, he knew, still coming in the dark. "Maybe this is far enough, ya think?"

"Shut up and pick him up, Jon!"

After one failed attempt (the corpse's shoe came off in Jon's hand) they lifted up the still limp body and, awkwardly, started walking with it. They had to go uphill first, and it was a struggle. The now yellowing autumn grass was thick. They grunted and strained and, finally, got up the first hill. Then they put the body down to rest, and to check their surroundings. The fickle moon had decided to hide behind another cloud, and it was hard to see anything at all.

"We've got to keep going due south, to the woods," Chief Thomas said as he grabbed and turned on his flashlight. "Those things were coming from the west. We can't veer that way, away from them," he said as he pointed his beam.

"There they are! Still coming our way," Darrin said as he shined his light to the southwest. "The bastards changed direction to cut us off. They're getting closer," he said.

The Chief's flashlight was pointed south in the direction they were going. The woods were still hundreds of yards away. "That's where we want to be," he said. Then he turned off the light and bent over the body. "Let's go!" he commanded.

Jon was watching the people approach in Darrin's light. When it went out he had their picture burned into his memory. The man had looked like a policeman. He'd had a determined, emotionless face. The little girl looked just like a little girl, only her eyes, at least with the light on them, were all black. "Maybe I could hold the flashlight with my neck somehow," he pleaded as he bent to get a hold of the legs. "I really think we need to, uh...see what's coming," he pleaded.

"You've got to be ready to shoot, Darrin," Chief Thomas said, ignoring Jon's request. "Are you ready to do that?"

"I don't know," Darrin said softly, " I mean...kids?"

"They're not kids! If you don't shoot, they'll kill you!" the Chief snapped back.

Jon only half listened to the exchange. He was sure he could hear them now, but had no chance of seeing them in the blackness. He couldn't think straight. He was scared half to death...but he was listening for them as hard as he could.

They got the body down the hill, up a shorter one, then another 50 yards or so on level ground. They walked as quietly as they could, but it was awkward, hard work.

This time they heard them, clearly, before they saw them. First to their right, the direction the man and girl were coming from, and then (almost immediately) from in front of them-the same frantic rustling of grass-close, as if someone was running through it.

"Down!" the Chief yelled, and all three let go of the corpse. A sliver of moon reappeared from behind a cloud the very second the body thudded to the ground, turning the pitch black night to a less dark, but still mostly impenetrable gray. They could see each other now, but barely. Darrin and the Chief reached for their flashlights as Jon spun around, crouching defensively, straining to see anything, in every direction.

The Chief's light came on first. Darrin's followed a few seconds later (he'd dropped it in his hurry). They both initially pointed their beams to the west, where the man and little girl were seen last. Nothing. The Chief swept his slowly to the south toward the woods. Darrin moved his in nervous, short zigzags to the west northwest, desperately trying to locate the people he knew were there...somewhere. Close. They had to be close.

The full moon came out completely. Suddenly, Jon could see the vague outlines of his house when he looked to the north, and the much closer woods, easily, when he looked south. The moon's glow had, in fact, turned the pasture, and everything else, an ethereal milky gray.

"You know, I think we could see better without the lights," Jon said, and as he did he heard them...could almost feel them-

and right behind him. No one had thought about them circling around and coming from the east. He held his breath and tried to find the courage to turn around. Then there was a hand on his shoulder.

Jon didn't turn around. He screamed and dove to the ground. The two flashlights whirled in his direction. They shone on him, then a step behind him and up. Sheriff Joe Blanton stood not two feet away from the prostrated Jon, looking down on him with what looked like a bemused, twisted smile. The little raven-haired girl next to him was giggling and covering her mouth with her hand, as though she were shy.

"Joe?" Chief Thomas asked with a shaking voice, "Joe, is that you?"

The Sheriff didn't move. The little girl did. She took two rapid steps toward Jon and began to bend down. Her giggle became a low growl.

★　　　★　　　★

Janice was standing in front of the living room picture window, crouched with her gun held in front of her with both hands in what she assumed to be the correct shooting position, when they heard the first shot. Marilyn, who was standing at the side of the window ready to pull open the curtains, let out a short scream. Janice flinched but successfully lowered her gun. By the time she turned around to face the direction of the pasture three more shots had been fired. Both women waited with held breath for more, but none came.

"Oh. My. God." Marilyn said after several seconds had passed.

Before Janice could say something reassuring there was a thump on the window again. This one was softer than the others, but was followed by a long scraping sound, as though someone was dragging their fingernails down it.

Janice turned back and jerked her gun back up. "It's still there," she said calmly.

They had had enough. For almost twenty minutes they had listened to whatever it was out there, hitting, banging on, and now scraping at the big window with the closed curtain. "We've been afraid for too long!" Janice had declared at the beginning of her argument to Marilyn that they should become proactive.

She didn't have to argue long. Marilyn too had had enough of it. Her fear had been overwhelming, but now, as the shock began to wear off a bit (or perhaps, settling permanently in), she was finding that there was an element of rage there. Maybe a little too much rage.

"Let's shoot the bastards!" she had declared to Janice's surprise. Janice had to back her up a bit.

Their plan was simple: Marilyn would jerk the curtains open fast, and at once. Whoever was out there would then suddenly be faced by a mean looking Janice with her gun pointed right at them. They would run away. End of story.

And if they didn't run? "Well then at least we'll know what we're up against," Janice had answered firmly.

Now with the ominous shots coming from the pasture behind them, and the scraping sound at the window in front of them, there was a moment of indecision.

"Maybe" Marilyn whispered, "maybe we should..."

"NO!" Janice commanded suddenly. She crouched again. "OPEN THE CURTAINS!"

Marilyn hesitated, then decided. She turned and opened the curtains as rapidly as she could, then stepped back and looked.

It was a woman with her face pressed up against the glass. Her mouth was open and her lips were stretched back to show long, almost feline looking teeth. Her eyes were rolled back so that only the whites were showing. One of her white long-fingered hands was pawing at the window, the other was holding a baby. A baby with the same doll-like, yellow-eyed stare as the baby Janice had seen in the hospital.

"CLOSE THEM!" Janice screamed, "CLOSE THE DAMNED CURTAINS!"

Chapter 34
October 11th 1:13 A.M.

"Right behind you!" Jon screamed.

Darrin whirled in time to see the dog begin its leap into the air. He fired his gun as he dove to his left.

Jon saw the muzzle flash only inches away from the dog's chest. It should have been dead instantly, but after landing on the ground it quickly scrambled to its feet and turned to renew the attack. The second shot, from Chief Thomas, almost blew its head off, and it collapsed like a sack of potatoes.

"I told you, Darrin! The head. It's got to be the head!" the Chief scolded.

Darrin didn't reply. For a few moments he didn't even move. He just lay where he was, looking at the dead dog. John walked over for a closer look. "I'm not sure...but I think we know this dog, Darrin," he said shakily.

That was enough to get Darrin up to his feet. And quickly. "Come on," he said sternly as he frantically turned and looked in every direction, "Let's go!"

They had walked, slowly and cautiously, half-way back to the house. Chief Thomas had continually urged that they walk together and very deliberately-to avoid being unprepared for the kind of surprise that they had just had. He knew that the first instinct would be to run (especially after the sheriff-little girl encounter they'd had), and that that would be even more dangerous.

Jon was still kneeling over the dead dog. He seemed dazed.

"Come on Jon," the Chief said quietly. "We're almost home."

Jon looked up. "I swear to you. This is the same dog that died out here two years ago." He started breathing hard. "What the hell is happening here?"

Neither of the other two offered an answer. They waited silently for him to somehow get it together, to get the emotions in check so that they could move on. There wasn't anything to say now. All three were in shock, at some level. All three were battling, each in their own way, just to stay sane.

"Oh God," Jon moaned as the other two watched everything around them, and waited. He wiped his face on his sleeve, forced a few deep breaths, then slowly stood back up. He cleared his throat. "Sorry," he said, "It's just that, well, cats and kids are one thing...but now we're shooting dogs?"

They walked carefully on, stopping only one more time. It was on top of the hill, before they made the final ascent down to the fence and then to Jon's back yard and house. They took the time there, once they were sure there was nothing between themselves and the deck, to take advantage their high vantage point to stop, turn around and look.

The bright moonlight let them see it all, though in the murky colors of a nightmare. They seemed to be everywhere. Most were congregating where the three bodies lay (bodies they could no longer see) at the far end of the pasture, just short of the woods. A couple were walking toward the dead dog. The three men stood watching, with as much wonder as dread... and horror. People. They were all real people, just a few days before! People they'd known and trusted as friends and neighbors. People who had once lived, laughed and loved...now silently, mindlessly bending over the most unholy of feasts.

"It's just, it's just, so horrible," Darrin choked out to finally break the silence.

Neither of the other two could answer. Chief Thomas was biting down hard and trying to control raging, wildly opposing emotions; a wave of grief and guilt about his wife Joanie, revulsion at having had to actually shoot a child, and an anger that burnt so deeply that it was all he could do to keep from running out there again and emptying his gun on them.

Jon just watched, and occasionally wiped away a tear.

"Look at the way they walk," Darrin said as he pointed. He was pointing to the two of them, what looked from their distance to be a teen-aged boy and girl, who were walking rapidly toward where they had shot the dog. It wasn't that far away. "I wonder why some of them walk faster than others?" he wondered out loud. "And some of them can, well... float, it seems like?"

Again, neither of the other two offered a reply. Darrin looked at each of them. Even in the relative darkness he could tell why. "We better get back," he said as he turned to lead the way.

"Hey, at least the girls didn't have to see any of this," he added a few moments later, as they started down the last hill.

★   ★   ★

"It was the most horrible thing I've ever seen," Janice said through her tears.

It had taken the men almost five minutes to get them to unlock the door. Marilyn had finally opened it after Darrin shouted loud enough (dangerous, but necessary) for her to hear. Even then she effectively blocked their entrance for another minute, as she leaped into her husband's arms right in doorway and refused to let him go.

The girls had locked themselves in the bathroom, and with the vent fan on (so as not to hear any more unnerving, threatening sounds) they had a hard time hearing them when the men had returned. Once all were in the house the story of the woman and baby was told, though in bits and parts at first.

But it was alarming enough to cause another armed search around the house's perimeter, and then some heavy lifting. They were getting too close; too brave and aggressive, they all agreed. Furniture was moved to at least mostly block off the picture window and the glass door leading to the deck, and two chairs were placed, one on top of the other, against the front door.

By the time they finished, any attempted entrance was made to be extremely difficult, or at least very noisy...even by a monster, it was hoped.

And now, gathered once again in the kitchen, they were listening to the shattered, emotionally exhausted Janice as she tried to describe the horror; which she told as much for herself as for the others.

"A baby! She was holding a baby! And it was just like the one we saw at St. Joseph's! And it was...changed. I could tell."

Jon, who was standing behind her, suddenly and very uncharacteristically (for him) reached his hands out and put them on her shoulders and began rubbing them gently to comfort her. "It's all right now, Janice," he said soothingly. But it only made her started crying harder.

"We need to start thinking about getting sleep," Chief Thomas said casually. He was, of all things, checking messages on his phone and therefore couldn't see the " *you must be nuts!*" looks he was getting from the others. "Darrin, how much gas do you have in your car?" he asked a moment later as he looked up.

"I don't know...a little over three quarters, maybe."

"There's stuff happening all the way to St. Louis now," the Chief said as he looked back at his phone, "and north too. Everybody's calling for help, reporting things. It looks like it is here, everywhere. The National Guard won't know where to start." He looked up again. "But you know what? No reports from the east, or south."

"That's because there's nothing there, east or south of Highland," Darrin said sarcastically. "Just corn fields."

"Maybe. But we're going to go that way. I mean you are," the Chief said. Everyone looked at him. He directed his look at Darrin. "We've got to get these women out of here, Darrin. Your wife..."

"That's sexist!" Janice bristled.

The Chief turned to her. "Maybe so. I don't give a damn though, Janice," he said calmly. "You see, I'm the Chief Public Safety officer here. And I say that when dawn comes the four of you are going to get in that damned car in the garage. And I say you're going to drive like hell 'til you get to Dixie, or the ocean, or some damned place where it's safe."

He stopped and went back to looking at his phone. The other four were temporarily too stunned to say anything. In the ensuing quiet they heard, again, the slight (but unmistakable) scraping sound at one of the windows again. Darrin stood up.

"Don't go," the Chief said without looking up. "Unless you hear glass breaking, don't go. If you end up shooting one we'll end of with dozens of them," He looked up at Darrin. "and you saw what that was like."

They heard a heavier sound, a thudding on the window. They all tensed, but it didn't repeat itself.

"My car is still at Hardees," Janice said, "We could stop there and..."

"No!" Chief Thomas commanded. Then he looked at her still stunned face and swollen eyes, and tried to be more patient. "Janice, I've only got one guy working tonight. At least I think he's still working. No one else showed up. This one guy, he sent me a message a couple of hours ago. He said the things are everywhere. They've multiplied. Spread. It's like the flu, like you said. He told me he saw them stop a car. It doesn't matter if you hit them. And then they..." he paused, and quickly decided not to go there. "Forget about your car, or going to your house, or whatever. Forget it."

"Then how the hell are we going to get out?" Darrin asked.

"Good question. Don't know for sure, but we've got to try," the Chief said coolly. "We're on the far eastern side of town. That's good, I think. When the sun comes up you get in the car, get out of this neighborhood, and head east on St. George Road. You'll be out in the country in two minutes. Then you keep on going."

"And what are you going to do?" Jon asked. He still had his hands on Janice's shoulders. He was still rubbing them gently.

"I'm going to create a distraction so that you can get away. Just like in the movies," the Chief smiled.

"I think he means why aren't you going with us, Chief." Darrin said. "What are you going to do here?"

All eyes turned to the Chief. He looked up at the kitchen clock then the other way, past them and out at the barricaded glass door. He obviously had no intention of answering that question now. "About five hours 'til dawn," he said. "I'll take first shift as guard. The rest of you try to get some sleep." He stood up, stretched, then started walking out of the kitchen to check the windows in the living room (and undoutedly to avoid any more questions) "Gonna be a hell of a morning," he added over his shoulder.

★   ★   ★

It had already been a hell of a night, and there didn't seem to be any cause for hope that the rest of it would get any better. But pure unadulterated exhaustion had set in; the one master that must eventually be served no matter what the circumstances.

They had to find a way to sleep.

After much debate on the issue, it was eventually decided that Marilyn and Janice would try to rest in one of the bathrooms, and Darrin and Jon would try to sleep in the other. One in the tub, one on the floor. The bathrooms had the advantage having fans running to create white noise. And locked doors. No little sounds could be heard. No monsters could get in. No nightmares. Maybe.

273

That was the hope.

It lasted exactly 45 minutes, until the electricity went out. Though Janice, Marilyn and Darrin stirred restlessly when it happened, they were tired enough to roll through it and sleep a little longer.

Jon woke up wide-eyed the second the fan went out.

He joined Chief Thomas, who was lighting a candle in the kitchen, a minute later.

"I guess now they've figured out how to turn off the electricity," he said as he walked in.

The Chief looked up. "Somebody has. Something happened. Not surprising, really." He held up the successfully lit little candle. "Got any more of these?" he asked.

Jon walked toward the cabinet above the sink as the Chief continued, "First the cable, then radio, then nothing working right. Static, or nothing at all. Probably be the cell phone towers next."

Jon handed him another, larger candle and a book of matches. "Can't say that I noticed," he said. "Something about dead bodies and ghouls everywhere kind of took away from my radio listening." He went over to the counter and tried to turn on the radio sitting there, just for the hell of it.

"Uh, isn't that a plug-in?"

"Oh. Right." Jon said sheepishly.

A long, mournful howling sound then. It came from the front of the house this time.

"A dog?" Jon whispered.

The Chief waited for it to end. "Can't say, but it was pretty close," he said.

A light tapping sound began on one of the living room windows. It was steady, rhythmic.

"I wouldn't bother," the Chief said as Jon took a step toward the living room. He sank heavily onto one of the kitchen chairs. "I mean, if you were going to go check. Won't do any good." He stretched his arms out and yawned. "I think they're trying to get us to run around. It's like they're probing." He yawned again.

Jon took one more look at his dark living room, then walked over to the table and took a seat himself. He had wanted to go check, but was glad to accede to the Chief. "Why don't you try to get some sleep," he found himself saying, "I'm up for a while. 'Course, you'll have to leave me a gun."

The Chief actually smiled. "Thanks, but I'll stay out here. Maybe doze off a little...while you're listening to the radio, maybe."

"Very funny," Jon said.

They listened to the tapping starting again. It was stopping and starting now, in no particular rhythm. It seemed harder now though, more insistent. For Jon, it was becoming alarming. He started to fidget.

The Chief seemed to be ignoring it. He was leaned back in his chair with his hands behind his head, looking at something up and far away, that maybe only he could see. "I think Janice was right, Jon," he said suddenly, "...and that priest. We shouldn't have quit two years ago, even if we didn't know what the hell we were doing. You know what I mean?"

Jon was listening, but his attention was definitely split. He stood up and nervously turned toward the living room. When he did, the tapping stopped. "I don't buy it," he finally answered. "I don't buy that there was anything more that we could have done." He started pacing. "I mean, and you know this, it was... Evil. It was a spiritual thing that we didn't understand. Weren't capable of understanding. And like I said before 'nothing you could shoot.'"

"And that's where we failed," the Chief said calmly. The tapping started again, and it seemed to be picking up, but the Chief seemed oblivious to it. "When they didn't stop Hitler, he just got stronger. When we didn't do enough to stop the terrorists, they just got stronger. Know what I mean?" Jon didn't answer. He had stopped pacing and was looking into the living room, and listening. "Same thing with this, this Pure Evil thing," the Chief went on. "We should have found a way. We shouldn't have pretended that..."

The glass of the picture window shattered with incredible force, and with incredible noise. Jon's first instinct was to run, but he ended up half jumping back and into the table instead. Chief Thomas froze for a second, then after Jon's rear end scooted the table he calmly reached for the gun and flashlight laying on it and rose to his feet.

"OH MY GOD!" Jon screamed.

"Easy," the Chief said as he stepped around the table, "They can't get in, Jon."

The first thing the flashlight spotted was Darrin trotting down the hall toward them, gun in hand. The light inadvertently blinded and disoriented him and he half crashed into the wall and almost dropped his weapon. He instinctively pulled his free hand up to his eyes.

"HOLD IT DARRIN!" the Chief yelled as he re-directed the flashlight while walking into the living room. Jon followed him in and by now there was more clatter and confusion as the girls staggered blindly into the hall behind Darrin. Chief Thomas pointed the flashlight at the window. At first there was just the confusing mass of furniture piled nearly to the ceiling in front of it. But as he moved the light slowly across the inanimate mass it suddenly landed on, went past, then came back to an animate, moving part. A man's hand and arm was sticking through, and it was grasping at the empty air, over and over again.

"Oh God!" Darrin exclaimed. He immediately turned to try to find Marilyn in the dark to push her back and away.

"Kill it!" Jon screamed.

Janice ran into Chief Thomas. He felt a gun hit his leg. "Janice put that down!" he commanded. She stared at the grasping arm held in the beam of light, and only held the gun tighter.

"I'll go out and get it," Darrin declared as he returned to the room.

"No. No you won't," Chief Thomas yelled. "Just hold on a minute, Darrin." He took a step closer and bent down and held the flashlight up to get a better sight line. When he had almost reached the hand itself he bent and looked up and past the arm. He saw the head, with its mouth opening and closing soundlessly, like a fish. It was inside the window, but it wasn't making any more progress than his arm and hand were.

"He's stuck," the Chief said as he stood up and backed away. "At least for now, he's stuck."

"Oh God!" Marilyn cried. She had just gotten her first look at the invading arm.

The living room lamp flickered, and then came back on, along with the kitchen lights, vent fans and every other light the group had automatically tried to flip on in their first moments of panic. Now, very suddenly, they could see the whole scene, from the shards of glass everywhere to the silent invader's struggles with the piled furniture.

There was a collective gasp. Janice raised her gun but Jon, firmly but gently, grasped it too. He whispered something to her and quietly took it away.

No one else noticed. All were taking in the stunning scene before them.

"We can't kill it," the Chief said solemnly, breaking the spell. "They'll be a dozen here if we do. Maybe more. And now we've got an open window." He and Darrin exchanged looks. Then the Chief looked at each of the other three. "We've got to leave," he said. "We've got to leave now. All of us."

Chapter 35
October 11th 3:47 A.M.

"I'll walk out the front door the moment you open the garage door. I'll cover you backing out of the driveway, then I'll head to my car," Chief Thomas said. The others nodded.

It had taken a while to get consensus. Darrin wanted to wait until dawn, unless the "...damned zombie gets free."

Jon was fatalistic on the one hand, but stubbornly and probably unrealistically optimistic on the other. He'd argued that he didn't see the since of driving into more trouble than they were already in (because "they" were everywhere), but he also maintained that the things would surely die off soon anyway, because, "...there's nothing left to eat!"

And he also kept mumbling, irrationally, about getting his window fixed.

Marilyn was more than ready to go. She only spoke once, in opposition to Darrin, and spent the rest of the debate detached from the others while carefully watching the uselessly waving arm and hand.

Janice went back and forth. As horrified as she was, there was something about just driving away from her town, her home, and even her poor car sitting alone at Hardees that disturbed her immensely. She didn't want to "just give up," and so kept saying so.

But when the electricity went off again, and stayed off, right after the Chief had received a text (from someone, but who??) reporting that at least three of the churches in town were burning... it quickly became unanimous. The unfathomable news of fire and being plunged again into total darkness with something so monstrous laying only a few feet away from them-focused their minds.

Now, they were ready to go. The street seemed clear, from what they could tell by flashing their lights up and down the darkened cul-de-sac. Yes, they were still in a numbed state, and frightened almost out of their minds, but they were ready to go.

"Chief, what are you going to do?" Darrin asked as the other three started moving toward the kitchen and the garage door beyond. "Are you leaving too?" He was pretty sure he knew the answer, but he wanted to hear it.

"Don't worry about me," Chief Thomas said dismissively.

Darrin didn't move.

"You better get going."

Darrin waited.

Chief Thomas could hardly see his Darrin's face, but he was aware that his stubborn detective was still standing, waiting. "I'm staying here, Darrin," the Chief said. "There's nothing for me anywhere else. Going back home loading up on ammo, then going to see if I can help anybody."

"And see how many you can shoot?"

"Maybe. At first. But help is on the way. They'll need somebody who knows what's what around here," the Chief said as he turned and walked past the waving hand to the front door. "You better get going, Darrin."

The girls were already in the car when he got there. They'd used candlelight to make their way. Jon was standing directly behind the car at the base of the garage door, ready to open it manually. Darrin opened the driver's side door, turned off his flashlight, and got in. "Ready when you are!" he yelled to Jon before closing his door.

"Better start it first!" Jon yelled back.

Seconds later the engine turned over, the garage door opened, and Darrin began slowly backing onto the driveway. Before he could stop it to let Jon in they heard an ear-shattering shot, then another. They saw the flash of the second one, but before they could even think to react, Jon was opening the back door to hop in, with a gun in his hand. He slammed the door shut and screamed "DRIVE!"

Darrin turned around instead. "What were you...how the hell did you get that!"

"Janice loaned it to me. Now drive!"

"What did you do?" Janice demanded.

"Shot the damned zombie in the ass. Now drive!"

All three looked at him, open-mouthed.

"He broke my picture window, so I shot him in the ass! Now drive!"

"Twice?" Janice asked.

"Once. Chief shot the other one. I don't know what he was shooting at. Hurry! Drive!"

It took only a few seconds to find out where the Chief's shot went, because they backed over the body. Darrin kept backing after the back tire ran over it, and soon the sprawling corpse was in their headlights.

And so was Chief Thomas. He ran up, jumped over the corpse and started frantically waving them up the street.

Darrin put it in drive, turned the wheel and hit the gas before Marilyn's scream had even stopped.

★   ★   ★

"Do you think he got out of there? The Chief, I mean?" Janice asked.

"Yeah. He's a tough old bird," Darrin answered a few seconds after looking at her worried face in the rear-view mirror.

She had strained to see him, turned around in the back seat, for as long as possible as Darrin had sped up the street and out of the Devonshire cul-de-sac. She saw him running for his car and thought she saw someone right behind him, but only for a brief few seconds before their car wheeled around the curve and onto Coventry.

And for the next fifteen minutes there wasn't time to worry, or even think about the Highland Police Chief. After the two block ride on Coventry (where they saw no one) they turned left onto Sunflower and immediately realized it was mistake. There were people, or zombies, or ghouls-whatever they were-everywhere. It looked like a street carnival for lobotomy patients, as Jon later characterized it.

Darrin stopped, and there was much yelling inside the car as he backed out double-time after one of them got close enough to claw at his window. Back on Coventry, he headed for Michael Road, then to St. George Road and east out of town.

The thinking was that there would be less of them out in the country, and that it would be safer to drive two-lane roads and avoid areas of population, at least until they were out of the "infected" Highland area.

And it worked...mostly. Twice animals (at least they thought they were animals) hit the side of the car hard, and it was especially frightening in the dark. And three times Darrin had to carefully swerve around people standing, unaccountably, in the road in the middle of the country.

But as they worked their way east, south, then east again they began to see things that gave them hope: lights on at some of the farmhouses, a car, then two pick-up trucks passing by in the opposite lane. And best of all they saw no people at all and just one animal; a frightened, but blessedly normal looking deer.

Finally, after a half-an-hour of driving they began, cautiously, to relax. A little.

"Where the hell are we going? Did anybody think of that?" Jon asked out of the blue. It was a question that would have been ridiculous under any other circumstances, but one that made perfect sense to all of them now.

"I say someplace to sleep. Anywhere. Just so it's safe," Janice volunteered. "But I really don't care," she added a moment later.

"Sleep now," Darrin said. "All of you. I'll drive for a couple of hours, then somebody can take over. Besides, we'll need gas by then."

His last sentence quieted, and disquieted, them all. The very thought of stopping, for anything, was still terrifying.

So they drove in silence, blissful silence for several minutes more when suddenly, the car radio came on. Full blast. For a few seconds there was absolute chaos. It could not have been more frightening. All four yelled and squealed in fright. It was so utterly surprising that it took Darrin a few seconds to even become cognizant of what was making the horrible, screeching sound. He swerved the car slightly, then finally figured it out, and mercifully turned the radio down as he slowly braked to a stop.

After a few seconds and a few deep breaths, he half turned in his seat and smiled at the others. "The radio works...Do you know what that means?" he asked happily, "We're out. We're out of the flash zone!"

It took a few seconds for it to soak in, but then there were hugs and shouts of pure joy-all coming from a car sitting alone in the middle of the open, lonely country, in the last dark hour of the night.

They had escaped the unimaginable.

★　　　★　　　★

They drove almost three more hours before stopping. They didn't want to stop. Even though the world around them gave, increasingly, every sign of being normal in every way (the sun was finally, gloriously rising, the radio chattered on with some banal but comforting local news story, work-day traffic was beginning to thicken-just like in the real world!) the collective combat-like stress they had suffered still made them cautious; even paranoid.

Darrin had at first avoided any place where people might be, and so zig-zagged through the country, heading basically east. Progress, at least as measured in miles, was slow. Eventually he reached an interstate highway (Illinois 57), and after a short debate, decided to take it south. Then he drove and drove as the others napped fitfully.

He passed cars. Cars passed him. The people in them looked normal. Everything looked normal. Wonderfully normal.

Paducah, Kentucky, he decided then. He had an uncle there. There they could stop, know they'd be safe...and finally, *finally* get some rest. He told Marilyn while the other two slept in the back. She gave him a forced smile, but didn't respond. Then she went back to sleep herself.

It was shortly after getting off of I-57 for another highway (24) that would take them to Kentucky when he decided to wake them and tell them that they had to stop.

"We need gas," he said, "We're almost dry. And we need to do a couple of normal things, like go to the bathroom, and eat something."

The others were too groggy to respond at first, but gradually he could see them becoming increasingly upset by his news. But no one said anything. Darrin saw in his mirror that Jon was suddenly sitting up tensely.

"Look, traffic is normal," Darrin said happily. "The guy on the radio is talking about high school football, for Christ's sake. We'll be fine!"

Janice nodded, but no one said anything.

"Besides," he added as he looked down at the gas gauge, "we don't have a choice."

What he didn't tell them was that the story of Highland, an hour before, had been on the radio too. Only now it was the story of the entire metro-east area, and even parts of St. Louis. The reports were vague and confusing. The media and government were certainly picking up that something had gone terribly wrong, but no one seemed to know exactly what. The speculation on what was causing the chaos centered around a supposed accident at Scott Air Force base, 20 miles to the south of Highland. But Homeland Security was denying that.

Darrin had listened to it all with the radio turned down as low as possible while the others slept. "It's all bullshit," he'd thought to himself when the report ended. He'd then turned the radio up, and looked for another station.

"How about stopping there?" Marilyn said, pointing to a billboard offering food and gas just a mile ahead.

"Fine," Darrin answered.

"Should we, uh, scout it out first?" Jon asked nervously from the backseat.

"How the hell do we do that?"

Jon didn't answer and Darrin took the entrance ramp and began slowing the car. Both Janice and Jon sat up in their seats as the service station/restaurant complex came into view. It was called "Marty's," the big sign said, and it looked like a normal Shell station with a restaurant attached. There were a lot of cars around it.

"Hey, we lucked out," Darrin said cheerfully. "No chain restaurants. Maybe we can get a home-cooked breakfast! What do ya think?"

Once again, no one responded. All three were nervously eyeing the gas station and the restaurant, and especially studying the people who were walking around.

Darrin pulled up to the first pump, put the car in park, and turned off the engine. None of them moved. Darrin unfastened his seatbelt, then did a half turn so that he could see all three of them. "Guys, I'm going to get out now," he said patiently, but with a bit of sarcasm. "I'm going to pump some gas. Jon, Janice, honey....go pee."

None of the three even looked at him, and when they made no immediate effort to get out of the door, he opened his own and stepped out into the fresh air.

★   ★   ★

He'd already pumped $20 worth into the tank when they finally got out. Or creeped out. They were quiet, sober-looking and tentative, but they did it. Janice and Marilyn waited for Jon to come around from the other side of the car. They stood looking at the station for a minute before moving.

"Go on, damn it!" Darrin commanded.

Marilyn turned to look at him. She looked pale.

"I'll meet you in there," Darrin said as gently as he could. "Nothing to be afraid of!"

Finally, they started to move. "We'll meet you in the restaurant, OK?" Janice asked nervously.

"Sure," Darrin answered. He shook his head as they walked away in a tight group. They were actually holding hands. All three of them. As though they were kindergartners entering a school building for the first time.

The tank was full less than a minute later. Darrin replaced the pump, screwed the gas cap back in then walked the short distance to the station and cashier.

"Good morning!" a pleasant looking gray-haired, older man said when he passed through the door.

Darrin smiled, and much more widely than he normally would have. "And good morning to you, sir!" he answered brightly. "I'm, uh..." he looked out to see the number, "...7. Pump 7." he said.

"All righty then," the man said as he looked down for the figure. "That'll be $37.17."

Darrin handed the man his credit card.

"Credit or debit?" the man chirped.

"Credit," Darrin answered as he took a glance around. "You know what, hold on to that for a minute," he said as he eyed the row of snack cakes. He was hungry enough to eat a bunch of them and breakfast too. "I think I'll pick up a few things for the road."

"Surely," the pleasant man said. "On a long trip are ya?"

Before Darrin could answer the cat was already on his lower right pant leg. He had seen only a quick, white blur out of the corner of his eye a second before. It happened much too fast for him to react to. He could only look, dumbly, down.

The cat had already sunk in its claws into his leg. With its ears laid back in anger, it screamed wildly then bit into him.

Darrin quickly broke through his shock, yelled out and kicked his leg wildly as the man came scurrying around the counter.

"Milky!" he screamed.

The kick was strong and the cat let go. It jumped back into the air, landed, then turned and ran as fast as it had appeared, screaming all the way to the back of the store.

Darrin was too stunned to react immediately, and it was the old man who got there and bent down to examine the damage first. "Jesus, I'm so sorry Mister," he said. "I'm so sorry!"

Darrin looked down at the balding gray head, and then at his own leg. He could see a spot of blood on his pants. "What...what happened?" he managed to ask.

"I don't know," the man said as he stood up. "I'm going to get some bandages. I'm so sorry!" he said again as he quickly began walking away.

The man went to the second aisle, grabbed the bandages, then walked back hurriedly, opening the box as he walked. "Damned cat!" he said. Then he looked Darrin in the eye as he offered him the opened box. His face was flush with embarrassment and distress. "He's never done anything like that before, I swear!" he said desperately.

Darrin took the box and bent down to roll up his pant leg and inspect the damage without saying anything.

"We had some sort of sonic boom, or some electrical sort of thing happen last night around dinner time," the old man said.

Darrin's head snapped up. "...and I tell ya mister, that cat's been plain crazy ever since."

THE END

LaVergne, TN USA
30 June 2010
187914LV00002B/2/P